# WITNESS SEEKER

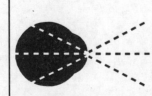

This Large Print Book carries the
Seal of Approval of N.A.V.H.

# WITNESS SEEKER

## STONE WALLACE

**THORNDIKE PRESS**

A part of Gale, a Cengage Company

GALE
A Cengage Company

Farmington Hills, Mich • San Francisco • New York • Waterville, Maine
Meriden, Conn • Mason, Ohio • Chicago

LIBRARY OF CONGRESS CATALOGING-IN-PUBLICATION DATA

Names: Wallace, Stone, 1957– author.
Title: Witness seeker / by Stone Wallace.
Description: Large print edition. | Waterville, Maine : Thorndike Press, a part of Gale, Cengage Learning, 2017. | Series: Thorndike Press large print western
Identifiers: LCCN 2017017332| ISBN 9781432839383 (hardcover) | ISBN 1432839381 (hardcover )
Subjects: LCSH: Large type books. | BISAC: FICTION / Westerns. | FICTION / Historical. | GSAFD: Western stories. | Suspense fiction.
Classification: LCC PR9199.4.W3424 W58 2017 | DDC 813/.6—dc23
LC record available at https://lccn.loc.gov/2017017332

Published in 2017 by arrangement with Stone Wallace

Printed in the United States of America
1 2 3 4 5 6 7 21 20 19 18 17

For the cowgirl who has consistently
ridden beside me on all my trails:
over heights of the hills and
occasionally through the flatlands.
I love you, Cindy!

# CHAPTER ONE

When you find yourself staring into the cold, black barrel of a Colt .44 aimed dead center at your chest . . . or maybe facing the double barrels of a twelve-gauge shotgun powered with enough discharge to blow your head clean off your shoulders, you'd better be prepared to make a decision.

You'd best know how to recognize the seriousness of your opponent's intent. Determine the look of purpose or desperation behind his eyes while keeping a wary watch on the finger as it either loosens or stays tense on the trigger and the thumb slowly brushes against the hammer.

Questions penetrate your brain. Is he primed to kill? Might he be bluffing? Or perhaps he's hoping for a stall, because he hasn't yet decided on his move? Maybe . . . if the situation warrants it . . . permitting you the chance to exercise diplomacy, which always is your objective.

Or in extreme situations, giving you precious seconds to defend yourself.

If you have the courage.

If you don't react in haste.

Lawman, lawyer, politician. Even, on occasion, gunslinger. You need to carry each hat and know which one to don for the situation at hand. And even then there are no guarantees. Because if there is one certainty in this occupation, it is that, before you walk into any circumstance, you're going against the odds. Like a crooked stud player daring to slap down a winning card pulled from his sleeve against a table of gun-toting gamblers who play for keeps.

You can never become too confident. Because each situation differs from the one before and the one to follow. Circumstances vary, as do the types of people you deal with. I reckon one of the key elements is that you've got to be a pretty keen student of human nature and of people in general. It's up to you to do the necessary detective work. Search beyond what seems obvious and find out all that you can about a person's family, background, personality. Education, if any. Religion. Virtues and vices. Strengths and frailties. Because when your services are called upon, you can be sure that you will run up against one of three categories of people: the submissive, the fearful, or the desperate. The submissive are the easiest to convince. They are usually tired of running, hiding out; the ones whose conscience has finally led them to make the right decision. The fearful pose the potential for danger but if you do your job right, state your purpose, and provide the proper assurances, they, too, can generally be talked into riding back with you to do their part to ensure proper justice.

In my experience, the desperate are the most threatening. They feel themselves cornered, frightened of retribution, and don't trust the law to protect them. Fear over their well-being can become so overwhelming as to provoke an impulsive action that could lead either you or them to a dirt bed on Boot Hill.

Yet if you are a professional, there remains an advantage. It comes through practice — often manifested by notches carved into your rifle stock or other such item, put there not to celebrate a kill, like the boastful marks made by a bounty hunter or professional gunman, but to serve as a visible reminder of each time you succeeded in your duty and walked away alive. Again, it takes someone with a bead on the twists and turns of human nature to make the proper call. Sometimes you decide right and your task comes to a satisfying conclusion; other times you watch that finger play on the trigger just a little too deliberately, and you'd better move quick and sure. If the aim of your bullet is dead-on, the killing will likely be judged self-defense. On the other hand, graveyards are full of people whose hesitation or reflexes were just a trifle off the mark.

An indecision or faltering I've learned through experience never to allow myself.

Those who I seek are not the desperados whose images are inked on wanted posters in towns like Tombstone or Dodge City. The people I track are mostly average folk, honest types: farmers, merchants, wives . . . even, on occasion, children. They serve a special, specific purpose, and as a professional I must never lose sight of that. They're people whose cooperation is necessary to bring lawbreakers to justice. Criminals who cannot always be easily categorized. Sometimes they are victims of circumstance or misplaced justice; other times they are a pure vicious breed. Lawbreakers of various backgrounds, but who ultimately share a corrupt purpose. They might be of the land, born and bred in untamed territories, intending to plunder new prospects among ungoverned towns and settlements — or they may be of the city, young and restless individuals seeking quick riches, determined to escape the restrictive confines of their eastern upbringing where laws have already been established and enforced, laws that those handy with a six-shooter might refuse to recognize or acknowledge — except by defiantly pumping bullet holes through their bold-lettered postings.

And to help curtail these lawless activities before they corrupt the expansion of the West is where I earn my pay. Tracking and using my skills of persuasion to bring in witnesses whose testimony can condemn a lawbreaker either to the hangman's noose or to serve a long prison sentence. Not an easy task with two equally dire outcomes awaiting the accused and the burden of whichever punishment weighing on the conscience of the witness. It is then that I have to reinforce my argument with the reminder that these witnesses carry a responsibility. They are the people who are helping to settle the frontier and have a duty to keep the territory safe not only for themselves and their families, but for future generations.

The other challenge I face is even more difficult and requires delicate handling. That is the occasion when I have to find a way to convince a witness frightened of reprisal. The fear of retribution can be just as intimidating as the knowledge of the condemned man soon to "ride the rope," or sentenced to live out his remaining years behind bars in a territorial prison. There exists a similar feeling of despair, oftentimes of hopelessness, a future clouded in uncertainty. And not without just cause. Because if there is one thing a man can bet his silver on, it's that western law can be as prickly as a cactus. In many of these frontier communities, very few judges and juries are what might be termed "unreachable" — especially when a fair verdict might be compromised by human temptation: a cash bribe either furnished out of pocket by the accused or provided by family, which presents an even more formidable problem, since that also brings into account the bonds of heritage and the blemish no family wants cast upon its name, no matter how deserving. Then there are those instances when justice promises to prevail and where not even cold hard cash can sway a decision, but where an outright threat can serve its purpose to influence — no, the proper word is *infiltrate* — one's commitment to duty.

These are considerations that accompany me on each of my assignments. Yet they remain thoughts that I must never dwell upon too deeply, otherwise they pose their own threat, which is to weaken my resolve. I must remain sturdy and steadfast in attempts at persuasion that even I might view as fragile guarantees, to ease, if not completely erase, the apprehensions of those I am paid to seek.

Still, despite such obstacles, I am regarded as one of the best at my job, and my record of successes has kept my services in demand throughout the frontier territories of the Southwest.

My name is Chance Gambel. My profession is Witness Seeker.

# CHAPTER TWO

Mine is a solitary occupation.

Aloneness has its advantages . . . but also distinct disadvantages. Too much time for idle thoughts to intrude upon the business at hand. Perhaps memories: remembrances of a past, either joyful or sorrowful and regretful. Maybe thoughts about a future in which you can finally settle down and watch the sunset with the satisfaction of not worrying about the uncertainty of tomorrow. Oftentimes just plain crazy thoughts flood through your brain. Your thinking becomes susceptible to the elements and the long, often monotonous trail. The days of travel and especially those lonely nights camping out under the open skies can heighten your uncertainty about what waits for you at the end of your ride. Those were the thoughts you had to be most careful of; dwelling on that kind of pondering can get you so twisted around with doubt and apprehension that you become no good to yourself or for the job you were hired to do.

In the beginning the lengthy periods of solitude got me to pondering a lot. Maybe because I was young and eager — ambitious — I wasn't troubled much by fear. While I'd certainly seen death — if only its aftermath at funerals and burials — awareness of my own mortality had yet to have real emphasis on my thinking. Mostly I reflected on the years behind me. My folks. My upbringing. The circumstances that took me away from my father's vast acreage in Kansas and saw me enrolled at various colleges in the East. I was enamored with poetry and literature and gave serious thought to becoming either a writer or a teacher. But I reckon those years of outdoor prairie life had a stronger impact on me than the notion of taking full advantage of my education did.

I finished my schooling, but my restless spirit soon motivated me to break away from the stifling environment of gentlemanly employment and landed me a virtual nomad, scouting about the Southwest. There were times when I marveled at how I went from baling hay and milking cows to excelling at classroom study to, finally, searching for trial witnesses along the various boundaries of the frontier.

My brain never relaxed, a phenomenon I first attributed to years of absorbing my studies, and which I regarded as a good thing. At least I was keeping my mind active, I reasoned. But I learned quickly that such prolonged and uncontrolled introspection could be detrimental, both to what I was musing about and, more importantly, by clouding my purpose. I had to keep my focus.

And the day came when this was driven home to me with double-barreled impact.

I had no qualifications for the job. In fact, I'd never even applied, but instead was approached — and trained under a former frontier scout named Calvin C. Birk. *Colonel* Calvin, as he preferred to be called, an indulgence I acknowledged without curiosity or question since he had served honorably in the Union Army and was deserving of respect. He was a man of bountiful energy and passion who knew his business. But once he made the fatal mistake of letting his attention wander while on what he assumed would be a simple assignment and rode head-on into an ambush. I'd followed his advice and kept a careful distance behind him that early morning and only heard the quick blasts of gunfire that shattered the stillness that, in thinking back, seemed unnatural, almost oppressive for the place and the hour.

The killer or killers of the colonel fled into the surrounding woods and lost themselves in the camouflage of the thick brush. I bolted forward on my horse to assist my mentor, who I found lying sprawled and bleeding on the dew-moistened grass. His chest had been blown away. I knew he was dying, and I was powerless to do anything for him. His gaze was wandering, unfocused, and with his final gasps of life he muttered words to me that did not reflect fear at the shadow of death, but instead expressed reproach at his own failing: "I let my guard down. They got me."

That was all. I felt the last staggering heave of breath vacate his body, and he died there on the spot. I confess I was filled with a strange amazement. I'd never seen a man die before, though I had my own preconceived notions about dying, as I had heard many stories told about the traumatic "passing of the soul." But Colonel Calvin did not depart this world in such a manner. True, his body had been blasted apart by bullets, yet he seemed oblivious to the damage they had inflicted. He never so much as winced in pain. It was more like a bewildered acceptance of what had befallen him.

As to his final words, he didn't have to say any more. I knew precisely what he meant. As I watched him die, consumed with helplessness, yet strangely emboldened by his bravery, I vowed from that day forward to keep my focus set, my intention firm. Oddly, even after witnessing such a sudden, violent death, I never considered surrendering this work I had more or less stumbled into as my profession. Instead, I resolved to use Colonel Calvin's fading words as my motivation. I determined that my work would become my one and only priority, my sole concentration while I was out on the trail following through on an assignment. I admit that moments of questioning occasionally intruded upon this decision. Took a lot of self-training, in fact, but eventually I mastered it.

Still, when I had the time to reflect, I pondered over those dying words he'd spoken. I knew Colonel Calvin had a family; he spoke of them often. He talked a lot, and it was only after his death that I started to wonder if he opened up to me as he did because he considered me a trusted friend — or merely a focal point on which he could express his innermost thoughts.

However he'd intended his talks — usually delivered at day's end before a desert or wilderness campfire — I learned a great deal about the man whom I had come to regard not only as a mentor but, indeed, almost a surrogate father — no disrespect intended to my own birth father, but rather as a man more geared toward my own present situation. After the bloody battles of war, Colonel Calvin had taken to becoming a wanderer, a man of his own means until he found his calling as a frontier scout. When he became restless in that endeavor, he took on the task of becoming a witness seeker.

Unwisely or not, he then decided to wed. He married late in life and his wife was young, his two boys mere children, aged four and two, the time he last saw them. His fondness for his kin was expressed often, yet his final thoughts, the words he said to me, were oddly not of his family. Instead, he reprimanded himself for his carelessness. He remained committed to his job till the end. I found it curious that he hadn't used those last ounces of strength to give me a message to take to his family, yet I reckon those dying words had their own relevance.

I knew he had left behind no funds for his wife and sons, nor would any pension be provided, since people in our trade worked independently — cash money for hire. We were not marshals appointed by the government or county sheriffs voted in by the citizens. We worked on the fringe of the law and did not receive a town or territorial salary. What we earned was what we carried. Some saved their money but most preferred to spend it, dispensing cash with reckless abandon, justifying their whiskey and female indulgences with the grim understanding that each payday might be their last.

To my knowledge Colonel Calvin was never careless with his pay, yet I was to learn his family would be left to make do on their own. I admit I considered throwing a few dollars their way, since I was free of family or any such responsibility beyond my own minimal needs and could well afford to do so. Yet I was to resist the urge. Selfishness, maybe. But I preferred to see it as a reflection of the independence I had taken upon myself. The irony was that there was a place for understanding and compassion in my work. But *only* in my work.

I divorced myself from indulgences such as sympathy or empathy in my personal life. Although Colonel Calvin was the closest to me, I had only to remind myself that there were others who shared my occupation who likewise had made errors in judgment and left behind destitute widows and children. I'd made a choice, and as part of that decision, I wanted no attachments to cause me worry and hinder me in my duty.

While steady progress was being made in the growth and development of the West, there were still territories where laws as yet undefined or properly enforced were challenged, and where the services of a witness seeker were needed to aid in establishing these rules. These were settlements and towns where legal protocol was not always observed and where one might not simply be handed a court summons and be expected to obey.

Most often, when a witness seeker was called upon, he would be armed only with the power of persuasion.

And trust that he was riding with a saddlebag full of luck.

# CHAPTER THREE

The assignment was unique to me, in that I had been hired privately. While the task involved my professional service as a witness seeker, which involved searching for an individual whose testimony might free a man accused of murder, on this occasion I would not be working as a representative of the law or serving a town committee. Rather, I was acting as an agent for the accused man's sister. The community itself hardly gave a damn whether the man in question was innocent or not. In fact, the citizens seemed to favor giving him the rope, as he was regarded as a brute and of no-account.

Normally I would have outright refused such an assignment. But the woman who hired me was a rich widow who had a special affection for her younger brother. She also paid me a handsome fee: an advance with the balance to be paid upon delivery. It was an amount that in total rightly appealed to my mercenary nature.

The travel I'd undertaken on this assignment provided its own challenge. Although it took only a half day's straight travel, the mountain terrain leading into the remote Bodrie Hills territory was tricky: high bluffs and ridges to cross, rocky inclines to navigate. Uncertain country I hadn't ventured through before, but then, it was rare that I ever scouted the same region twice. Each journey provided a new adventure.

Fortunately, I was a skilled horseman and my animal, a big, sturdy bay, had traveled a lot of distances with me. Funny as it might sound, we understood each other. The hill treks that followed our descent from the natural mountain path and through the box canyon were steep with narrow passages. They required cautious treading, and the clearing I came to once my mount and I emerged from the forest of trees and dense underbrush was discouraging to my purpose. There wasn't much foliage to hide me directly from sight or even keep my body protected in shadow.

As I halted at the edge of this clearing, I decided it better to dismount and go the rest of the way on foot to the house where

23

the person whom I sought resided. I unsaddled but didn't tether my horse because I knew he would wait for me — and if, by chance, something should happen and I didn't come back, I didn't want to leave the fate of my mare to the discretion of my killers.

This required weighing two choices. I did not want to come upon the house too suddenly, nor did I want to sneak up on the place and catch anyone by surprise, thereby risk startling someone into an abrupt response. Most importantly, I had to be watchful in my approach so as not to present myself as an easy target for a scattergun, which seemed to be the weapon favored by those who took refuge in hill country.

I reminded myself that few of those people were professionally trained when it came to defending themselves. Oh, most could use a gun all right, but their main advantage came by catching a person unawares. Whether through prior information or by some queer intuition hill folk seemed to possess, it was possible your quarry might be waiting hours or even days for you to show up. A fellow might be cleverly hidden at some concealed vantage point with gun loaded and ready, primed to get the drop on you. If you were lucky enough not to be shot dead, you'd best be ready to negotiate . . . and pray they were of a mind to listen.

My head was free of all intrusions as I crept toward the small shack. I'd come across many ramshackle dwellings during my travels, and this ranked among the worse. From what information I was able to gather through my investigation that puzzle-pieced me to this destination, I knew a family lived there. Reclusive, not welcoming to strangers even under the best of circumstances. I'd also been told the man I was seeking had been taken in by the resident widower father and his brood. While the specifics were not clear, from what I was told, this shelter was provided as payment of a long-ago debt.

Therefore, I proceeded with caution, finally taking a moment to figure out my next move by secreting myself next to a thick growth of shrubbery maybe twenty yards from the west side of the house. It was a good location, for if I had to sit out till the sun finally went down, this would be where the last filtering light would set before the night shadows took over. I admit to giving in to a mild case of nerves, which I usually did by this point. But I could live with that without compromising my self-respect.

25

All I had to do was remind myself that just a few years earlier I would have been surrendering to total trepidation.

At least my hands felt steady. No trembling. It was just my gut that felt knotted. It was always an uncertain situation when you were dealing with people who have spent their lives in virtual isolation. They didn't feel obliged to abide either by the law or the rules of fair play. They could kill you as easily as they would shoot a rabbit for supper.

On the other hand, they could be friendly, hospitable types. But from what I had been told beforehand, that was not the reception I could expect from these people, which was why it seemed a mite curious to me that they had permitted the man I sought to take refuge with them. What was the debt he'd been paid? I pondered.

That was a question I hadn't the luxury to dwell upon. What concerned me at the moment was that beyond looking at me as an intruder, these hill folk might consider me a threat. Since I wasn't authorized by the law to be on their property — if that really made any difference to their way of thinking — if they decided to shoot me, they could justify doing so and say I was trespassing, a punishable-by-death transgression to these people. And it was a sure bet that whatever justice existed in these parts would side with them.

As was my practice, I prepared myself for a hostile reception. I always thought about Colonel Calvin and that one moment of overconfidence that had cost him his life. As I searched about the property (there was no side window facing me from the west side, so I could not see if there was any activity inside the house), I kept in mind the likelihood that I might be spotted first. As careful as I was, I knew hill people were skilled trackers — had to be; otherwise, they would never eat — and could sniff out and sneak up on their prey without giving any warning until it was too late. For a second I hesitated to turn my head, fearing I could look behind and find myself staring into the barrel of a scattergun. Might even be the kids I'd first encounter, but that made no difference as far as keeping up my guard. With hunting for their supper the only way they'd get fed, I didn't doubt that even the young'uns were skilled shooters — if only with a squirrel rifle, and just as quick to use their weapon on an unwelcome stranger.

It had been hot for most of the day. Of a sudden the air had taken on mugginess, foretelling the coming of some rain. It wasn't long before my clothes felt damp and sticky. I pulled off my Stetson and wiped along the sweat-band, snapping off the moisture with my forefinger.

As it was late in the season, dark would come early. And when night descended in these parts, it fell heavily. The colorful hues of twilight would soon give way to a blanket of black. I hadn't wanted to arrive so late, but the traveling conditions had been rough and unpredictable. Of one thing was certain: I could not begin my ride back to the town of Malachi, some thirty miles away, in pitch darkness. The trails would be impossible to traverse. My two options were either to backtrack to where I'd tethered my horse and camp out for the night and return to the house at daybreak, or announce my presence while there was still light. With luck, I could present myself and state my purpose for being there convincingly and perhaps be invited to spend the night and ride out with my witness come morning.

The skies were becoming thick with clouds and the night starting to deepen, and I would have to make a decision quickly. I never carried out my business after sunset. Too much of a risk that my appearance in shadow might be misinterpreted, and I could be shot full of buckshot before I could give my reason for coming. That was especially so out here in the wilderness.

This time I sought a man named Ed Chaney. He was a former bank clerk with his own checkered past. He was fired from his post for some small-time embezzling, but had been spared prosecution by a sympathetic boss — though, naturally, his services at the bank were no longer required. Unemployed and soon broke, he took up card playing, with which he had no luck. His fortune worsened in a saloon back room, where he sat with two surly poker players. Both were drunk and one accused the other of some fancy deck maneuvering: drawing four jacks against a full house. This resulted in an argument, leading to an exchange of gunfire that left the "cheat," Ridge Sutter, dead on the floor.

Apparently, Ed Chaney ran from the room in a panic while the besotted killer, Matt Simmons, was promptly arrested. Simmons claimed not to remember what happened but swore that if he had pulled the trigger on his companion, it was in self-defense. Possibly it was — only there was some question as to who had fired the first shot. Chaney could provide the answer, but he had made himself scarce and was nowhere to be found. And as Ed Chaney was the *only* witness, it was his testimony alone that would decide whether Matt Simmons, who had the reputation of being a drunkard and quick-tempered bully, would walk free of a murder charge — or walk up the scaffold to face the hangman.

If the killing truly was in self-defense, then I could not see Chaney having anything to fear. He would not have to worry about any reprisal from Matt Simmons — in fact, he'd probably find himself with a new best friend. But there was the possibility that what Chaney witnessed was outright murder — perhaps impulsive, fueled by alcohol, but a cold-blooded killing nonetheless. And Simmons's reputation around Malachi certainly lent itself to this conclusion.

These were the thoughts I had to consider. It made the difference between Ed Chaney going back with me willingly or him and maybe his "protectors" putting up resistance.

By now I had determined that Chaney must be inside the house. Maybe they all were. But I once more reminded myself that some of these hill folk possessed keen senses and might already know that I was outside nestled behind the brush, and they could be waiting for me to show myself.

I decided my safest choice was to announce myself from a distance. Instinctively,

I reached toward my gun belt where I gripped the handle of one of my .44-caliber Colt Dragoon revolvers. I didn't withdraw the pistol, but my fingers remained poised and ready to do so if the need occurred.

"Chaney, Edward Chaney!" I called out. Then I waited.

Quiet. For what seemed the longest time there was nothing but silence. A faint breeze blew by but it passed as a whisper, barely rustling the shrubbery behind which I kept out of sight. A mental timepiece ticked within my head, and still no answer to my call.

I realized that Chaney might have thought I was the law — or someone sent by Simmons to silence him. Or maybe that I was Simmons himself. He had to be made to understand that I had come neither to arrest him nor bring him harm.

Simple enough. *If* I could convince him of that.

I called out again. "Ed Chaney, I'm here to talk with you. If you like, I'll drop my gun belt and walk toward the house unarmed."

That was an option I wasn't keen on carrying out, but I had to let him know I wasn't there with threatening intent.

I glanced up toward the sky. Growing

increasingly darker as those deep gray clouds were starting to gather in bunches overhead, it looked to bring rain as I had expected. I didn't relish sitting out the night under a downpour. But I wasn't getting any response from Chaney or whoever else that might be inside the house. Not even a round of buckshot over my head to let me know my presence was not welcome. It was possible the house was empty, but my gut told me otherwise, and that was an instinct I could usually trust.

I figured they were waiting for me to show myself. Which I might have to do if my calls were not soon acknowledged. And if I did, I would have to leave my gun belt behind to keep my word that I would approach the house not heeled. While still not certain of what the outcome might be, I had to let Chaney know he could trust me.

I waited just a little longer. What decided me was a light splash of rain against my face. Then another. The raindrops were beginning to fall, pattering against the earth. If what I saw overhead was any indication, a good storm was brewing, and I was out in the open on high ground.

I cupped my hand around my mouth and shouted at the house, "I'm going to show myself, Chaney. Won't be wearing my side arms, like I said. I'm trusting that neither you nor anyone else will draw a bead on me." I waited, then added, "Would like for you to assure me of it, though."

I hoped I could rise to my feet and hold myself steady but I knew that if a scatter-gun was aimed at me, as my instincts told me was likely the case, once I came in view I'd make an easy target and wouldn't have to worry about the rain as I would be blasted dead on the ground.

I had just begun to pull from my crouch when a voice called out from inside the house, "What do you want here?"

Although the tone was brusque and not welcoming, I felt instant relief at finally being acknowledged. We had established a contact, however slight and tenuous. It lessened the chance of my being shot dead once I showed myself whole.

At least that was what I hoped.

I yelled my reply. "I told you, just want to talk . . . preferably outta the rain."

I promised not to bring my revolvers with me, yet I didn't want to leave them or my fancy leather gun belt exposed to the rain. My only option was to bury my guns and belt as deep as I was able under the protection of the shrubbery. But if the rain got heavy, the foliage wouldn't provide much cover. Still, I had no choice. I had just started to lay my Colts and gun belt under a leafy mound when I instinctively felt a presence getting nearer. I glanced out past the scrub and saw a short, stocky man, bewhiskered and bespectacled, wearing bib overalls and a cap, walking toward me through the rain. I stood up cautiously. The man stopped several feet from where I was and regarded me curiously through his rimless glasses.

"I'm Chaney," he said gruffly.

Before I could answer, a clap of thunder rumbled through the clouds. I glanced upward at the sky.

"Weather's getting rough," I said neutrally, though hinting at my preference to move our talk indoors.

"Better if'n yuh say what you have to out here," Chaney answered. His voice was flat.

The rain felt chilled in the cold evening air and, because I hadn't anticipated expecting this shift in weather, I'd left my slicker back with my horse. Chaney likewise wore no outer protection but appeared unconcerned. And why shouldn't he be? All he had to do was turn and walk back inside the house. My comfort was of no concern to him.

The rain came down harder. Judging by

the sky, it didn't look to let up any time soon. This was not an environment in which I felt comfortable speaking my piece and attempting to express the sincerity of my motive. I sensed that Chaney just wanted me to say what I had come to tell him and then be gone. It seemed doubtful he was prepared to give my words the consideration they warranted. Still, I couldn't wait any longer. I could sense his impatience.

"I've come to ask you to ride back with me to Malachi," I said.

Chaney blinked but otherwise his expression didn't change. "You the law?"

"No. I'm not the law."

Chaney carefully removed his spectacles and with his fingers began to absently wipe the moisture from lenses that looked as thick as the bottom of a whiskey bottle. It was a curious and pointless effort against the continuing rain. Yet it was also a telling gesture, onc of those that I was quick to detect in a person. He wasn't just wary of my presence. There was something he was trying to hide.

"You'd best explain," he said, refitting the eyewear over his face. The lenses were instantly splotched and streaked with raindrops through which I doubt he could see me clearly.

The weather was getting nasty, so I spoke to the point. "A man's gonna hang unless you come forward as a witness."

Chaney regarded me as if he didn't understand. But I damn well knew that he did.

"Speak in his defense," I said to clarify.

"What makes yuh think I know this man you're talkin' 'bout?" Chaney asked.

"You know him," I said bluntly. "Matt Simmons."

I waited for a reaction. Judging by his attitude I didn't think he'd say anything, but I did count on a look or a subtle gesture I could recognize. When it finally came, it wasn't quite what I was expecting. Chaney looked momentarily distressed and his body seemed to hunch as he lowered his bespectacled eyes to the water pooling around his boots. He was silent. The next sound I heard was a roll of thunder.

Finally, he raised his eyes and met my gaze. His voice was quiet, yet held a mild accusatory tone. "You kin of his?"

"No," I replied.

"Then — what's your interest?" he said, speaking more strongly.

"Professional," I said.

"Professional?"

"Yeah."

I didn't want to say more unless absolutely

necessary. Through experience I'd found it usually worked better if I could gain a measure of trust from my witness before revealing wholly who I was. Otherwise they might feel themselves cornered and prove harder to convince. "Witness Seeker" was a term still not generally known to most people. Some might even suspect it was a fancy handle for "gunslinger."

Chaney eyed me speculatively, and I could read what he was thinking. For the first time he looked nervous. He interpreted "professional" as maybe meaning "killer."

"Just so you should be knowin', mister, there's a pair of rifles aimed right at yuh," he said as he straightened his body.

That wasn't a startling revelation; I'd known it all along — or at least had a strong hunch. What I did find interesting was how he spoke the words so quietly he was almost talking in a whisper. Given the distance we were from the house, I couldn't see the point in his keeping his voice low. I myself could barely hear him. No one inside the house surely could. Curious.

"I haven't been hired by Simmons," I told him. " 'Fact is, never even met the man. Don't know him."

"Then I'm askin' yuh ag'in, why the interest?"

"All you need to know is I'm working on behalf of someone who doesn't wanta see a rope placed 'round the neck of an innocent man. Here to convince you to come back and just speak the truth."

Chaney regarded me cagily. "You got a summons?"

"Malachi won't issue a summons — 'specially when the citizens seem dead set on seeing Simmons hanged. The law's not too particular about this one."

"So you're askin' me to go with you of my own choosin'?"

I didn't have to answer him.

Chaney was quiet for what seemed a long while, as he considered what I was telling him and maybe debating if he could trust my word. I'm sure he was also wrestling with whether it was in his best interest to comply.

In the meantime, we both were getting soaked by the rain.

Finally, grudgingly, he said, "All right." He seemed suddenly agitated.

I wasn't sure what he meant.

"Well, yuh'd better come inside," he said in a grumble. "Otherwise we'll both catch our death." He removed then refitted his spectacles back onto his face, squinted his eyes through the thick lenses, and glanced about, searching. "Take it yuh didn't walk up here. Where's your mount?"

"Back aways," was all I would tell him.

"Can't give it shelter," Chaney informed me. "Don't have no barn."

I nodded.

I knew my horse would be fine — and protected from the weather where he was. Not to mention safe from these hill inhabitants who conceivably might consider horse meat a tasty supper. Put me at a bit of a disadvantage, being at a distance from my mount, but I was harboring the hope I wouldn't need a quick getaway.

I did say, "I'd like to bring along my side irons. Don't wanta chance 'em getting rusted out in this rain."

Chaney nodded slightly. "Yeah, all right. Just keep 'em holstered and carry the belt in both hands to the house where they can see yuh." He paused. "Keep in mind those rifles are gonna be followin' yuh till you and me get ourselves indoors."

Again the tone in his voice was odd. Maybe it was just in my imagination, but it almost sounded as if he were speaking to protect me.

It felt good to be out of the rain and sitting next to a warm fire provided by the wood stove — which looked to be the only luxury the family enjoyed. Chaney even gave me a swig of powerful corn whiskey right from the jug that did a fine job heating up my insides.

His "protectors," on the other hand, made me a mite uncomfortable. There was an old man pushing back and forth on a rickety rocking chair, two scrawny adolescent boys, and one plain-faced but not wholly unattractive girl. She had to be all of twelve and was dressed in the same worn denim material as her brothers, none of whom uttered a sound beyond odd, muted giggles, but who frequently pierced me with squinty-eyed stares. Eyes that looked permanently narrowed, as if from gazing up into sun-bright skies for too long. It was clear not one of them had ever had a day of schooling.

While the boys' long-barreled rifles weren't directed at me, the guns never left their sides. I had to keep my own weapons on the table they used for eating, next to their mess of sloppy supper dishes. Not only did I not like having my side arms at a distance, I wasn't keen on having those two feeble-minded boys paw my guns and fancy leather belt with their filthy hands. I was mighty particular about my possessions.

But there wasn't much I could say without running the risk of insulting their "hospitality." I knew they wouldn't take kindly to being told to mind their manners.

Besides, I had to stay focused on why I was here.

Chaney remained standing, sipping on a cup of coffee that had been brewed atop the stove. I would have preferred if he'd been sitting. I never felt comfortable having to look up at the person I was talking to, and that was especially so in this setting. I had a feeling Chaney detected my unease and wasn't about to oblige me by taking a chair. I sensed he might be testing me to see if I could be taken at my word. He still might believe I'd been sent by Matt Simmons to silence him.

If that doubt was still swimming around inside his brain, it likely would prove difficult to convince him otherwise.

"You wanta know the truth?" Chaney finally said, emphasizing his words. "I can't rightly recall who fired first."

That wasn't the answer I was hoping for. Chaney admitting his ignorance in the matter made my job a whole lot tougher.

"It's a fact," he said, heaving a breath. "Thought about it some . . . but reckon my mind's gone a-blank."

"In that case, Simmons is gonna hang," I said pointedly.

"Don't got no love for Simmons," Chaney said with a reflexive tightening of his jaw. "Don't even know the man outside of that night. 'Fact, as I remember, it was him that took most of my money."

"No reason to let an innocent man swing," I said.

Chaney gave me a hard look. "I told yuh . . . I don't recall. And it ain't nowhere near right to let a guilty man go free, neither."

"You aiming more in that direction?" I asked him. By now I realized I was starting to tread into marshy territory.

"Can't say. Can't recollect." Chaney took a quick sip of his coffee then walked over and tossed the rest into the stove, the splash momentarily weakening the flames. "Best I could do for yuh is toss a coin."

"You were gambling that night, too," I said.

Chaney just shrugged.

I'd run into this type of situation before — where the witness swore he had no memory of the crime. It provided a convenient "out" that I could neither prove nor disprove. Whether it was true in this instance, I couldn't determine. I could go by my gut feeling, but while I usually put faith in my hunches when it came to crimes of less severity, I didn't feel quite so confident when a man's life was in question. I needed to know definitely. Or as definitely as Chaney was willing to say.

Per the arrangement I'd made with Matt Simmons's sister, for which I'd been paid half the fee, balance on delivery, I was expected to bring Ed Chaney back with me, even if it was only for him to declare his memory loss before the court, where perhaps he might be "encouraged" to remember through the efforts of Simmons's legal counsel. But if he had nothing to offer, as he was claiming, it wasn't going to be easy to persuade him to ride alongside me back to Malachi.

Since I'd been paid well, I even considered offering him a cash incentive. I debated the idea and decided that such an inducement would be my last resort.

Chaney didn't seem particularly troubled by his lack of recall. Unfortunately, I could well understand it. Matt Simmons meant nothing to him, whether he was guilty of cold-blooded murder or innocent by reason of self-defense. As for Simmons himself, I'd quickly learned, from the few Malachi residents whom I'd overheard talking in saloons, that he was a miserable and mean-spirited person. His cruel disposition caused me to wonder why his sister, who struck me as a kindly, demure lady, would go to the trouble to hire me and pay me an admirable sum to help her brother's case. I reckoned it had to do with family responsibility. Or maybe the disgrace of having her brother publicly hanged.

Chaney cleared his throat. "So you see, Mister . . . Uh, you never did say what your name was."

"No, I didn't," I replied straightly.

Chaney gave me a peculiar look. Once more I had aroused his suspicions, but I had no other recourse. When it came to my business, for practical reasons, I never offered my name. If pressed, I'd allow them to refer to me as "Seeker."

He waited a bit before he resumed what he was saying. "As I was tellin', there ain't no point in my goin' back to Malachi with you. Nothin' I can say would make a difference."

I exhaled a slow breath and decided to play my trump card.

"Might a hundred dollars sway you?"

Chaney again regarded me with a suspicious glint in his eye. But he didn't say anything. The room fell silent; the only

44

sound to be heard was the steady squeaking of the rocker where the old man sat.

"A hundred dollars. Straight cash," I repeated.

Chaney turned and looked long and hard at the others, particularly the old man. He kept his gaze directed on him for what seemed a long time. I started to get a queer, uneasy feeling as my brain played out an unsettling thought.

"You got that hundred dollars on you?" Chaney asked as he pivoted his head back toward me.

I took particular note of how he asked the question. His voice sounded a bit tense.

"Nearby. Part of it," I replied, which of course was a lie. I had five hundred dollars stuffed into the pocket of my trousers. But that was absolutely the last thing I was about to admit.

"Seems a smart move not to walk into a situation you're unsure of with money in your pocket," I added.

Chaney gave a slight nod. "Reckon so."

That was when the old man finally talked. He stopped rocking in his chair and edged his upper body forward. He was a skinny weasel, but a threatening presence nonetheless. He spoke very slowly and his words came out in a rasp. "Kept it with your horse,

45

I figger?"

Even the three kids were beginning to look eager, as if they'd been starved and were just told that a large supper was being laid out on the table for them. I trusted them no more than I did their pa. Instinctively, my eyes crossed the room to the table where my two Colts lay.

"Hunnert bucks y'say?" the old man said.

The offer wasn't intended for him so I paid him no mind.

The old man scratched the whiskers on his chin as he squinted at Chaney. It was as if some private message was being exchanged between the two. Kind of like the feeling I had got before.

I could no longer hear the rain pelt against the roof of the house; it had either tapered or ceased altogether. I glanced out the far window. It was pitch black outdoors. The light inside the shack was dim and muted, provided by the kerosene lamp resting on a small table next to where the old man sat in his suddenly still rocker.

I spoke against my better judgment.

"Too dark to go out now," I said directly to Chaney. "Come sunup, you can give me your decision. You agree to ride out with me and I'll pay you fifty tomorrow and the other fifty once we get to Malachi. I assume you have a horse."

Chaney shook his head. "Sold it."

I looked at him blankly. He might be telling the truth, but how could I know for sure?

Chaney could read my doubt.

"Yeah," he said, at once exhaling a regretful sigh. "Needed quick cash and took the offer of a horse buyer who came through these parts. Didn't figger I'd be needin' a horse since . . . Well, I wasn't plannin' on goin' anywhere any time soon."

I noticed how his gaze flickered toward the old man.

"Kinda makes it rough," I muttered.

"Reckon it does," Chaney agreed, leveling his bespectacled gaze back at me.

"Not easy getting through these parts," I said.

Once again I cast my eyes on my revolvers. The two young boys sat just across from them. Unless their reflexes were as slow as the dull expressions they had pasted on their faces, it would be a gamble — a longshot play against the house — to try and rush across the room and make a grab for the pistols. I wasn't too concerned about Chaney — I figured I could get by him easy enough. He wasn't that close to me and seemed slow and lumbering. But the old man had his rifle stretched across his lap

47

with one hand slowly caressing the stock, the other closed around the barrel, his fingers pumping against the metal. He was sending me his own message. His daughter sat on the floor next to his rocker, her position reminding me of a dog resting beside its master. She looked half-asleep and shouldn't be difficult to deal with.

But it was never wise to underestimate.

Chaney spoke up. "Maybe we can still work somethin' out."

I gave my head a shake. "Can't double up. Like I said, the trail's too treacherous." I paused before adding, "But I'm sure you know that."

"Well, then I guess there ain't nothin' more for us to talk 'bout," Chaney said heavily. He gave me a strange look. He seemed uneasy, and this attitude made me curious since it seemed all the cards were in his favor.

"But no sense *you* ridin' out tonight," he added. "Can't offer yuh much by way of comfort. Ain't no adequate sleepin' arrangement, as you can rightly see. But you're welcome to stretch out on the floor." He turned toward the old man. "Ain't that so, Henry?"

The old man just nodded and tossed Chaney and me a miserable look.

"And if'n you like, one of the kids here can fetch your horse and bring it into the yard," Chaney offered.

Yeah, I thought. I was sure they'd be happy to do that, and in the meantime search out the saddle bag, where they probably thought I'd left the money. I sat quiet. I wasn't about to agree to his suggestion, but if I told him just to leave my horse be, they'd know for certain I was suspicious of their motives.

I was tired, true, and I doubted I'd find my way back to where I'd left my horse in the total darkness that blanketed this part of the country. But my gut was rolling at a fever pitch. I knew the moment I shut my eyes, I stood a good chance of getting my throat slit. My mistake had been mentioning the money. I should have gambled and waited until daylight.

These people weren't going to let me leave until they first checked my person for the cash. I suspected that, as slow-witted as Chaney's friends appeared, they were dubious about my claim the money was with my horse. Five hundred dollars would be a mighty tempting sum of money to these people. My life to them wasn't worth a fraction of what I had folded in my pocket. Easier to dump me somewhere deep in the bush and let nature take its course on my remains.

If I stayed the night, it promised to be a long one. I couldn't allow myself to fall asleep, and even awake, I would have to stay watchful and alert. I didn't trust the old man or his kin not to attempt a move at even the slightest suggestion that I was getting drowsy.

I didn't much care for the quiet that insinuated itself into the house like some creeping plague, especially since the only sounds that reached my ear were the deep, raspy breathing of the old man whose crinkled eyes remained steadily focused on me, the continuous squeak of his rocker, and the occasional mournful howl of wind trying to penetrate the feeble framing of the house. The combination of these sounds was most discomforting.

"Think I'll just sit up for a spell, maybe have some of that coffee," I finally said in an attempt to break the silence.

"Ain't tuckered out after your long ride?" Chaney queried with another of his curious looks.

I suspected he was wise to me. He could see that I didn't trust any of them — and no lie would convince Chaney otherwise. And as simple as his hill friends were, I'm sure even they — especially the old man — could read into my doubts. To their eyes, I was helpless, and they could make their move at any time. The way it looked, there wouldn't be much chance for me. Physically I was certain I could subdue any of them one-on-one, but they wouldn't be looking at a fair fight. The extent of their struggle with me would be a simple finger tug on the trigger of a rifle.

For the moment my only defense was not to show any hint of apprehension. Even if they possessed the slightest idea that I might be able to protect myself, it was an advantage I wanted to maintain.

Chaney's gaze rarely veered from me. I reckoned he was waiting for me to start to doze, give in to a shut-eye that, under different circumstances, I would have surrendered to. I don't know if it was the fatigue setting in, but catching those eyes focused on me, I gradually fell victim to another strange and troubling thought.

I made sure my face didn't reflect my concern over this disquieting, if as-yet unsubstantiated revelation, but Ed Chaney seemed to interpret what I was thinking. I caught his expression. It hadn't changed in any definite way . . . except for the almost imperceptible shifting of his eyes behind those thick spectacles. Something had connected between us.

He slowly started to rise from his chair, his stare as leveled on me as mine was on him.

I felt the urge to speak before Chaney did, but I resisted. I sensed he had the need to come clean. And when the words finally came, he delivered them not dramatically but in a flat, impassive tone of voice.

"Reckon yuh figgered it out by now," he said.

"Shoulda figured it out sooner," I said in return.

"Done what hadda be done," Chaney said unemotionally, without any hint of regret or apology.

I played it a little rough. "To your way of thinking."

He paused before acknowledging. "Yeah, to my way of thinkin'."

I was starting to understand the reason for his hesitation. And if there had been any doubt, all I needed to do was shift my gaze to Henry and his boys and catch the glint of greed in their eyes.

"A lotta money was sittin' on the table that night," Chaney offered pensively.

I was quiet. He looked at me with an expression that seemed to demand I say something.

Finally, I obliged. "What about Simmons?"

Chaney gave me a half smile. "Passed out drunk. But I was starin' at all that crumpled cash and knew it could solve a whole lotta my troubles."

"Maybe bring you some, too," I couldn't resist saying, even as a knot started to grip at my belly, a growing apprehension at what this confession might lead to.

Chaney ignored my remark.

When he next spoke, his words came in a low mutter. "Could use that hundred dollars you was talkin' 'bout."

The hundred-dollar incentive I'd offered was worth little more than two bits in the pocket, and I knew it. And Chaney knew that I knew it. He'd pretty much admitted he had killed Ridge Sutter and grabbed the money from the card table.

I was gathering a suspicion but couldn't know for certain what he'd done with the cash. All I did know was that he seemed mighty eager to add another easy hundred to his poke.

And it had already been established to my way of thinking that Chaney and his hill protectors weren't going to be too particular how they collected.

I nodded directly at him and spoke with a bravado I somehow managed to muster. "Deal still stands."

Chaney's eyes shifted over to the old man, who just kept watching and rocking in his chair with an empty expression, without saying anything, still caressing his rifle.

"Means nothing to you that an innocent man's gonna swing?" I next said.

Chaney didn't answer. He plainly didn't give a damn.

The cards were face up on the table. I was a dead man. Made no difference whether I willingly handed over the money in my possession. I now knew too much. More than I expected or cared to learn under the circumstances.

"I'm not the law —" I started to say.

"Already made that clear," Chaney interjected.

I finished. "But people know where I was headed."

Chaney bit his lower lip. "Yeah?"

I answered with a slow, deliberate — and completely untruthful — nod.

Chaney looked momentarily uncertain before he came back with, "You're bluffin'."

I forced my face not to change expression.

"Trail ain't easy to find," Chaney then said.

"I found it," I told him.

Chaney's jaws looked to tighten before he said, "So . . . we just move on."

"Haven't so far," I countered.

"No need . . . up till now."

"Can't do much spending . . . not holed up in these hills."

"No . . . reckon that's a truth."

"Been wondering about that," I said as I tugged at my earlobe. Perhaps interpreted by Chaney as a meaningful gesture, as he seemed to be watching each of my moves with distinct interest.

Of course I was watching him, too, though I hoped with more subtlety, altering my gaze occasionally so not to appear too obvious. I took note of the restlessness starting to grip Chaney. That, together with the odd behavior he had exhibited from the beginning, told me plenty, and it was no longer mere guessing on my part. Whatever money he'd stolen from that card game was no longer in his possession. The questions I had asked myself were answered, the pieces fitting together nice and neat. Why had these hill folk taken Chaney in so willingly? Why had they protected him? Why did Chaney ask me inside when he could just as easily have shooed me away? Why did he really want that paltry hundred dollars I'd offered him, and why did he ask for it so that the others could not hear?

It all became clear. For a reason I could not understand, Chaney owed these people — and had paid them from the money he had taken the night of the killing of Ridge Sutter. He himself was penniless.

So as I figured it, he'd satisfied a debt, killed a man in the process, and now, in a strange sort of way, was as much of a prisoner to these people as I was myself.

Chaney cast me a look — a quick flickering of his eyes, but telling in its intent. Once again he had reached into my thoughts. It was my understanding of the situation that he had been waiting for. He began to take slow, casual steps across to the table on which my weapons lay, which the dirt-grimed hands of the two simpleton boys were fondling. While his move struck me as curious . . . in those next moments before anything actually happened, everything became clear — and I was ready.

Chaney grabbed one of my pistols and tossed it toward me. I caught the Colt in both hands, slamming the metal into my gun hand. I twisted my upper body as I rose from the chair, aimed and fired twice in quick succession. Both of the boys fell dead, dropping like stones.

Chaney held onto the second gun and made his own move on Henry. But the old man did a strange thing. Before he died, head flung back with a bullet in his neck, he'd swung the rifle he had been holding over to the daughter I had assumed had been dozing. She suddenly popped open her eyes, twisted her mouth into a grimace, and tugged on the trigger, blowing a big hole through Chaney's midsection. To Chaney's credit, either intentionally or in reflex, he got off his own shot, and the girl sighed before she died with a bullet in her brain, perishing with a look of wonderment forever locked in her eyes.

Kinda sad, actually. Don't know why I thought it, but that expression should have been reserved for the kiss from her first beau — not an acknowledgment of her young death.

Chaney groaned and dropped flat, his body holding still only for a moment before excruciating pain set in, and he writhed about on the floor, hands clutching at his gut.

He spoke in a gasp, expectorations of blood accompanying his words. He was rightly scared, and what he said came in a panic. "My God! Belly wound. Ain't gonna make it."

I knew that to be true. It was unfortunate, hard for a man to accept that he's going to die. But what troubled me most was that my work had ended. His dying guaranteed I would not be paid the balance of my fee. That was hard for *me* to accept.

Yet . . . maybe it wasn't totally finished. I might still see a payment for my efforts. The odds were good he knew where the stolen money was hidden. There wasn't much to bargain with at this point other than my offering Chaney the option of a quick death. Otherwise the man was looking at a misery that might go on for hours if a well-placed bullet did not provide a swift *adiós*.

His eyes grew large. "You can't let me die!"

Wasn't much else I could do for him.

His voice was desperate, pleading. "What more d'yuh want? Told yuh all that matters."

The son of a bitch *had* saved my life, but after what I'd endured, I found it hard to offer much by way of comfort or solace.

"Not quite," I said bluntly.

"You . . . saw how it was," he said. "Couldn't do no more. Hadda go along with 'em . . . long as necessary. Till the time was right."

"You coulda come clean when we were

outdoors," I said stiffly. "None of this had to happen."

"And you . . . you'da been dead." Chaney managed to chuckle balefully. "Rifle barrel aimed straight at your chest."

I dismissed any notion of expressing gratitude. It wasn't difficult for me to determine why Chaney hadn't allowed me to be killed. He'd had no personal interest in my well-being. He just wanted to make his own getaway from these people, and hoped that I would be able to help him.

"One . . . one of 'em kept watch on me all the time I been here," he said. "I knew they was waitin' to kill me. Stalled 'em by tellin' 'em more money was comin' . . . only never counted on it bein' someone like you that showed up."

"You had to be sure I wasn't the law."

Chaney gave his head a quick, painful nod.

My voice was cold, my tone flat, as I remained practical. "And now I ride away empty-handed."

"They'da been after us. We — we couldn'ta gone far on just one horse. Hadda hold out till sunup. But saw how they was lookin' at yuh. Hadda make the move 'fore they killed yuh for that money yuh said you brung."

I kept my eyes on Chaney.

"Then maybe you would have killed them anyway to get at my poke," I conjectured.

"Dammit, I saved your life!" he blurted.

I noticed how a sly look etched across Chaney's face.

"You sayin' I still *owe* yuh?" he rasped.

"Depends. Could take you days to die," I said flatly. But I doubted that would be the case. The closer I observed his wound, the more I could see that Chaney's time would soon be up. That girl's shot had done its damage. I watched gouts of blood that seemed to gurgle from his belly wound. She wasn't doing him any deliberate favor when she fired her gun, but in the long run, I reckoned she had. Not that I was about to tell him that. I needed him to think his agony would go on a lot longer.

A look of anger twisted Chaney's features.

I drew a breath. "Can't say I envy you what's comin'."

Chaney struggled with his words. "You son of a bitch. You — you're as corrupted as they was."

I took another breath but spoke easily. "Reckon I'll never know for certain that you weren't planning to toss me outdoors for buzzard meat. But for whatever reason, didn't turn out that way. Now I'm the one surrounded by dead folk, and you're lying here waiting to join 'em in maybe what might be the Hereafter."

"Dammit, what is it you want?" Chaney said through clenched teeth.

"You're sure 'nuff a dead man, so you can't bargain for your life," I told him outright. "But since it's not gonna do you any good in what time you've got left, might as well give your soul an even break by compensating me for my troubles."

Chaney's lips tightened. "Never put no worth on my soul."

In a strange way I admired his truthfulness. To my way of thinking, even the staunchest nonbeliever had to give some consideration in those final moments as to what might be waiting for him. I could tell Chaney really didn't give a damn.

I clicked back the hammer on my Colt Dragoon revolver and lifted it so that Chaney could see it. I could tell by his expression that he understood what I was offering him.

His voice was growing weak. "Can't tell yuh . . . 'cause I don't know."

He grasped hard at his bleeding belly as his torso tensed suddenly and then his legs kicked out as his body squirmed. I admit it was a distressing sight, though I wouldn't express my upset to Chaney.

He was dying fast.

He had to know his time was limited. Still, he managed to push out what sounded like a mocking laugh. "Sure . . . and you can ride back and tell the law it was me that shot down Sutter and took the money. Ain't much chance in that now, is there?"

"Nope," I said with a sigh of resignation. "And reckon with my word being all that stands between Simmons and a hemp necktie, his fate's pretty well sealed." I sighed again. "Still, could at least make my efforts worthwhile."

Chaney sat bolt upright with a suddenness that plain startled the bejesus out of me.

"You got all you're gettin' outta me!" he exclaimed.

And with those words, his eyes rolled white. He fell back and died, staring sightlessly into his private eternity.

I had saved myself a bullet.

I needed the next several minutes to recover from my ordeal. It wasn't just the prospect of my coming so close to death that disturbed me; it was also that I had never before reacted with such cruel harshness, as I just had with a dying man. I reckoned I believed him about the intentions of Henry and his kin, but there still remained some doubt I couldn't entirely erase. In a way that was good, since it provided me with a justification for my actions.

I got up and walked over to the table. I wedged the revolver I held into its holster and strapped on my gun belt, which pocketed my second gun. Then I afforded myself my first good look at the carnage strewn about me.

A houseful of dead people. I'd been around corpses before, but never so many, and never in such a remote surrounding. An eerie feeling came over me. Just moments before there had been five people sitting in this room, not folks I wanted to be around, but each had been breathing and had a heartbeat. Now all were dead and the room was quiet. Just as quiet as it had become outside now that the storm had lifted and a calm settled over the land. I couldn't help but absorb the overwhelming silence and stillness, especially since I'd be sitting out the night with all these bodies, waiting for the first rays of sunrise so I could find my way back to my loyal horse and leave.

I had to occupy my time somehow, so I decided to search the cabin to see if I could find the money. It was doubtful that much

— if any — of it had been spent. But even as I did my cursory seeking, I knew the undertaking to be fruitless. If those people really had taken the cash from Chaney in receipt of a debt, they would never leave it in these sparse surroundings where Chaney could easily find it. They were simple, primitive folk, but probably not stupid when it came to money.

It was more likely they'd buried it somewhere on the property — or found some other significant hiding place, like maybe stuffing it into the hollow of a tree trunk. But with all the trees in the area, that, too, would require more searching than I felt capable of.

In any case, it was doubtful I would ever find the loot, even if I ripped up the terrain over the next ten years.

So when daybreak came, I saddled my horse and rode out in the damp yet refreshingly cool of the morning, my pockets empty, leaving five bodies exposed in that shack in the hills. I figured someday somebody might care enough to follow the trail I took to give them a decent burial. But whether or not that was the case, it made no matter to me.

What did trouble me was that it was now apparent an innocent man was going to

64

hang, and there was nothing I could do to prevent it. Chaney had confessed his guilt to me, but my word alone wouldn't be worth spit in a courtroom. I knew the truth, but that would be scant satisfaction to Matt Simmons's sister. Maybe if her brother hadn't achieved such a bad reputation among the townspeople . . . maybe what I could tell the citizens might hold some value.

*Maybe.*

It made no difference. It was all guess-work, and I dismissed such thoughts from my brain. What held significance was that I had failed in my task. I'd been unsuccessful before . . . and most of the time after delivering a witness, I'd ride off uncertain of the outcome. But uncertainty is a darned sight less troubling to the spirit than surety. And in this case, I knew with surety that a man would be condemned to death unjustly.

I needed to remedy my disappointment. And after a brief return to Malachi, I determined there was only the one way to do that.

A tried and true method that always produced the desired result.

Little did I know that this time my stop-over would be much different and that, once again, I would find myself riding into an uncertain and downright precarious situation.

# CHAPTER FOUR

"You ever have to gun down one of those desperados you were after?" I heard myself being asked.

I detected the eagerness in the voice, which was heavy with accent, and had likewise noticed a slight quirkiness in the speaker's manner as he prepared to broach what was foremost in his brain.

I knew where he was headed with his question even if he was mistaken in assuming that I pursued outlaws and rustlers. Sometimes desperados did fit into the equation, but they were never my purpose. But I wasn't going to correct him . . . or even oblige him with an answer. It hadn't even been a month since my Bodrie Hills ordeal, from which I came away virtually empty-handed. (Though after I explained the details, Miss Simmons was "considerate" enough not to ask me to repay the advance money — "For expenses," as she justified it.

Having come close to my own demise I refrained from expressing my "appreciation" for her kind generosity.)

Anyway, I was in no mood to talk about my profession. The man sitting with me in my hotel room wasn't a friend, not that it would have made any difference. He was just someone I'd started talking to while idling over a few afternoon drinks in the cantina. An *hombre* who simply had appeared at my table, *sombrero* in hand, and introduced himself as Francisco Velasquez. He seemed inoffensive at the time, and I found him amusing and someone with whom I had no objection passing away a few lazy hours on this hot afternoon. We conversed easily . . . until he invited himself back to my room. I tried to remain cordial, but there was only so much I would acknowledge, and that was little indeed; most of what I might reveal would not be expressed through words. I merely gave an enigmatic half smile that I could see frustrated my companion and further whetted his curiosity. He would likely interpret the smile I provided as a "yes," but he wouldn't know for sure.

He cleared his throat and shifted uncomfortably on the patterned cushion-backed chair in my hotel room.

I finished packing my essentials into the valise, then turned to him, glancing at his still-expectant features through the late-afternoon sunlight filtering through the single window.

"Seems everyone wants to know the worst about my business," I said.

He tried to justify his curiosity. "It is just that it is a, how you say, unusual type of work that you do, *Señor.*"

"Man makes his living however he knows best," I said.

"Yes, I understand. Best for *himself,*" he replied cleverly.

I nodded my reply.

He was a walnut-skinned, tight-featured Indian, square-jawed, with prominent features: narrow dark brown eyes set wide apart, a straight aquiline nose, a broad mouth, and wide-gapped front teeth. I assumed he was either a *Tzotzil* or *Tzeltal,* perhaps come to Santa Rosina from the Chiapas highlands. He gave me a queer look, but I could tell what he was thinking. As happened with most people, the judgment he had passed upon me could not have been more wrong. I was a witness seeker. Not a bounty hunter. I got paid for bringing them in alive, not with their corpses draped over a saddle. If killings did occur, as had happened in the Bodrie Hills, it was never part of the plan.

Call it a quirk in my personality — or maybe an odd pride — but I never contradicted what these Mexicans imagined about me or how they often misjudged my work. If thinking I was a bounty hunter gave them a moment or two of excitement, who was I to let them think different? Life could get pretty damned dull in these dusty border towns.

There was one final detail to take care of, and this would surely set my companion's imagination afire. I had to prepare my guns. I carried two, in a dual-holstered gun belt. They were attractive specimens, ivory-handled, single-action .44-caliber Colt Dragoons, each with a gleaming silver-plated cylinder and barrel that I cleaned and polished frequently. I'd never had the need to draw them during my Mexico stopovers, but just the fact that I was packing a pair of well-maintained firearms gave rise to more than a few eyebrows. Part of the mystique I carried, I suppose.

I deliberately avoided looking at Francisco, but it didn't matter. I could feel his gaze sliding after me, following carefully and inquisitively as I went into the cabinet to fetch my guns, laid barrel to barrel on the inside counter surface. His tentative re-action provided me with my own amuse-ment, a momentary humor I rarely encoun-tered in my line of work. I was surprised he stayed with me throughout the cleaning and inspecting of my side irons — but he did, and as I progressed, his curious expression gradually gave way to what might be inter-preted as subtle fascination. I maybe should have offered him a drink of whiskey from the bottle on the corner table, a reward for his patience in sitting with me through the hot hours of the afternoon, but once I was set, both Colt revolvers holstered in my silver-beaded leather gun belt, I ushered Francisco from the room, locked the door behind us, offered a pleasant *adiós,* and left him standing downstairs in the lobby. I sauntered out onto the street to keep an ap-pointment I anticipated would prove more appealing than spending any more time with the little Mexican.

My destination: a little dust-washed can-tina where I was to meet a delightful diver-sion named Constancia.

Just about seventy miles south of the Rio Grande in this border town known as Santa Rosina was where I liked to relax after my work was done. The village provided me with a sense of isolation even though I could always be found there by anyone seeking my services — and, I confess, most often I could be found in the company of an accommodating *señorita.* I appreciated the Mexican sunshine, the liquor, and the music provided by the mariachi, most particularly their haunting strains of *La Paloma,* which never failed to put me in a reflective mood. The players always knew when and where to find me when I was in Santa Rosina. Like clockwork, come sunset I would be seated outside the cantina at my usual table, blanketed by the shade provided by the wide canvas overhang, sipping at my drink. The musicians in their white pants and shirts, each wearing a straw hat, would, as if by magic, suddenly appear through the deepening shadows of approaching nightfall and serenade me with their songs.

In years past the mariachi had earned good wages providing entertainment at celebrations at the haciendas of wealthy Mexican landowners. But following the revolution, most were now forced to travel from town to town to eke out their living. The group that had found its way into Santa Rosina looked poor and well traveled when I first met them. They were tired and dusty, yet the music they produced in no way reflected their despair. Unlike other patrons who would humiliate these gallant musicians by tossing them coins, which they would then have to retrieve from out of the dirt like peasants, I would lay my *pesos* respectfully onto the table and one would step forward gratefully to accept my contribution. It was then that I would find my way to the *señorita* of choice with whom I would share that night, my desire fortified by the potency of the local beverages, yet my urges tempered by the romantic music of the mariachi.

Because I was a Yankee, I was appealing to the girls of Santa Rosina — all of whom equated the United States with great wealth. Although Santa Rosina was situated less than a hundred miles from the border, sitting just east of the Chihuahuan Desert, to most of the people of the village it was as if a whole different world existed north of the Rio Grande.

It took me a while to understand their thinking, but after a few visits to Santa Rosina, it became clear to me. We each had our own way of how we perceived paradise. What I saw as an escape, many of the locals regarded as a type of desperation. At first I was immune to the poverty that had settled upon Santa Rosina following the revolution.

73

I saw only the remnants of the prosperity that once had existed there. But, as with the mariachi, many of the people of the village had also suffered loss. I soon became acquainted with these unfortunate circumstances, which was why I made it a point of returning to Santa Rosina once I was finished with an assignment. Whether my mission was a success or not, I found a peaceful respite in the village, and I was glad to show my gratitude by spending my American dollars on the various pastimes Santa Rosina had to offer, which, though limited, suited my needs.

I walked outside into the glare of the late-afternoon sun, its still-shimmering whiteness reflecting against the adobe walls of the cafés and merchant shops that populated the main *calle* of the village. I was well known in Santa Rosina. Hardly had I stepped from my hotel before those locals out and about acknowledged me either with expansive greetings in Spanish or simply by flashing friendly, toothy grins.

I welcomed their friendship, but I also recognized the need to maintain a careful distance from these people. By nature I was a loner. I wasn't always successful in my efforts to express this preference, as with Francisco, whom I soon discovered had followed me outdoors that afternoon like a loyal dog trailing its master. I was still learning that there were those in the village who had a tendency to misinterpret my generosity and cordiality as an invitation to become my steady companion. I had to politely discourage anyone from getting *too* close — not the least because I suspected the camaraderie they offered had more to do with benefiting from the *dinero* they presumed I carried on my person.

Fortunately, this had yet to become a serious problem. My past and the details of my profession remained mysterious enough for most not to become too assertive. No one in Santa Rosina took offense when I stated my desire to be left alone.

Even the *señoritas* who helped to fill some lonely hours understood that our affairs were to remain casual, that I was not interested in pursuing a commitment. I enjoyed physical intimacy (after all, I was a man who frequently spent long periods alone), but just as often my need was simply for the companionship of a female. We would sit in a café, have a drink or a meal, and talk — yet at other times we might scarcely share a word between us. I didn't think it appropriate to discuss my work with a woman, so most conversation revolved around the village itself.

In this way, I gained an education about the history of Santa Rosina and some of its people. I came to learn about the revolution that had affected much of the country. I was told about General Diaz and how officials betrayed suspected traitors to the general's armies to demonstrate their loyalty to *El Presidente.* I discovered that, besides poverty, there existed much bitterness in Santa Rosina. A large number of the people who now resided there had fled from other villages in fear of being wrongfully accused as sympathetic to the revolution. In the fury of such a rebellion, this was not an uncommon occurrence. Punishment was swift and harsh, and the tragedy was that in some instances the innocent numbered equally among the guilty as those who fell before the rifles of a firing squad.

I did not know what it was about Francisco, but my initial annoyance at his shadowing presence strangely turned into gradual acceptance. Normally by this point I would be devising ways to be rid of him. Especially since he seemed to be more insistent on ingratiating himself with me than had other villagers with whom I'd made an acquaintance. My suspicions were naturally aroused at whatever might have been his intentions.

Therefore, I decided to test him. I summoned him over to the village plaza, which was normally where the women of Santa Rosina congregated with their babies under the shade of the wide, leafy trees that bordered the grounds. At this time of day the plaza was quiet, as the womenfolk had returned to their homes to await husbands who had either been out in the sun all day performing manual field labor for starvation wages or spending hours in the company of cronies under the pretense of seeking work that did not exist. Where Francisco fit into this setting I could not know. He was a mystery. He seemed *in* this environment but not necessarily *of* it.

He eagerly followed me, maintaining his obsequious manner, his wide-gapped teeth flashing against the slowly fading sunlight. I'd decided on a bold, perhaps even risky, move, but one I deemed necessary, since my curiosity had been piqued. I took out several dollars of the money in my pocket and wordlessly thrust the bills toward him. Francisco stared at the money, American currency, the cash value of which he perhaps could not determine, but still looked tempting to a poor man. After several moments, he slowly lifted his eyes toward me. My expression was grim and fixed. I would not provide even a hint beyond the obvious as to what I intended by my gesture.

So far Francisco seemed to be passing my scrutiny. He was not eager to accept the bills that were his simply for the taking. All he had to do was reach out his hand. I wouldn't have taken the money back. With my expression still firm, I looked him directly in the eye and rocked my head once in a swift, deliberate movement, encouraging him to accept my offer. His eyes narrowed, and he regarded me quizzically. Then, as if I were trying to pass him a scorpion, he backed away suddenly and gave his head a stubborn, determined shake. The look on his face was a blending of hurt and insult.

"I no want your money, *Señor,*" he said adamantly.

"I'm offering it to you," I told him with utter sincerity.

"No, *Señor,*" he muttered.

I waited a little longer to see if he might finally succumb to temptation.

Francisco studied me. "Ah, *Señor,* I see it in the way you look at me. You are suspicious. Suspicious of why I choose to be with you."

With a mild shake of my head I replied, "Not so much *you, amigo,* as your motives."

Francisco looked puzzled. "My . . . motives?"

"*Sí,*" I said.

All at once Francisco wore an expression
of enlightenment and he blurted, "Oh, motives, *Señor.* I have no motives — not how
you think."

"No?"

Francisco spoke to the point. "What I
want . . . is simply to ride with you. Learn
from you what it is that you do."

I studied the little Mexican, at the same
time trying to determine exactly what it was
he was after. I frankly didn't know how to
interpret his suggestion, yet at the same
time, I found it difficult to hide my amusement. Merely from a physical standpoint, I
doubted he could possess the endurance
oftentimes needed in my work: the long,
arduous treks across difficult, at times perilous, terrain, trekking through formidable
mountain passes; the uncertain and extreme
shifts in weather, when one minute it is so
hot you can hardly breathe, then in the next
instant the air turns so cold you almost see
the breath freeze before you.

Sudden powerful winds were always a
concern, too. They could whip up without
any warning. A strong gust from a Santa
Ana would blow a man of Francisco's slight

physique over the side of a treacherous mountain pass as if he were a bundle of straw.

And, of course, there were other considerations. Personal . . . mainly my need not to have a partner trail along beside me. I wasn't so much opposed to the companionship, especially on the lonely campouts at night when the silence could become oppressive and some conversation would be appreciated to repel intrusive thoughts and help promote sleep. My chief concern was that I retained the memory of my friend and mentor, Colonel Calvin. Despite his advice, I had grown close to him (as I know he had with me) and his death and the guilt I still endured from not being able to prevent it had affected me deeply. I was hesitant to take on the responsibility of another partner. Alone, I had only myself to be concerned about. I'd long ago decided I was satisfied with that.

Still, I could not ignore Francisco's determination. He seemed genuinely interested in learning my trade. What I did for a living was not what one might call an enviable business. The compensation varied but it was usually on the low scale — that was, if you got paid at all. Not frequently, but often enough, I delivered on my promise only to be refused the fee, with excuses given for a variety of reasons. Since I worked independently and my dealings were often with the law, what recourse did I have other than to accept the piker's word that payment would be forthcoming?

The sad fact was that my hair had grown gray waiting for many of those accounts to be settled.

Back to Francisco. I began to detect that I likely could have been misjudging him. His small, fragile appearance aside, Francisco might have been a lot tougher than I was giving him credit for. Through my travels I had come across big, burly men whose toughness lay only in their boasting. On the other hand, I'd seen mere wisps of men who were prepared to take on brutes easily twice their size. The outcome of such confrontations rarely varied, but I was impressed both by the bravery and tenacity of the underdog. So I could not make a judgment based on Francisco's size. His fortitude could easily compensate for what he might lack in physical strength.

But I knew nothing about the man. If I were to consider bringing him along on one of my quests, could he be trusted? Over the years, dealing with all sorts of characters and personalities both honorable and corrupt, I'd become skilled at forming accurate appraisals of people, and I had to admit the answer to my concern was almost immediate:

Yes, I could trust Francisco.

I nodded thoughtfully and could see the glint of expectation in Francisco's eyes.

Still, I held on to my reservations and wasn't ready to commit.

I squinted and looked solidly, intentionally, at him. Once more he grinned, his unevenly spaced teeth seeming to grind together in an expression of utter purpose, urging me to give him that one chance to ride alongside me — to allow him the opportunity to justify my trust if I decided to do so. Yes, it was a gamble, I reckoned. Still, I couldn't overlook the fact that if he was sincere in his desire, in a predicament he could prove an advantage . . . much like having an extra pair of Colt revolvers at the ready, prepared to protect my back.

But my dilemma persisted. Such a consideration went against my natural leaning, and I could not allow myself to be too quickly swayed. In all those years after my mentor Colonel Calvin was killed, I rode alone, ever mindful that those bullets that might miss me could strike the one who straddled the saddle next to mine. I didn't want to be responsible for leaving another family destitute. I knew that many of the Mexicans of Santa Rosina had large families, most with no means of supporting their brood.

If Francisco had a wife, if he had children, I could easily make my decision. He would have to find some other way to earn his livelihood. The welfare of his family would not be thrust upon my conscience because he was impulsively seeking a quick way to provide for them. If I were to take on a partner, he would have to be a man with no obligations. Someone not distracted by the need to support a family. Someone whose pay would be spent solely for his own benefit and not intended to put food on the children's supper table.

In short, someone driven by the same motivation as I was.

I invited Francisco to join me at the cantina. I ordered a glass of Mexican beer while Francisco declined a drink. He boasted to me that he never drank liquor. While I did not voice it, I was impressed; another positive attribute.

The *señorita* with whom I had planned to spend the evening, the raven-haired, dark-eyed beauty named Constancia, would arrive shortly, but there was still time for Francisco and me to have a talk.

I'd never met a man who kept his eyes so steady upon me as Francisco did as I waited for my glass of beer to be brought over. I suppose this was not a bad thing, as I interpreted his unwavering gaze as his having nothing to hide. Wandering eyes generally warned me to keep on my guard. But because Francisco's eyes were wide-set and beady and somewhat unsettling in their concentration, I still felt wary and kept my defenses up. Caution was necessary in my profession, and I reckon it had become ingrained in my everyday behavior.

"I think we would work well together, *Señor,*" Francisco finally said.

My beer had yet to come, and until it did and I had the opportunity to refresh myself, I was not quite ready to engage in our conversation.

Francisco seemed impatient. It showed more on his person than in his words, in a sudden if subtle restlessness. Again this presented itself as a test, as I saw it. Patience was another requirement in my work. If he was of a restive nature, Francisco would be of no value to me — or, ultimately, to himself. I wasn't sure if it was intentional or not, but I had begun to keep a mental track of his virtues and vices.

Finally, my drink arrived. I chugged back

a long swallow. The beer had a powerful flavor and was potent, but satisfying to my taste. Francisco looked at me, tilted his head toward the narrow *calle* where one or two *sombreros* were lowered, and said with a barely concealed disgust, "The peasants of San Rosita should soon be waking from their siesta."

I didn't comment, but found it intriguing how he referred to his fellow Mexicans as "peasants."

I indulged myself to another healthy swallow of beer.

"Kinda late in the day for napping," I then said, speaking the words with no particular inflection.

Francisco spoke firmly. "Not in this village."

I gazed at him. I understood what he meant. For many in Santa Rosina there was little else to do but sleep. There was virtually no work, and with money so scarce among the villagers, there was rare occasion for entertainment or diversion. I also now understood why Francisco had said what he had about the "peasants." He wanted me to know that he did not want to be counted among their number; he was not to be looked upon like other men of the village. While many had simply surrendered to their circumstances, losing ambition or settling for day labor, Francisco wanted me to understand that he kept alert and was seeking new opportunities.

Once more he said, grinning amiably, "You and I would work well together."

"We would?" I replied vaguely.

Francisco nodded his head vigorously.

I gave a noncommittal shrug.

"Why do you lift your shoulder in that way?" he asked me, indicating my gesture with a sharp nudge of his head.

"Not convinced I need a partner," I said simply.

Francisco stared at me with his penetrating brown eyes.

He spoke directly. "You want me to convince you, perhaps?"

I responded with a slight, cynical smile.

Francisco's face took on a thoughtful expression as he rubbed dirt-stained fingers along his jaw.

"I don't know how I can convince you," he said.

I took a last slow sip of my beer, then slid the empty glass to the side of the table. I gestured to the waiter to bring me another.

"How do you expect me to prove to you that I am a dependable man, *Señor*?" Francisco asked with intent. "A man upon whom you can place your trust."

"Doubtful that you can," I returned.

"*Señor?*" He was requesting an explanation.

Finally, I obliged him.

"You're a Mexican," I said forthrightly.

Francisco didn't respond, though he wore a tentative look, unsure as to what I was insinuating by my blunt remark.

I did not feel it necessary to say more.

Francisco edged forward in his chair, looking to assume an aggressive posture.

"Are you saying that I cannot be trusted?" he said, quietly indignant. He gestured with an abrupt hand movement toward the street. "Perhaps is it because of what I point out about the others? That to your eyes I am as lazy and of no account as are they?"

When I still didn't speak, he said, "I assure you, *Señor,* if you have such concerns, they are unfounded."

"I regret if what I said offends you —" I started to say.

"How can I not take insult at your words?" Francisco interrupted.

I softened my tone but spoke earnestly. "I keep watch on all that goes on 'round me. As much here in Santa Rosina where I come to relax as anywhere else my travels take me. In short, I am a careful man. And I am also a suspicious man. That is how I must be. Careful and suspicious of the person I ride with, if that was to be my decision, as well as for myself."

The tension seemed to ease from Francisco, and he settled back into his chair, his gaze reaching into the distance, his expression contemplative. After a while he turned his eyes back to me and he spoke his words slowly.

"Yes," he said. "I — think I am beginning to understand, *Señor.*"

I responded with only a nod. The waiter brought over my second beer. Before I took a taste, I lifted my glass in acknowledgment of Francisco's understanding.

I'd made my point and pretty much thought that was the end of the conversation. But I was wrong. I continued to underestimate Francisco's determination.

He said, "Perhaps it might make a difference to you to know that I fought in the revolution."

His words were spoken with purpose, and he stimulated my interest, mildly.

Francisco appeared pleased that he'd gotten my attention. He offered more, coloring his words with pride. "Yes, *Señor.* And from my time participating in the revolution, I learned that a man cannot fight alone. With the type of work you do, you need a *compadre* at your side. A man on whom you can depend. And, yes, that man must also know that he can depend on *you.*"

"And . . . you see yourself as that man?" I commented, maintaining my position of doubt.

Francisco's words came with utter earnestness. "I do, *Señor.*"

Then, just moments later, before I could even decide how to respond, a strange expression came over his face. Francisco's eyes glowered, threatening to put me at my defense. They shifted away from me, veering off to the side.

And in the next instant, in a move so swift it barely had time to register with me, Francisco leaped up from his chair and pulled out a knife he'd had concealed under his shirt. He tossed the knife with such speed and precision that I heard the *whoosh* as the blade whizzed past my left ear. I heard a scream followed by a groan. I'd recovered sufficiently by then and twisted my head in time to see the body of a man stiffen with a grimace twisting his features, the knife dug deep into the chest — directly piercing the heart. A wash of crimson blossomed from the wound, spreading a pattern of blood across his white shirt. The man remained standing for only a few seconds before he dropped face forward into the dirt, the impact of his fall thrusting the knife into his body to the haft. The still, hot air shattered with screams and wailing from the women who were witness to this scene. Shaken, I remained practically oblivious to their sounds.

Instead, I looked with astonishment at my companion.

"You bring along your guns, but they do you no good when someone comes at you from behind with a knife," Francisco remarked in a calm voice.

I found it difficult to regain my composure after what might have been an attempt on my life. I confess I also felt embarrassed at having been spared a sudden death by this man whose capabilities I had questioned. I pretended not to hear his comment.

Francisco sat himself back in his chair. He looked at me, his expression fixed yet hard to decipher, then his eyes shifted beyond where I was sitting, and he stared at the fallen body for a long while before the noise, confusion, and activity heightened about the cantina and the dead man was surrounded by curious onlookers.

Finally, he said, "Do not blame yourself, *Señor*. You had no way of knowing. I, on the other hand, was expecting it."

I straightened in my chair and spoke with a deliberate calm. "You — expected it?"

"Yes," Francisco replied.

I waited for him to explain, but Francisco didn't offer anything more. Therefore, I asked him outright, "How did you know?"

He smiled at me — not a grin this time, but a subtle, clever smile that almost seemed to overwhelm the simple, peasant-like quality he had exhibited since I'd met him earlier that day. His whole attitude seemed to change.

But what I found most curious was that, after he'd tossed his knife into the man's chest, he completely disregarded his action. It was of no further significance to him. He might just have killed a chicken for supper. What I also thought intriguing was how he calmly stood up, pushed through the crowd, momentarily vanishing until he once more reappeared, wiping the blood from the blade of the knife, then resting the weapon openly and boldly in the sash tied around his waist. He had brazenly killed a man, his action was seen by many, yet he appeared to have no fear of the consequences.

"You considered me a mere *paisano,*" he said, and there was authority in his voice. "The truth is, I knew before you arrived here in Santa Rosina that there was a price put upon your head."

I suppressed my apprehension at hearing this with a frown. Francisco paused as a slight twitch edged the corner of his lips.

"I suspected the attempt on your life would be made this day," he said.

"And . . . that's why you've been following me," I deduced.

"*Sí.*"

Before I could completely collect my thoughts to ask any more questions, Francisco spoke with emphasis. "The village is no longer safe for you."

I tried to figure out what was happening. But I could only think in a blur. It was a reminder of when I was a child and came down with a fever and for days during my waking periods nothing seemed as it should. There was no reason any man in Santa Rosina would want to see me dead. I'd never had professional dealings in the village — or anywhere else in Mexico, for that matter. I tried to penetrate the confusion whirling about in my brain but couldn't come up with an answer. The best I could manage was that it had to have something to do with my work. But what precisely? I'd always taken particular care to protect myself when on assignment. Not even the witnesses themselves, those who at times traveled beside me for many miles, knew who I was. Neither my name nor where I was from, or where I would be going afterward. My identity was always a secret.

Francisco stood up abruptly.

"We should go," he said.

"The *Federales* are going to have questions," I said grimly.

Francisco looked unconcerned as he smiled. "Yes. And they will be questions I will have to answer. There won't be any problems." His next words interested me. "They will be glad to be rid of him. The dead man is a known assassin."

"Assassin?"

His voice went grave. "Yes, *Señor.*"

I gave Francisco a speculative look. "Maybe you'd better tell me just who you are and how you knew —"

Francisco spoke before I could finish.

"There will be time for that later," he replied. "For now it is best that you ready yourself to depart Santa Rosina."

The shock had begun to dissipate, though I remained disorientated by what had just happened. My head swam with questions I needed to have answered. A man had tried to kill me. Or had he? As I considered the matter, I had only Francisco's word; my

93

back had been turned at the time a blade was supposed to be thrust into me. I pivoted my head to take a studied look at the body, searching specifically for a weapon lying next to the dead man. Through a parting in the crowd I spotted none and my curiosity grew. I'd just seen the one weapon, the knife that Francisco had used to kill the man. How then could Francisco be certain of the man's intention? Yes, perhaps he recognized the man as a paid killer. Maybe he did possess prior knowledge of an attempt on my life, but those were possibilities I could not know for certain. And the question that kept winding through my brain was: Why would anyone hire an assassin to kill me? I doubted the man had a personal motive. I could not recollect ever tracking a Mexican — or an Indian, for that matter. It seemed that all of the people I had been paid to seek were white-skinned. This deepened the mystery and frustrated me further.

Before I knew it, Francisco was gone; he had disappeared amidst the confusion. I forgot about the *señorita* I was supposed to meet. I doubted Constancia would keep our appointment anyway, once she saw what was going on in the street. No girl of such reputation wanted to walk into trouble. I got up and started back toward the hotel, not a far distance, but I was careful. If what Francisco told me was true, how could I be confident that there might not be another assassin in hiding, waiting for me to pass by?

It was a strange feeling. I always kept alert and vigilant when tracking a witness, and of course I always traveled those last miles as I neared my destination with a heightened sense of caution. But what I felt this afternoon was more of a sense of trepidation. I justified this uncertainty as I realized it was *I* who might have become the hunted.

The witness seeker becoming the one sought. In a strange way I also came to more clearly understand the apprehension of the people I searched for in my work. The fear they must have felt at my approach, not knowing who I was or why I had come for them. Was I friend or foe? The oftentimes great lengths they went to protect themselves.

I kept watchful as I walked the final steps along the cobbled *calle* to the hotel, keeping an eye out for any suspicious looks that might come my way. That would be easy for me to detect with everyone's attention now focused on the activity outside the cantina. I would be of no interest to anyone — except for that someone who might ·want me dead. Although many in the village recognized me, at the moment I was merely a passerby. I kept my glances subtle, my stride sturdy and confident, and did not notice anything among those people who I passed that gave me reason for concern.

I felt more at ease once I stepped inside the lobby of the hotel. However, the desk clerk, Manuel, seemed nervous and impatient behind the counter. He was a fidgety man at any time, but right now he seemed particularly restless. He could hear activity out on the street and demanded to know the cause of the commotion. He'd scrambled out from behind the counter and practically jumped on me when I entered the lobby. I simply told him that a man had been killed. He pressed me for details, but I lied and said I didn't know anything more; I'd simply been out for a stroll and hadn't seen what happened. He looked doubtful; then, quickly, his features shifted into an expression of distress. He took hold of my arm with a firm grip. I politely removed his hand.

"Such a thing is not common in our village," he said, his voice quavering slightly. His eyes grew large and he swallowed past what must have been a lump in his throat. "Rarely is a man killed unless . . ." He halted long enough to cross himself. "Perhaps — it is a return to the revolution."

I'd heard this from him before and said nothing to relieve his panic. There was no point. The revolution had never reached Santa Rosina, which was why so many had fled to the village from other parts of the country. Manuel should have known that, but it had occurred to me a while back that he himself might have been one of those thrust from his home. Perhaps he harbored memories of that tragic time. That would be reason enough for a man to live in fear.

What I knew for a certainty was that his worry would have been better justified had he known that the man whose forearm he had clutched could pose a more real threat to his well-being than a phantom army. If someone truly intended to see me dead, it was unlikely a nervous desk clerk would be spared to later serve as a witness.

"Has anyone come asking for me since I've been away?" I asked Manuel. I spoke casually so as not to add to Manuel's distress — or betray my own tentativeness.

He looked perplexed by my question. "Someone you were expecting, *Señor*?"

"No, someone just asking," I said simply.

Manuel cast another anxious glance outside. There was still a lot of noise coming from up the street. Then he wagged his small head from side to side and answered quickly.

"No. No one has come asking for you."

I was careful not to alter the inflection in my voice. "You're sure?"

"Yes. I haven't been away from my desk all afternoon."

I nodded and started to walk toward the staircase. Once more I felt a hand take hold of my arm. I turned and saw that the desperation had not faded from Manuel's eyes.

"*Señor,* I beg your pardon but I still ask you —"

I interrupted him and spoke reassuringly. "There's no revolution, Manuel. You can rest easy. Whatever happened out on the street I reckon was just a private quarrel. Perhaps too much tequila."

He didn't look entirely convinced, but there was nothing more I could say to put him at ease, so once more I gently pulled free of his grip and stepped away from him. I climbed the stairs to my room on the second floor. I could feel Manuel's eyes following me, as if he suspected I knew more but was keeping it from him. Of course that was true, but I didn't have the time or inclination to deal with the anxieties of a nervous desk clerk.

Despite Manuel's assurance that no one had come into the hotel seeking me, I wasn't about to enter my room without first taking precautions. I walked lightly down the narrow hallway, quietly approaching the door to my room so as not to alert anyone who might be waiting inside. Then I gently tested the door handle to make sure it was locked, as it was when I'd left with Francisco. I inserted my key into the lock, twisted the handle carefully and, as I did so, I stepped aside and withdrew one of the revolvers from my holster. I waited for several seconds before I swung myself into the room, my body braced against the door, gun firm in both hands, poised at the ready.

My eyes darted about the room. Quiet . . . and everything seemed to be in order. I kept the shutters closed during the day in an effort to keep out the midday heat, so most of the room was in shadow, with faint shafts of light filtering in through the slats.

I saw nothing to concern me.

The tension eased from my body. I locked the door behind me and sat on a chair I positioned against the back wall, facing the door, and a distance away from the one shuttered window that, when open, overlooked the main street from the second floor. I wasn't particularly concerned about anyone trying to get in through that window, but still thought it wise not to make myself vulnerable to any possible point of entry. If someone truly wanted to see me dead, there was no telling to what extreme he might go.

I sat in the late-afternoon gloom and waited to see if Francisco would return. He knew I would have plenty of questions for him.

He would also know that I would expect the right answers.

It had become dark, and I struck a match to light the lamp on the table next to me. It had been several hours since I had last seen him, and Francisco had not returned. My suspicions about the man grew in my solitude and through the lengthy wait. But whether he returned or not, I'd made the decision to follow his advice and leave Santa Rosina come morning. I would ride out at sunup when the streets of the village would not be crowded and I could keep a good eye open for any peculiar activity. I still didn't know if I had been marked for death; I would need to settle that question with Francisco.

All I knew was that I would be saying *adiós* to Santa Rosina with regret. It was unlikely

I would ever return to this village to take my rest between assignments. If what Francisco said was true, some enemy as yet unknown to me appeared to have learned of my visits to the village and had hired a professional killer to murder me. The attempt had failed but how could I know for sure the threat was over, that another assassin did now not hunt me? A killer I would never recognize among the many faceless Mexicans, intending to execute someone's revenge for a reason I could not determine.

As a young boy growing up on a Kansas farm, I was full of oats and always rarin' to go. My restless nature often proved difficult to corral. Patience was a quality I had in short supply and was something I'd had to develop and nurture. Through practice and stubborn determination, I eventually learned to master it. Establishing patience was a vital component of my profession. I could apply it well and effectively.

But here, now, in just a few hours, I felt my endurance start to crumble. The same thoughts and questions had turned over and over in my head since that crucial moment at the cantina, cluttering my reason and even starting to cause me physical anguish, as my head began to throb. The longer I waited, sitting alone in my room, the more my brain struggled to make sense of what was happening, the more the answer eluded me.

I doubted I would get any sleep, but after a while fatigue set in and I began to doze. At some point I snapped fully awake as, ever so faintly, I heard the outside handle of the door begin to twist. I'd rested my Colt on my lap, and I hastened to reach for it. I lifted the gun and aimed the barrel straight at the door. I cocked the hammer. I would not act recklessly, but I wasn't going to give whoever might be on the other side of the door the chance to make his move first. If it came down to him or me, it would be him who would fall dead courtesy of a bullet.

I waited, beads of perspiration I could not attribute to the Mexican heat dotting my brow. The heat had settled upon my room even with the window shutters closed. I refused to surrender entirely to apprehension, though once more I faced the disturbing possibility of the pursuer becoming the pursued.

My finger tensed slightly on the trigger.

Silence. The turning of the door handle ceased. I remained seated, not daring to utter a sound that might alert whoever was outside my room that I was waiting, armed and ready.

Then — a slow, precise knock.

"*Señor?*" a voice spoke. Quietly. Deliberately quiet.

I instantly recognized who it was. The peasant-like utterance was unmistakable.

It was Francisco.

I felt a moment of relief, but still intended to remain on my guard. Francisco had not yet earned my trust. His saving my life, in fact, had lessened my confidence in him. The sincerity behind that act had yet to be proven. Perhaps I was thinking in the extreme, but how was I to know that he himself was not part of a plan to kill me?

Again, in a voice slightly above a whisper: "You can open the door, *Señor.* It is only me: Francisco."

I didn't respond. Instead, I rose from my chair and stepped gingerly across the room to the door, holding myself next to it, listening. Might there be someone else standing with him in the hall? Someone waiting to make a move once I opened the door to Francisco? I held myself so still and quiet that not even my breathing could be heard, pumping out the air silently and shallowly. Caution, patience. I'd become adept at the practice of both, though never in such a circumstance, where I might be the one being sought.

Francisco had become just as silent on the other side of the door. He, too, seemed to be waiting.

The question was, whose patience would give out first?

# CHAPTER FIVE

While standing inside my room waiting out those indecisive moments, a strange, unexpected thought occurred to me. I wondered if I might finally have begun to pay a price for my profession.

When on the trail I was motivated solely by the job I was hired to do and, of course, my fee. Both kept me focused on the task at hand. But I had neither my work nor the promise of pay to occupy me at the moment, just a damned uncertainty. Something drawn out of the pit of my gut that, of a sudden, I was forced to acknowledge. An unwelcome intrusion that released doubts I'd never considered before, let alone taken time to reflect upon. For the first time I questioned the profession I had chosen.

Only once before — and briefly — had I harbored misgivings about being a witness seeker, and that was when Colonel Calvin was killed. But I overcame that hesitation and, in fact, both learned and grew from his death. Even the close call I experienced with the murderous clan in the Bodrie Hills was a professional risk for which I had prepared myself when I accepted the assignment. But what I might be facing now was different. This might be a direct threat from an enemy I did not know. A foe I could not recognize, whose motives were unknown to me.

A man can never be the same when he discovers his name is on a bullet. I could not be confident that I would ever again be effective at spending days, weeks, months tracking witnesses, using my proficiency to trail them, my powers of persuasion to convince them to ride back with me to what were often tenuous outcomes. That required a strength, a determination I'd always been able to call upon and put to task. I took pride in being a professional. That part of my approach had now been compromised, and there was no guarantee I could ever again retrieve it, given the events of the afternoon and the cloud that might now hang over my future.

I debated if witness seeking was even where I wanted to return.

One thing was definite. I needed to know at this moment where I stood with Francisco. If I could trust him. He needed to speak again. To say something — *anything* — so I would know the man standing outside my door was someone I could feel confident letting into my room.

Whoever the man who called himself Francisco Velasquez was, I knew there was more to him than what he had thus far revealed to me. There was as much mystery to him as he saw in me. I now realized he was a clever man who had effectively created the disguise of a poor illiterate for a reason yet to be determined. What was important was whether he considered me a *compadre* or a man whose killing would matter as little to him as swatting a fly.

One of us had to acknowledge the other. It was then I decided that, if I were to maintain pride in myself and my reputation, I must unlock and open the door and face whatever awaited me on the other side. I hefted my Colt Dragoon and regarded it with respect. Only a few men had fallen under the discharge of its barrel; in each instance I had been given no choice. Such might be the case now, and I had to accept that possibility. Yet I hoped Francisco would not force me into such a decision.

I drew a breath and turned the door handle, taking a step or two back as I did so, my gun firm in my hand, trigger finger ready to respond to any sudden aggressive move.

I suspected Francisco knew my intention, for he too seemed cautious.

"It is all right," he said. Then he slowly maneuvered himself into the room.

He looked about in the gloom before his eyes fell upon me holding my pistol on him. Instead of displaying surprise or fear, he nodded approvingly. The nod and the genuineness of the grin that accompanied it allowed me to relax my own apprehensions.

I steadied myself and, wordlessly, lowered the Colt, sliding it smoothly back into the holster.

Francisco shut the door behind him.

"You're wise to be careful," he said. "But it would be wiser still for you to be packing."

I patted my holster. Francisco understood the gesture, though his interpretation of "packing" was different from mine.

"I suspect a man such as you travels light," he said.

I spoke to the point. "Never mind that. I need you to answer some questions, starting with what you know about what happened this afternoon."

He gave an agreeable nod.

"You already admitted our meeting today was not by chance," I began, phrasing my sentence not as a question.

"Perhaps not."

"What I find curious is I've come to this village many times . . . and I can't recollect ever seeing you."

"Santa Rosina is not my home, *Señor,*" he replied simply.

"How is it that you know of me?" I next asked, my tone firm.

Francisco took a moment to reply. When he finally spoke, his words were direct. "I know because someone has signed your death warrant."

I purposely showed no reaction.

"This does not trouble you?" Francisco asked, cocking his head inquisitively.

I didn't answer. I did not know or trust Francisco well enough to admit my true feelings in this matter.

*"Señor?"* he urged.

"I find myself troubled by many things . . . Francisco," I finally said, speaking his name with deliberate emphasis.

"And does that include me, and the reason I am here?"

"Yes," I said.

Francisco sighed deeply. "This man who tried to kill you, *his* reason is known to me."

I said nothing as I watched him steadily.

Francisco, too, was quiet for several moments. He looked to give thought to what he was about to say.

"No, *Señor.* As I told you, it was not by chance or through coincidence that we met today," he said.

I nodded.

Francisco wrinkled his dark-skinned brow and began to move about the room. I watched him and held back the urge to set my hand next to my gun belt.

He ceased his pacing. Then he pivoted his head in my direction and pierced me with his gaze.

"In fact, *two* men were set to kill you today."

Before I could absorb completely what he had said, he thrust another jolt at me.

*"Witness seeker,"* he said.

At hearing Francisco refer to me — with a deliberate emphasis — by my professional title, I tensed. My fingers dropped instinctively to my holster and the gun grip. Francisco seemed to anticipate my move and raised his hands in a pacifying gesture.

"It is better that you know what I know," he said.

The aggressive curve of my fingers relaxed. I eased my fingers back from my holster. But my gesture was slow and I held my hand close to my gun. I hadn't stayed alive this long by surrendering to trust or carelessness.

Francisco breathed out slowly, and just as slowly he rocked his head. I was uncomfortable with him standing and gestured for him to take a seat in the chair where I had been sitting. I felt more secure when his back was to the wall. He obliged me, and we walked around each other in a tentative half-circle. I moved to the opposite end of the room where I remained standing and could keep watch of his every move.

Francisco regarded me with what I interpreted was an amused — or perhaps ironic — expression. "I didn't come to kill you."

I don't know why, but I believed him, though I wasn't ready to admit that to him. He still had a lot more to say before I could let him know I was convinced. For now it was best if he accepted that I still had my doubts. Better for both of us if he understood I wasn't ready to relax my guard.

The quiet that passed between us signified our unspoken agreement.

"I ask you to hear me out before you pass judgment," Francisco said.

"I'll listen," I returned patiently.

He spoke without reservation. "Yes . . . it

is I who was that other man who was supposed to kill you."

Earlier that confession might have earned Francisco a bullet. But now I wasn't surprised by his revelation. If Francisco had hoped for a different reaction, he must have been disappointed. My face hardly changed expression.

"This does not come as a surprise to you?" he said.

I merely smiled and gave my head a slow shake.

Francisco looked perplexed by my calm acceptance of his admission.

"And you killed your *amigo*?" I questioned.

Francisco's features relaxed. *"Sí."* His voice was steady.

I regarded him speculatively. "So that you might kill me yourself?" I ventured.

"No," Francisco replied. "I told you the man was an assassin, a professional killer."

"As are you," I dared further.

He did not respond to the bluntness of my accusation. He hesitated, and his face took on a strange, almost distant look.

What he said next did startle me.

"The man . . . was also my brother."

I maintained my composure but gave him a hard look.

"It is true," Francisco said, speaking without emotion.

I kept my voice even. "You . . . killed your brother?"

"*Si.*"

I couldn't make sense of what he was telling me. "Killed him . . . to prevent him — *your brother* — from killing me?"

Francisco offered me the faintest nod.

"Someone you've never met before today," I said.

Francisco didn't answer, though the expression on his brown face shifted. Traces of guilt, and shame, shadowed his features. Perhaps even a hint of regret. But I could not detect any particular sorrow. There seemed no indication of sadness about what he had done.

As I usually did when I crossed into Mexico, I had brought along a bottle of American whiskey. I hadn't opened the bottle, but now I thought this was the right time. Francisco watched me sort through the sack that contained the whiskey. I showed him the bottle and he sighed appreciatively.

A puzzling thought then occurred to me.

"I thought you didn't drink?" I said.

"Now might not be a bad time for us both

to share a glass," he replied with a slight smile.

I didn't bother with glasses. We drank straight from the bottle, passing the whiskey between us. I admit I wasn't being entirely generous. I hoped the liquor would free him to say more of what I needed to hear. I could not comprehend how a man could kill his own brother to protect a stranger. Neither could I understand why he was showing no grief over what he'd done.

His next words came unprovoked in answer to my curiosity. "You find it hard to understand why I shed no tears."

I regarded the alcohol remaining in the bottle and took another swallow.

"My brother killed men freely," Francisco said. "When our sister was murdered, he vowed that her death would not go unpunished."

I blinked. "Your sister?"

"Yes," Francisco acknowledged, a twinge of emotion beginning to seep through in his voice. "Our mother's daughter. A beautiful, spirited girl named Felicia." He swallowed, and the muscles in his jaw grew taut. "Did I say *murdered, Señor*? No, that is putting it too mildly. She was *slaughtered.*"

Francisco stopped to bow his head and cross himself twice in quick succession. I then heard him mutter what I assumed was a prayer for his sister's soul.

Soul? That was a notion that eluded me. According to the Bible and the religious upbringing my parents imposed upon me as a child, we each were possessed of a soul given us by a supreme creator we recognized as some heavenly being known as God. A God who, to my youthful understanding, was loving and merciful. An attractive concept, but I surrendered that notion, as I had seen damned little kindness and compassion during the years I'd worked my trade. Tragedy and despair were what I had become familiar with. This unfortunate girl, Felicia, was just another example of the unfairness of life. How could one accept the love and mercy of a God who could allow such a terrible thing to happen to one so innocent?

But I wasn't allowed to dwell upon a question for which there seemed to be no answer, as I was about to learn a disturbing truth that affected me directly.

*I* had played a part in the girl's fate. As Francisco was to tell me, it was I who had convinced Felicia to speak against the crimes committed by her husband. My memory was jogged, and I instantly recalled the events as if still fresh in my brain. Yes, I distinctly remembered. I had comforted her with words of encouragement as I escorted her back to the town where the trial was to be held. And with my duty completed, I had left her under the protection of the law, which, ultimately, provided her with no protection. Her husband was set free due largely to his wife refusing to testify against him.

Yet instead of gratitude, he still harbored hatred at what he saw as her betrayal. After just weeks, he found her . . .

I did not know this at the time. My work was finished. As always, what was to come afterward was of no consequence to me. My only concern was the pay packet I'd hoped to be rewarded with.

Yet now, here in Mexico, where I had always come to relax and forget, I was reminded of an assignment, a quest that had ended tragically — one that apparently had made me the target of an assassin.

Francisco became quiet, allowing me to contemplate this terrible revelation before he resumed.

"My sister was not a full-blooded Mexican, as am I . . . as was my brother. *Our* father was of the *Tzotzil*. He died when my brother and I were very young. He died bravely, standing alone against many soldiers while others deserted him. Cowards they were. Offering their support until they knew they could not defend their cause and then scattered like rats. But my father — he did not run."

Francisco halted, inflated his chest proudly, and went on. "Our mother is an American. Yes, *amigo,* while it might not appear to you, I am a half-breed. The man my mother remarried was also from your country. The child my mother conceived with this man was our half-sister. She was not Mexican; she was white-skinned, like you. But she was family to us."

"I can respect that," I said.

"Yes, I see that you do," Francisco replied softly.

I spoke to the point. "But you and your brother hold me responsible for the death of your sister."

Francisco answered me just as directly. "Yes."

I frowned. "Your brother is dead, yet you still insist I leave the village."

*"Sí."*

"Then my life is still in danger," I presumed. "There are others who want to see me dead?"

"My brother took the spilling of your blood upon his own hands," Francisco explained. "He looked on it as his duty . . . *our* duty, his and mine as Felicia's brothers. Though my own grief is deep, I cannot agree with that in my heart, as I respect that you were only doing your duty and should not be faulted for what happened afterward. But now that my brother is dead, others will be hired to take his place. To finish what he could not."

"And who is the one behind this . . . vengeance?" I asked.

Francisco answered me without hesitation. "Our mother."

I wasn't especially shocked to learn this, not after what Francisco had told me about his family and the close bond they seemed to share. It was something I personally could not relate to, as my parents had no other children and I had never been particularly close to either my mother or father. But I could appreciate the loyalty Francisco spoke of within his own kin.

"Our stepfather died soon after the tragedy that befell my sister," he said. "He died never recovering from the death of his only daughter, a child who was the lamp of his life. He died a man broke of spirit, *Señor,* but not of wealth. He left an estate of value. My mother inherited all of it. And I tell you, my friend, that wealth brings her no comfort and serves only one purpose."

It wasn't necessary for Francisco to elaborate what that "purpose" was, and I certainly did not need to hear any more. But I still wondered why Francisco had betrayed his mother and killed his brother when he himself must hold some hatred against me for contributing to the death of his sister.

"It's important that I know, Francisco," I told him. "Know why you apparently have spared me."

"Killing you would prove nothing!" Francisco exclaimed, appearing to take offense at my demand and fairly spitting out his words.

I felt a twinge of unease at his outburst. Despite his passive exterior, I sensed there lurked a man of explosive temperament inside Francisco. I also realized it wouldn't take much to set off that charge of dynamite.

He quickly regained his composure. He looked at me with apology and exhaled. "My sister was murdered, and the man who killed her was set free. He was freed by your courts because when she sat before that man — her *husband* — she could not speak as a witness against his crime. But before that, my sister went into hiding. You found her." He hesitated and looked at me squarely. "You can also find her killer."

The situation with Francisco was becoming clear to me. His finding me that afternoon. His questions and curiosity about my work. His wanting to join me as a witness seeker. Yes, it all was beginning to make sense. Except for him killing his brother, which I found difficult to understand. Francisco appeared to be a religious man, yet he had committed a sin that was condemned in the Bible. I wasn't much for religion, but one didn't have to respect a person's belief to recognize the enormity of such a crime.

I found myself in a difficult position. While I had not yet been asked directly, I had a strong hunch what Francisco expected of me. If that suspicion was correct, it would not be easy to refuse him. The man had saved my life . . . and had killed his own brother to do so.

Yet there remained a troubling uncertainty. I couldn't be sure he was speaking the truth. How could I be confident that this man, whom I had come to know just over these past hours, did not have his own vengeful scheme in mind. Perhaps he had killed his brother as a way to earn my trust?

How could I even know that the man he had killed outside the cantina truly *was* his brother?

And if all that Francisco was telling me *was* true, did I face the threat of becoming the prey of other paid assassins?

Too many questions clouded my thoughts.

"The man I speak of was last seen in Chesterfield City," Francisco said abruptly. He added with an emotion perhaps intended to encourage my decision, "The man who murdered my sister."

I looked at him, not saying anything.

He added sturdily, "The man we seek."

"That *we* seek?" I echoed his words with only mild expression.

His reply was simple yet confident.

"Yes, *Señor*. As you well have figured by now: *we*."

# CHAPTER SIX

"I owe you a debt because you saved my life," I told Francisco. "But what you're asking is not something I do."

"You do not seek people?" Francisco said slyly.

I gave my answer straightly. "I don't seek people so they can be murdered."

Francisco lowered his head and gazed at the floor. After several moments he lifted his face. He blinked. "Then you are rejecting my offer?"

I didn't answer. I wanted Francisco to first consider my words — and perhaps recognize the unspoken implication.

He scratched furiously at his greasy scalp. "I think there is more, *Señor.* I think maybe it is that you do not trust me. Is that it?"

He'd answered the question himself. I didn't say so. Instead, I kept my expression blank, yet firm.

Francisco looked at me for a long time

before his lips parted in a grim smile.

"I understand, *Señor,*" he said, his tone expressing neither offense nor disappointment. But he added, "Yet maybe you should keep in mind that there seldom is complete trust in any partnership."

True. But I wanted him to know exactly why I harbored doubt.

"Hard to feel confident teaming with a man who could kill his own brother," I said.

Francisco started to speak, but I interrupted him.

"And then to feel no regret at doing so," I concluded.

Francisco's expression became pensive. "Perhaps. But maybe if this man you doubt had not done what he did, it would be *him* who is now lying dead."

I noted how he had phrased his words; as if he were speaking about someone else, excluding himself from the act that did not appear to weigh heavily on his conscience. I looked tightly at Francisco, waiting to see if he would explain his curious statement.

"True, *Señor,*" he said. "I told you my brother was a killer. But that is not all. He was also a wanted man, sought by the *Federales* in many places throughout Mexico. He even had a reputation, a name given to him. He was called by many *El bruto*. A man who would kill without hesitation any who he felt had wronged him. Yes, he would have killed you. And once you were dead he would have killed me."

I responded with an involuntary lifting of my eyebrows. "You?" I said quietly.

Francisco smiled wanly. "Yes, *Señor.*"

"You told this to the *Federales*?" I asked him.

Francisco gave his head a shake. "The *Federales.* They know all they need to know."

I waited for him to say more, but he seemed unwilling to expand on his comment.

"My brother's body will be taken to the catacombs," he then said, finishing his sentence with an emotionless sigh.

I was vaguely familiar with this procedure. The assassin would not receive a proper burial. Both his crimes and the value of his infamy would preclude a sacred interment unless a hefty price was paid. Instead, the corpse would be put on display in a cavern below ground where tourists and the morbidly curious would pay plenty of *dinero* to see it. The "exhibition" could go on for several years due to the conditions that would help to preserve the body.

My expression must have registered my

distaste at such a ghoulish enterprise because Francisco tilted his head in a curious manner. He wore a very thin smile as he studied my face.

He said, "Apparently, *Señor,* despite your many visits here, you still do not quite understand the peculiar ways of this village."

Nor did I particularly want to be educated on such matters, I thought to myself.

"To bury the dead properly and with respect is costly here in Santa Rosina," Francisco explained. "As you have seen for yourself, the people are poor. Many barely have enough food, there are those just outside the village who live in shacks that cannot keep out the rain, and they grow sick. Children and the elderly, they die. Yet there are those who are wealthy, who own land, more land than they require for their own use. Greedy, yes. They look for ways to profit quickly. Building cemeteries on their land is one such way. But for families to bury their dead in these cemeteries . . . it is not a right. No, *Señor,* it is a *privilege.* Those of Santa Rosina and many of the neighboring villages must make a regular payment if they wish for fathers, mothers, sons, or daughters to stay protected beneath the ground. Yet many cannot pay the fees

125

these corpse landlords demand. When that happens, the bodies are pulled from their graves and placed within the catacombs where visitors may come to see them — at a price. *Sí,* I could have had my brother given a proper burial, but that would have cost me. And cost me a great deal more due to his, how you say, reputation. And why would I pay such a fee to ensure the eternal comfort of a man who intended to murder me? So . . . instead it is I who have been paid. And paid well."

I kept my eyes focused on Francisco. I really had nothing to say. First Francisco had killed his brother. Now he was admitting that he'd also profited from his death. My opinion of Francisco was that he was an intriguing, if not a wholly principled, fellow.

Francisco noticed the critical way I looked at him, and he tried to justify his reasoning. "Yes, *Señor.* You may think it wrong of me, but my brother no longer has earthly concerns. I ask you, what does he care what becomes of his corpse? I, on the other hand, could find a practical use for the money."

"I imagine you could," I finally said, failing to rope in the cynicism in my tone.

Francisco grimaced and then spoke rapidly. "No, no, *Señor,* you do not understand.

I have no need of personal wealth. My family is very rich. What I speak of is a, how you say, business arrangement. Between us."

I furrowed my brow.

"You're paid for the work you do, is that not so?" Francisco said.

I found myself answering perhaps a little too quickly. "Paid well."

"Yes," Francisco said. "And I am willing to pay you well."

"You're . . . saying you want to hire me?" I said, finally speaking the words I'd avoided saying outright.

"Yes, *Señor.*"

"To help you find the man who killed your sister?"

"Yes, *Señor.*"

"So that when we do find him . . ."

"Yes, *Señor.* I will kill him." Francisco spoke this admission without hesitation or emotion. A simple cold acknowledgment.

I gave my head a slow shake. My gesture was in response to the blunt honesty of his intention, not a direct refusal of his offer. That still had to be decided.

"It is justice I seek," Francisco said in a firm voice. "The courts will not give him justice. They set him free before, and it was then that he murdered my sister."

I spoke my own words in a gentler tone.

"You tell me the courts freed him because your sister would not speak against him."

The intensity in Francisco heightened as his voice rose in pitch. "Yes, that is true. My sister made a mistake, but she did so out of fear — and she did not deserve to die for it." His attitude softened. "My family knows he is the one who killed Felicia, but we have no way of proving it. The courts would not even listen to our case with no evidence other than our word. Justice must be served another way."

I still didn't know what to say. I was indebted to Francisco. I owed him my life, even as I now understood that the reason he'd prevented his brother from killing me was because he needed me — or, more precisely, my *skills* — to lead him to the man responsible for his sister's death. Yes, it was a private proposition like the Bodrie Hills assignment — and how that venture had almost turned out wasn't lost on me.

I was still uncertain about my future as a witness seeker, yet I confess I was tempted by a practical concern. I was broke and needed money. I doubt I would even have considered the offer if I had been compensated for my efforts by Ed Chaney. That money would have seen me make due for a long while.

Another consideration was that the climate in Mexico had become decidedly unhealthy. I had to leave the country. Whether I could trust Francisco or not, if I were to accompany him on his mission of revenge, I would have to take him at his word that he would honor his promise to pay me. I would need a substantial stake, regardless of whatever direction my life would now take.

I asked him straight out, "You'll pay me?"

Francisco nodded his head vigorously. "Yes. Of course."

"With cash. Not with a knife in my back?" I said, adding a deliberate skepticism to my words.

Francisco laughed a little. "I make no guarantees about the knife in your back. After all, who knows what we may encounter along the way? We have many days' ride ahead of us, and then possibly more to come. But if we are successful . . . the money will be paid."

"Depending on the outcome?" I said warily.

Francisco raised his hands, palms open in a noncommittal gesture. "Who knows what that outcome will be, *Señor*? To make such a promise is foolish." He paused to consider for a moment, then he grinned deviously. "But if you accept my offer, now it is *you* who will have to trust me."

He was right. The arrangement Francisco proposed presented a curious turn of events. If I agreed to what he was proposing, the cards would mostly be in his favor.

I decided to produce a high card of my own that might even out the play a little more.

"If I agree, I receive half payment upfront, cash on the line," I stated flatly.

Francisco's grin dissolved, and his dark-skinned features turned serious. "You wish to be paid before we start?"

I nodded. "Payable before we ride outta Santa Rosina."

As Francisco spoke, he began to slowly twirl his hand in what appeared an impatient or frustrated gesture. "That is how you generally do business?"

"Let's say in this case I'd prefer to work with a guarantee," I told him. "Just good-faith money to make me feel a mite more comfortable with our arrangement."

"Like what might be called . . . an *insurance,* maybe?" Francisco said wryly.

"Call it whatever you like."

Francisco was quiet before he exhaled. When he spoke, his face did not alter expression. "As I figured, *Señor,* you are a clever man."

"Not 'specially," I said with a smile. "Just careful."

Francisco responded with a look that was not easy to interpret. "I suppose on that we shall see."

"You wanted to convince me. It's only right that I should convince you," I told him.

"That . . . is the only guarantee you ask for?" Francisco asked carefully.

I gave him an enigmatic smile. "No. Not the only one. Reckon you understand."

"I suspect we both understand each other, *Señor,*" Francisco answered. "My only other guarantee, if I was to make you one, would likely make no difference to you." He widened his arms in an exaggerated gesture. "And why would you accept my word in any case? No matter what I say to you, you will hold on to your doubts."

Francisco spoke precisely what I was feeling. I didn't even have to acknowledge. In fact, if I were to wager on anything, it would be that he'd kill me once the opportunity presented itself. That was the uncertainty clutching at my belly. But it also tempted me with a strange, yet compelling, sense of competition.

I needed money, and at the moment my options seemed limited. At the same time, my mercenary nature led me to suspect

131

there could be yet another way I might profit from this venture. I understood that rewards for fugitives in Mexico were often large. If Francisco's brother was as notorious a character as Francisco had said he was . . .

I considered everything carefully. There was a good chance that Francisco had collected a handsome sum of money for betraying his brother. If so, I intended to see part of it added to my fee. But that would come later. It was simply another practical financial consideration. I wasn't about to overlook a welcome bonus to my payday. And I figured it would be well earned.

Of course if I agreed to go along with Francisco, my main concern was never to lose sight that this was not a typical assignment. There was a personal angle that involved me directly, and not in a way that would contribute to a good night's sleep. There was a price on my head, placed there by the mother of the man who now wanted me to ride beside him. Naturally that made me wary of Francisco's intentions. He admitted that he had shared a close bond with his sister. A frightened girl I had tracked, to whom I spoke with a practiced confidence, offering a reassurance I knew I could not truly guarantee. I did not know until today the tragedy that resulted from those assurances. That in itself was not unique. Rarely did I know the outcome of any of my missions. In truth, I did not want to know. I delivered the witness per my contract, collected my pay, and took my rest in Santa Rosina while waiting for my next assignment.

While I'd never given it thought, it occurred to me that during my time as a witness seeker, I'd cared little for the people with whom I came in contact. Neither they nor their welfare had ever been my concern. They were merely a part of my job. My primary motivation was just to take the money and enjoy the pleasures that lay ahead in Mexico. I was like most men, I suppose, and could admit without shame that I worked for the dollar. What was difficult to accept was that through my mercenary nature, I had become callous and selfish.

Maybe . . . by agreeing to ride with Francisco, there could come the added dividend of easing my conscience over the guilt I felt, not only for Felicia, but now for others I might have persuaded from the safety of their anonymity to uncertain fates.

"Francisco." And without saying anything further I held myself straight . . . before I gave my head a single, steady nod.

Francisco's face took on a hopeful expression. "You are telling me you have agreed to come?"

"Yes."

*"Bueno!"*

I gazed fixedly into his eyes as my way to solidify our pact.

But Francisco had his own idea. He regarded me thoughtfully.

"Do not you *Americanos* seal a bargain with a handshake?" he said.

"Yeah," I replied as I stepped toward him. I added solemnly, "It's a bond of honor. A commitment that an honest man would never break."

I spoke with all the integrity I could muster to see if the words might prompt even slight resistance from Francisco.

The little Mexican never flinched. The look on his face was serious and determined. He stiffened his posture, military-style, and thrust out his arm, which reached toward me, ramrod straight. It was an impressive gesture, but I still wasn't ready to trust him completely.

I think he understood my reservation even as he clasped my hand.

The man Francisco sought was named Silvano Ramos. He was the person who had escaped justice and then took out his vengeance on his wife, Felicia, Francisco's half-sister. From what Francisco revealed, Ramos had beaten her savagely before he killed her. Many times in the telling Francisco had to stop, pained and angered by memories and his own visions of how his sister must have suffered before the brute ended her misery with a gunshot to her head, and then committed a final indignity upon her by his discharging the remaining bullets into her lifeless body.

"When we saw her at the undertaking parlor, *Señor,*" Francisco concluded softly, his face twitching at the memory, "we could not even recognize her."

He took a lengthy pause and then he sighed. When he next spoke, his manner had become less emotional, but the words were stronger, more determined. "*El Diablo, Señor.* If the devil truly walks this earth, it is in the form of Silvano Ramos." He stopped and sighed again. The tone of his voice softened, yet his intention remained firm. "I live with the memory, but I do not dwell on it. I wait for my time when I will come face to face with this *hombre.* That will be the first time I will see him since that terrible day when I sat in the courthouse. It will also be the last."

I could usually maintain my composure, and I held myself stoically while listening to Francisco tell his story. But my poise was merely a facade, for on the inside I was seething. My gut twisted into a knot. I'd known of criminals who had committed the most heinous acts for which even hanging had seemed too generous a punishment. But it was difficult to conceive of any man doing to a woman what Francisco had just described happened to his sister.

It was just as hard for me not to feel some responsibility for the horrific act. While it wasn't easy to accept, I could almost understand why the girl's mother wanted to see *me* dead.

And perhaps that was also true with Francisco.

"We will ride out in the morning," Francisco stated.

"Early," I agreed. "Before sunrise."

"But until then . . . do we stay awake and keep watch on each another?" Francisco asked.

Whether he was being facetious or not, under the circumstances his was a question I could not afford to consider lightly. Yet . . . more reasonable thinking soon lessened any hesitation about sharing his company on this night. Still not the most comforting arrangement, but if his plan *was* to kill me, he'd wait until much later, after I'd fulfilled my part of the bargain. He needed my experience, and my reputation as a seeker was impressive. I rarely failed in a task. I had the feeling Francisco had checked that out long before he had arranged our "meeting" that afternoon. Therefore, I was valuable to him. I would be kept alive at least until the end of our journey, wherever that took us. Because whatever his intention in that regard, there was someone he needed to see dead first. My troubles would begin once we found Silvano Ramos.

There was another matter, though; one with which I could not yet burden myself. While not bound by law, I debated whether I could stand back and watch a man be killed in cold blood, regardless of how deserving he might be of such a punishment. The prospect presented a dilemma. Because the bitter truth was that Silvano Ramos would likely not be prosecuted for his crime. Even if Francisco was of a mind to bring Ramos in alive to be legally tried, he had no proof other than his own conviction that the man had killed his sister. In my thoughts I could picture us finding the killer and him surrendering graciously, willing to accompany us to trial . . . but only so that he could laugh in our faces once the court threw out the case for lack of evidence.

No, we would find him . . . and Francisco would kill him. I could see no other outcome. And perhaps that was when I, too, would be killed. If murdering Silvano Ramos outright was Francisco's intention — as it surely had to be — I would be a witness to his act. The irony was that, while the courts would set free a cold-blooded killer like Ramos, my word against Francisco could see him hanged.

# CHAPTER SEVEN

Opening the shutters, I gazed out through my window at the scattering of stars shining over the vast Mexican landscape, which in the distance took on its own haunting splendor once the sun had set and the burnt orange twilight deepened over the western horizon until wholly consumed by nightfall. It was my favorite time of day, when I would often find myself waxing poetic. I would stand outdoors and savor the balmy caress of the desert breeze.

Tonight, however, was different. I would wait out the night inside my hotel room, where the air felt heavy and the room itself grew relentlessly dark, relieved only by the somber glow emanating from the kerosene lamp I kept lit that sat next to me on the table. At first restless, Francisco finally stretched himself out on the floor across the room. I offered him a blanket from my bed, either as a covering or to use as a pillow, but he refused. He said he had no need for such comforts. I wasn't about to argue with him. To each his own. From where I sat in my chair, I could watch his every move . . . provided I kept myself awake. I'd made the mistake of drinking earlier. Two glasses of strong Mexican beer, along with some whiskey, and I could feel my eyes becoming heavy-lidded.

A glance at my pocket watch revealed that it was not yet ten o'clock. There were still many hours to go before dawn. Even though I could use the rest, I was determined not to give in to sleep. I watched Francisco periodically pivot his head in my direction, each time his mouth splitting into a grin I couldn't decipher, but which to my weary eyes seemed to project a decidedly ominous intent.

Was he waiting for me to fall asleep?

I knew that we understood each other: neither of us trusted the other. But who had the advantage as we waited out the night? It looked as if Francisco might have the edge. I had to blink frequently to keep my eyelids open; they were becoming dry from want of sleep. Yet each time Francisco shuffled on the floor and turned to me, he looked as alert as I'd seen any man. From my time spent in Santa Rosina, I'd learned that

Mexicans did not need long periods of sleep. They could get by on *siestas,* napping during the hottest period of the day so they could be refreshed during the cool hours of evening when most activities throughout the village flourished.

That put me at a disadvantage. Under normal circumstances I would participate in the street festivities at a cantina or café — or at least entertain female company in the privacy of my room. But these weren't normal conditions. I had no diversion to keep my brain stimulated. Only a companion whose ultimate motives remained unclear.

Francisco's voice rose softly. "You should try and get some sleep, *Señor.* The morning comes early. I can keep watch — if you would like."

I looked at him without answering. His words and the way he spoke them did not fill me with assurance. While I knew much of my unsettledness was caused by fatigue and the events of that afternoon, and that if I would just allow it, I could surrender to sleep without threat or worry, the man's mere presence made it difficult for me to relax.

Francisco would have been a fool not to recognize the mistrust I had for him. The question I now asked myself was, did he derive any pleasure from my wariness?

My thoughts were suddenly interrupted by a pounding at the door. I reacted with a start, pushing forward in my chair, my posture ramrod stiff. I sat perfectly still, quiet, and waited to hear if the knocking might continue. Seconds later came another loud series of hammering. Whoever was outside my room was determined and persistent.

I again checked my pocket watch against the light of the tableside lamp. It was almost ten-thirty. I expected no visitors. By now Francisco himself had sat up from the floor. He turned to me with an expression of concern. I watched his hand slide into his pocket and slowly withdraw a derringer. I suspect we both considered the possibility that whoever was standing in the hallway might be someone who had come to finish what had been thwarted that afternoon at the cantina.

Francisco continued to stare at me. The look of seriousness on his face gave me confidence that, in this instance at least, he was on my side. If trouble was waiting for me on the other side of the door, I could count on his backup. I rose slowly from my chair and took a few tentative steps toward the door before Francisco's whispered words halted me.

"*Señor,* keep in mind it is not likely an assassin would announce himself in such an obvious way."

Sensible words, though I wasn't completely convinced. I'm sure my expression conveyed my uncertainty.

"Then I would suggest you move aside," Francisco said quietly as he motioned with a tilt of his head to the faint slant of light peering through the gap at the bottom of the door. The blob of a shadow was just visible, indicating that whoever was there stood directly in front of the door. I was impressed by Francisco's keen eye. The sound of my approaching footfalls might encourage the discharge of a fatal bullet straight through the door.

I leveled my Colt Dragoon and edged off to the side. Francisco likewise slid across the floor, skating on an elbow like a one-armed man toward a corner, where he positioned himself to take aim with his small handgun.

We glanced at one another and then, with my body pressed up against the wall, I reached for the door handle, cupping my hand over it. The look in Francisco's eyes urged me to make my move swiftly. To catch the visitor off-guard and gain the advantage. Francisco had a precise aim on the door. I hoped that was where he intended to hold it. Once again a flash of misgiving coursed through me. All he had to do was shift his aim, and he could drop me before I'd have a chance to defend myself. But that doubt passed quickly. I felt confident that Francisco wouldn't try any tricky move. Not now.

I nodded to Francisco, then silently inhaled a breath. My first twist of the handle was slow, but then I turned it all the way with a flourish and swung open the door, maneuvering my pistol in the direction of the caller.

I breathed out through clenched teeth.

I'd forgotten about the *señorita* with whom I'd made a date that night. But evidently she had not. She stood in the hallway, eyes wide and lowered at the gun pointed at her, her face pale, almost white, a striking contrast against her black hair; her mouth agape, she understandably looked stricken with fear.

The girl named Constancia.

She stood frozen to the floor. When I saw she was not about to move, I had to take her by the arm to bring her inside. She looked ready to scream or pass out. I wasn't

144

sure which reaction might come, but I certainly did not want either to occur out in the hallway.

I heard Francisco sigh. I turned to see him shake his head as he put his derringer away. I was gratified to notice his relief. It reinforced my confidence that he wasn't yet ready to see me dead.

I guided Constancia over to a chair near the door and sat her down. I noticed her hands trembled. I debated offering her a swallow of the whiskey still left in the bottle or simply pouring her a cup of water from the pitcher. I decided on the water, though by this time it was usually warm and hardly refreshing. Francisco and I had made good use of the whiskey. Hardly a taste remained in the bottle. I decided I could appreciate a final swig and took advantage of it.

Francisco looked indifferent to my indulgence. Constancia, on the other hand, had a greedy look on her face. As she watched me take that last slug from the bottle, she screwed her features into an expression that made a person think she was perishing from hunger and that the last scrap of food had been snatched from her hand. But that wasn't all. She went further when she suddenly shifted into a rage, cursing in Spanish. Then she tossed the cup of untouched water she'd held in both hands off to the side, shattering the cup against the wall. The faintest growl escaped her lips. Whatever the noise she made, it was predatory and instantly painted Constancia as less attractive in my eyes.

Francisco watched in silence, his face set in an empty expression that suggested the girl was my trouble and that I alone would have to deal with her. He confirmed that when he hummed out a lengthy breath and rolled over onto his side. Within seconds he was snoring. I knew he was only feigning sleep and his gesture irritated me, but he was right: Constancia wasn't any of his concern. At that moment I wished she weren't mine. She looked hostile and downright determined. She demanded a drink. It appeared she was ready to raise holy hell to get one.

I didn't need *that* sort of disturbance after the day I'd had.

"Water, *phooey*!" she fairly spat at me. "I come here after you leave me to sit alone to wait, and the best you can offer me is water." Her accent was thick, her voice husky. It had seemed softer and more pleasant earlier that day when we had arranged this rendezvous.

I lifted a shoulder. "It's all I have now."

"No," Constancia said steadfastly. "If you have no whiskey here, we go out like you promised. We have some drinks, we dance, then we come back and we have our own party."

I heard Francisco murmur, "*Señor,* I suggest that you throw caution to the wind."

I couldn't tell if he was serious or not. In any case, I didn't need to listen to his advice. The young *prostituta,* who had impressed me earlier that day as a quiet and even shy girl, was displaying another side I did not find appealing. She was a spitfire, energetic and doubtless passionate. What she could not know, and what I was not about to tell her, was that if we walked through the dark streets of the village visiting dance halls, she was accompanying a man who would be presenting himself as an easy target for another attempt on his life.

I wasn't willing to chance that.

What also was important was that I planned an early start, and I doubted I'd manage that with Constancia sharing my bed. If I was right in my guess, she had a flaming desire that would likely keep me awake till past sunrise, allowing me no rest prior to my journey. Still, in a way it was regrettable, because under different circumstances the evening could have been interesting and exciting.

I had to bid her *adiós* and didn't know how to accomplish that without the risk of Constancia raising a fuss. In the mood she was in, it wouldn't take much to inflame her already volatile mood into a pure fury. With no liquor available and no intention on my part to fetch her any, she might either fly into a rage or become mulish. If she decided to give vent to her considerable temper, she could cause enough of a ruckus in my room that I'd be asked by the hotel to remove her from the premises. After all, the establishment had the comfort of at least one or two other guests to consider.

I didn't want to have to use physical persuasion, but if it reached that point I could not see me having much choice. Evidently I could forget about Francisco lending a hand. And I doubted that Manuel, the desk clerk, would be of much help. If he showed up at the door, he would be nervously apologetic about requesting that Constancia leave the hotel, but doing the dirty work would be my responsibility.

To prevent such an unpleasant outcome, I attempted another tactic. I pulled some money from my pocket. I didn't have much to offer since my resources were minimal, but maybe I had enough *dinero* to satisfy her. After all, that was our arrangement. But no; she regarded the money I held in my hand with an expression of disgust. She looked almost ready to spit on it. In anticipation of such a move, I pulled my hand away. Her eyes shot daggers at me.

"What do you think I am? I don't take money as if it is charity," she said in a tone of self-righteous indignation. "You pay for my time, I give you my time."

I was astonished. I'd never before dealt with a whore who had integrity. Of course, this put me in a spot. She made it plain that she wouldn't take the money without earning it; she was also making it clear she would not leave until she *did* earn her payment. A ticklish situation. I was sure I could hear Francisco snickering from the floor.

"I could have gone elsewhere tonight," she went on. "Constancia had plenty of other offers. But no. I wait for you outside the cantina and you no show up. Now you owe me for my time. We drink tequila, we dance, then we come back here. And then, after we have a good time, tomorrow, then I'll take the money you owe me."

I jerked my thumb at Francisco.

"We're not exactly alone," I reminded her.

Constancia shrugged and frowned. The dim lighting inside the room seemed to accentuate lines burrowed into her face that I hadn't noticed before.

She boasted, "What does that matter to me, to share a room with one man? I've shared a room with a dozen men."

Here was information I did not need to know. Between this admission and her hellcat attitude, any attraction I'd felt for this *señorita* dissolved into dust.

"Maybe your friend, too, would like a little time with Constancia," the girl said in a sly, suggestive voice.

I refrained from commenting. I waited to see if Francisco would stir from his pretend slumber to respond to her offer. Instead, what I heard was another obvious, practiced snore. I was sure not even Constancia was fooled by the forced sound emanating from somewhere deep in his throat. But Francisco was not her problem. That remained my privilege.

Constancia's eyes searched about the room. Finally, her gaze settled on the chair where I had been sitting. She moved briskly across the floor and seated herself firmly, her posture stiff and determined: legs crossed, arms tightly folded across her chest, taking no pains to hide her obstinacy. She would not leave unless I picked her up kicking and screaming and deposited her ungentlemanly out the door, dropping her onto the street like a sack of turnips.

Or . . . unless I capitulated to her damned stubbornness and followed through with our arrangement — which I was not prepared to do. In any event, it's hard to attempt intimacy when there's a price on your head.

Yet how things now stood with Constancia, I wasn't sure which would be the worse outcome.

It was an unarmed Mexican standoff between a determined *prostituta* and me. I had the distinct feeling her pig-headedness was such that she would not budge from the chair all night. Which meant that, either way, I wouldn't get a moment's shut-eye.

In my business, it was essential to keep my wits about me. I'd need to stay particularly alert on tomorrow's ride, simply because I couldn't know if someone along the trail might have a rifle trained on me, hoping to collect the "bounty" put on me by Francisco's mother. Keeping vigilant extended to my partner. I could try and convince myself all I wanted, but anything could happen along those long empty distances the two of us would be traveling.

Just the two of us. Alone.

Finally, I heard Francisco speak — in a vague mutter, with just a hint of resignation to his voice.

*"Señor,"* he said, "you need the rest more than I do. Suppose I take the *señorita* off your hands." I turned to him and noticed that he had lifted himself onto an elbow and was looking at the girl, whose own expression remained cold. She'd heard and likely had taken offense at Francisco's rather indelicate phrasing.

Francisco might also have realized his poor choice of wording as he was quick to add, "That is, of course, if the *señorita* would flatter me with her company."

Before Constancia could answer, Francisco, perhaps anticipating a severe response, said to the girl, "You did say you were not opposed to allowing me to share your pleasures tonight."

Constancia's features began to soften, but she remained hesitant. I understood the reason for her resistance, just as I didn't question her insistence that we go out. In Santa Rosina, it was considered almost a badge of honor for a local *prostituta* to be seen around the dance halls with an *Americano.* At least among her own kind. Other whores would look at her with envy, and village shop proprietors often were more respectful when the girl came into their establishments the following day to peruse the fancy trinkets and other merchandise more frequently to be purchased by tourists. Then these merchants would treat the girl like a customer and not as a peasant, as they knew there was likely *mucho dinero* to be spent.

"I still want to be paid what the *Americano* offered to pay me," she insisted.

I looked at Francisco, then back at Constancia. I nodded. It was only fair I pay the American price — not the pittance locals paid, and then not always in money. With the village being so poor, often vegetables or even services were given in exchange for a night of pleasure.

Yet Francisco's generous offer puzzled me. It was the second time today that he had come to my . . . rescue. I was beginning to grow fond of the little Mexican, but could not yet bring myself to trust him completely. The main reason, of course, was I was not convinced he did not hold me responsible for the death of his sister. But maybe it also was because he was overly accommodating. I had a problem accepting the apparent good will of people. The irony was that with the people I sought, when I located them, I had to convince them to accept the sincerity of my word and hope that their trust in my assurances would be justified. I reckon most times it was, but as had been brought home to me today, there was at least one instance in which someone's trust in me had been misplaced. As for myself, even when I believed intentions were honorable, I had to remain wary. That hint of suspicion was always with me; it had become carved into my character.

"We will not be coming back tonight," Francisco said as he sidled up next to me so that I could hand him the money without the transfer looking too obvious; a needless gesture, given that Constancia knew whose *dinero* it was. He added quietly but with emphasis, "But I will return in the morning."

"I don't want to leave any later than sunup," I told him, pressing the bills into his hand. If Francisco was true to his word about paying me, I'd get the money back — and a lot more.

Francisco didn't say exactly what time he would be back. Instead, he offered a comment. "I think you will be safe until then."

I didn't much care for his remark. I detected a patronizing tone, as if he were suggesting I needed him around for protection. Issuing a subtle reminder of how he had saved me from an assassin's blade that afternoon. I could accept that, just as I

154

didn't object to having someone watch my back during our long ride into Texas. But I didn't appreciate Francisco assuming I was dependent on him for my safety. I'd proven my own ability not a month before during what had happened in the Bodrie Hills. I doubted that even with the time he claimed to have served in the army, Francisco had ever found himself so close to death as I was in that little shack. Where after the smoke had cleared, five people lay dead, and I was the only one to walk away.

Still, I didn't respond to his comment. I just tilted my head in an empty nod.

Constancia seemed reluctant to lift herself from the chair. She also looked petulant, the resentment now drained from her face. She almost resembled the *señorita* I had met earlier in the day: sweet, girlish. Her change in attitude made no difference to me. I, however, had offended Constancia's dignity. To be seen with me, a well-known *Americano,* was a symbol of status. That leveled a black mark against me in her book, but I had other concerns to deal with. Besides, I doubted I'd ever see her again. I would not be coming back to Santa Rosina.

A necessary but regrettable decision.

True to his word, Francisco returned to the

hotel before sunrise. I had sat up for most of the night, drifting off only for brief periods of light sleep, and was opening my eyelids once again after a short doze when I saw a silhouette standing in the doorway just as the faint golden tones of dawn began to appear on the horizon. Even though I had given Francisco a key to the room, I was groggy enough to be startled at seeing an intruder whom I did not immediately recognize. I instinctively reached for the Colt revolver on the table next to me.

Responding to my action Francisco spoke immediately, though his words were not in greeting.

"She had no interest in me, *Señor,*" he said. "A couple of drinks and she let me know she could now accept your money in good faith." He sighed expansively. "I suppose my pride is hurt, but I expected no less."

I relaxed and my mouth twisted in a half-smile at what he said.

"But she care for you even less, *Señor,*" Francisco added with a bit more cheer.

I stifled a yawn. "*I* expected no less."

Francisco halted, tilted his head to examine me. "You no get any sleep."

A second yawn escaped me. "I'm fine."

Francisco's forehead creased and he spoke

with concern. "No, *Señor.* We have a long ride ahead of us. Many days of travel. You can't get a good start today without rest."

"I can put in a good day's ride as well as you," I said, my pride leading me to speak boastfully.

Francisco was prepared to challenge my boast. He regarded me speculatively — rather, he scrutinized what was likely the haggardness of my appearance.

"Maybe. Maybe not," he said. "But no, I don't think so." He stood straight and puffed out his chest. "Look at the two of us. Who is the more fit to go?"

The chest he was expanding didn't do much to improve his scrawny physique, but the little Mexican had a point. I didn't know if he'd gotten any sleep after Constancia left him for more promising prospects, but since he was just now getting back to the hotel, I guessed he'd likely been awake most of the night. I hadn't fared much better, although I'd at least managed to capture moments of shut-eye. Yet Francisco looked as hearty and alert as if he'd just returned from a restful vacation.

I admit this troubled me, because not long ago I'd been able to go for long periods with little or no sleep and appear just as vigorous as Francisco did now. It was stubborn pride, but I became resentful anytime I detected a weakness in myself. I particularly disliked Francisco standing there, maybe taking note of a vulnerability in my character. It was important that Francisco have no reason to question my stamina on our journey . . . and maybe later use it to his advantage.

If that was his intention.

Francisco suddenly snapped his fingers. "I have just what you need that will perk you up."

I was only slightly curious as I watched his hand reach into the small bag hanging over his shoulder. He withdrew a little pouch and dangled it in front of me.

"What the hell's that?" I asked him.

Again came the affable grin I'd come to associate with Francisco. "Tobacco, *Señor.*"

He announced it with the same enthusiasm as if it were some carnival prize he had just won. I was less impressed. I wasn't much of a smoker outside of the occasional cigar I might reward myself with at the end of a successful assignment, but neither was I a stranger to Mexican tobacco — or its supposed "stimulating" effects.

Francisco could tell I was doubtful.

"You no smoke any tobacco like this, *Señor,*" he said. "Oh, no. This is specially grown from special fields. A few puffs, put

158

you right on your feet."

I'd heard about some of the "special" tobacco the peasants smoked. More likely to knock me right on my ass.

Ever cautious, I suggested to Francisco that he smoke some first.

"But I no need," he protested.

"But it no hurt," I said, mimicking him.

Francisco briefly considered. Then he spoke in a hesitant voice. "No . . . I suppose it no hurt."

"All about trust, Francisco," I said as a reminder. "Do I trust that tobacco's safe to smoke?" I lifted my shoulder in a questioning gesture.

"I try to do you a favor and you think it is a trick," Francisco said, sounding offended.

"Well, as I see it, *amigo,* we're gonna have a lot of opportunities to test the trust between us along the way."

Francisco's face brightened a bit. "With you having to trust me more than I you, *sí?*"

It was rather a juvenile comment, but I saw no harm in agreeing if it made Francisco feel better. I replied with a nod.

"That is fine, *Señor,*" Francisco said with a grin.

With that, Francisco sprinkled a generous amount of the dark tobacco onto rolling paper and built his cigarette. He produced a wooden match with which to light it, drew a few deep puffs, and within moments the room grew heavy with a stench so strong and vile it could choke *el toro.*

I instantly determined that either Francisco wasn't a smoker or his tobacco wasn't as pure as he had claimed. The expression on his face turned sour almost from the moment he took his first inhale. Not unexpectedly his upper body began to heave and, after valiantly trying to subdue it, he started to cough. Heavy coughing that seemed to come from deep in his chest. After several moments his eyes turned watery and he regarded me with a desperate, pleading expression. I wasn't sympathetic and responded with an upward thrust of my head to urge him on. He drew another tentative puff, coughing all the while as his brown, tanned complexion actually appeared to take on a greenish tint.

Finally, he gasped, *"Señor . . . please."*

He hadn't smoked even half of the "cigarette" but I took pity on him. I nodded. He tossed the cigarette to the floor with a flourish and stomped on it with his *huarache,* as if he were crushing *la cucaracha.*

I had to wait almost five minutes for him to finally stop coughing, during which time, between spasms, he swallowed all the water remaining in the pitcher. I kept my eyes on him, and I smiled. When he finally settled and lifted his face to look at me, he was not happy with my amusement.

The smell of the tobacco was overpowering and I hastened to open the shutters to allow in the fresh predawn air, turning to him as I did so.

"And that's what *you* had in mind for *me*?" I deadpanned.

He spoke in all innocence. "I — I didn't know, *Señor.* I swear to you the tobacco is good . . . but perhaps . . . it has been sitting in my pouch for too long," he said, his words croaking and halting as he expelled a few final short coughs. He took a deep breath and regarded me sheepishly. "I think maybe I throw it out. *Sí?*"

"I don't care what you do with it, *amigo,*" I replied, and I thrust a thumb at myself. "But I ain't smokin' none of that locoweed."

"Not locoweed, *Señor,*" Francisco said, his face etched in a miserable expression. "But maybe better if it was."

I nodded. *"Sí."*

I decided what I needed most to invigorate me was some coffee. The problem was, it was too early for any of the cafés in Santa Rosina to be open. We would be gone at least a good hour before their doors opened for business.

There was a knotted Hessian cloth sack on the floor next to the door. Francisco must have brought it with him when he came in, but I just now noticed it. It was a fair-sized burlap pack and looked to be about half-filled with supplies.

I nodded at it.

"Our goods, *Señor,*" Francisco said. "For our travel. Not all that we'll need, but enough for us to get started. Naturally we will have to make another stop along the way. I know of a trading post just north of the border." He seemed a trifle hesitant to speak the rest, and I suspected the reason. It had to do with some extra *dinero* I knew he carried with him, that he wasn't too eager to have me know about.

"I picked these up yesterday," he explained quickly, with a slightly nervous edge to his voice. "*Sí,* after my talk . . . with the *Federales.*"

I neither commented nor did I give him a questioning or knowing look. He appeared relieved at my tactfulness. Besides, at the moment my main hope was that he had thought to purchase some coffee. I could benefit from the powerhouse kick from a strong cup of java and told him so.

Francisco looked pleased with himself.

"I like coffee, too, *Señor,*" he said. "Plenty strong and black, and I bought us the best blend Santa Rosina has to offer."

That sounded agreeable. I figured we could afford a stop once we were some miles from the village, out in the open country with a view of all that surrounded us — where we couldn't be sneaked up on by any bounty-hungry varmint who might be following our trail. There we could build a small fire and brew a cup of the much-needed eye-opener.

"Looks as if you thought of everything," I said, my tone of voice perhaps suggesting more beyond the obvious.

Francisco just looked at me and grinned.

# CHAPTER EIGHT

Before we started on our journey I thought it only fair to clarify a point with Francisco. I didn't think it would make a difference as far as he was concerned, but I wanted to be candid with him so there would be no misunderstanding later on.

"I'm a seeker, not a tracker," I said as I packed the rest of my travel gear into a gunny sack.

Francisco hefted the Hessian cloth sack containing our supplies over his shoulder.

"I do not understand what is the difference," he said with a puzzled frown.

"As a seeker, I usually know where it is I'm going. I don't need to 'track,' like, say, a bounty hunter."

It was apparent Francisco still did not quite comprehend.

"*Señor?*"

I tried to explain simply enough for him to understand. "I rely on information. A few questions to the right people usually set me on the right trail. I'm not hunting criminals, just ordinary folk. They might go into hiding because they're frightened, but they generally don't take pains to cover their tracks like a fugitive might do."

Gradually it looked as if Francisco was beginning to catch on. He spoke his words precisely. "So . . . these people to whom you ask the questions . . . they tell you where they are? They . . . the ones that you hunt."

"Seek," I corrected him. "But yeah, they give me leads. Doesn't always pan out, so I might have to start over. Search out fresh sources. Sometimes takes a lot of patience and a whole lot of doggedness."

Francisco looked concerned. "But we might have to *track* Ramos — not as you say *seek*. He *is* a criminal."

"Might at that," I agreed.

Francisco knitted his brow. "It is doubtful that just questions will do us much good, if he has gone into hiding."

I gave a vague nod.

"And this you no can do?"

"I told you from the start I can't make any promises. Texas is a big state. Lotta territory. Like you said, depends mainly on whether Ramos suspects he's being sought."

Francisco spoke in a firm voice. "A man

165

like Silvano Ramos must always, as you *gringos* say, be keeping a watch over his shoulder. I will tell you about him so that you will know his advantages. He has the size and strength of the bull, *el toro.* The speed and agility of the mountain lion. And he has the cunning of a wolf. He is, in short, a most challenging adversary."

Listening to this description of the man hardly filled me with confidence. But I'd made my position clear. My obligation went no further than leading Francisco to where Silvano Ramos might be. It was not my purpose or my intention to involve myself in any way after that.

Of course, Francisco might have a different thought on the matter.

What neither Francisco nor I could know as we packed our mounts and set out toward the Chihuahuan Desert, then to cross Río Bravo del Norte, and onward through into Chesterfield City, was that the man we sought, Silvano Ramos, had already initiated a reign of terror across west Texas, forming a gang and robbing and killing relentlessly and savagely. Two Texas Rangers who had set out after the outlaws had been found strung up by their feet on heavy tree branches, their throats cut so that their heads were nearly severed from their bodies and, for added effect, their eyes gouged out. Having tasted torture with his own wife, it seemed Ramos had developed a craving and a peculiar talent for bloodlust. He was not content just to murder his victims; first they must be made to suffer unspeakable cruelties.

Had we known that the Rangers had begun a massive manhunt for Ramos and his bloodthirsty band, I wondered if Francisco would have abandoned his own course of revenge. I likewise contemplated whether I would have refused his offer to join him on this undertaking — especially upon learning that Ramos was not alone and that the men who rode alongside him were as mean and vicious as he was. Questions to consider, but by the time we reached Chesterfield City and discovered these facts, the more immediate concern was: Had we committed ourselves too deeply to simply turn back?

While I won't deny the idea had crossed my mind more than once during those first days of travel, I never presented my fear that we might be embarking on a much more dangerous mission than we had anticipated to my *compañero*. I admit I would not have argued with Francisco if he had proposed that we give up our quest. But I would not be the one to offer the suggestion. Once more I would have to wrestle with my stubborn pride, which always proved to be a formidable adversary. If I were to abandon Francisco, my own conscience would brand me a coward.

While I could confess to many faults, I never considered myself a coward.

When I tracked people in my official capacity as a witness seeker, I never knew for certain what I was riding toward; could never be sure of the subject's capacity for violence, since fear and self-preservation could provoke mighty powerful responses. Sometimes the danger that presented itself could have fatal consequences — like what happened to Colonel Calvin, my mentor and friend, and what came close to happening with me in the Bodrie Hills. But I'd never gone into a situation where I knew beforehand, with an outright certainty, that the person I sought was a killer.

But discovery of the Ramos Gang's rampage was still days ahead. For the time being Francisco and I rode our ponies onward, occasionally traveling by night as well as by day. We stopped to take advantage of whatever shade we might find along the way and to conserve the strength of our mounts, as well as ourselves, during the hottest periods of the afternoon. By contrast, the desert air grew bitterly cold come nightfall. We didn't make much distance those first days as we figured out our best riding periods, finally determining the most beneficial traveling hours and pacing ourselves accordingly.

When we rode at night Francisco would bundle himself in a long, color-patterned wool *serape,* while I kept my own body warm by wrapping myself snugly in a plain woolen blanket. Once we felt we had put in enough miles for the day, we would dismount, feed and water our horses, build a fire, and brew coffee.

While the ride was frequently uncomfortable, I confess I felt a mounting apprehension as each day passed and we came nearer to our destination. It appeared quite the opposite with Francisco. The closer we got to Chesterfield City, the more I could detect my *compañero*'s eagerness. Eager, perhaps even restless, but not impatient. For he, like myself, knew that Chesterfield City would likely provide us with only a lead, and that the odds were against us finding Ramos in or near the town. But that was sufficient for Francisco. He looked upon each mile we traveled as another step nearer to fulfilling the obligation he felt he owed his sister.

We didn't speak much during our ride and talked only a little more when we stopped to camp. Our conversations were usually brief and perfunctory. Francisco initially had impressed me as a man with much to say — at least that was how he came across that first day I met him. Of course, I now understood his talkativeness; there was much he had to find out about me, and there were things about himself he felt it necessary to reveal. But now that he had acquired my services and our journey was underway, he developed a more quiet, serious disposition. He seemed preoccupied much of the time.

At first this change in his personality was curious and even a mite intimidating. Gradually, though, I came to respect and even appreciate his lengthy silences. But I did have to wonder what exactly was going through his brain. Most of the time his expression remained set and impenetrable, as if he'd built a wall around himself and his emotions. I understood that much of his thinking was likely focused on what lay ahead. I'm sure he thought a lot about his sister: her violent death and the terror she must have endured during those final hours as Ramos brutalized her. Perhaps he offset those thoughts with memories of the better times they had shared as brother and sister. Yes, once or twice I caught just the glimmer of a smile cross his lips. A pure, untainted smile that could only come from a pleasant recollection. But whatever else went through his brain, I was sure he spent much of those long, monotonous hours riding across the desert sands and grasslands, through the patches of yucca, creosote, and mesquite, planning his vengeance against Silvano Ramos. Francisco was a man consumed with hatred, of that there was no question, though I had to ask myself as I studied my *compañero* if he would be a match for the man he sought. At that point I still knew little about Ramos — only the vile and vicious nature of his crime, but that was sufficient to provide insight into the man's character. He was a mad dog. He would likely prove a challenge to any man who dared to confront him.

I had no doubt that Francisco would carry through on his promise to kill Ramos if given the chance. It was not just because he had informed me of his purpose with such extreme passion. I also had only to remember what I had witnessed outside the cantina in Santa Rosina. If a man could kill his own brother and barely bat an eyelash, he would have no hesitation about executing someone for whom he felt such venomous hatred. In fact, I was convinced he could carry out the task both with ease and satisfaction.

Francisco possessed two advantages that could make him a potent adversary against a conscienceless killer. He carried torture in his brain and vengeance in his heart, both characteristics reflected by the intensity that frequently flared in his eyes, a look that became more familiar and pronounced as our journey progressed.

One of the questions that stayed with me as we rode those many hours in silence was how precisely Francisco planned to kill Ramos should we find him. Would he ambush him, kill him in cold blood, or might he want to warn Ramos of his intention and call him fairly to give him a chance; have Ramos look him in the eye so he would understand why he had been marked for death? At the same time, he could give himself the satisfaction of watching the man who murdered his sister die slowly and painfully. The same tortured death that Ramos had delivered to Felicia. Those seemed to be the only two options available, and I could not guess which course Francisco would choose. Each would produce its own result: either a personal judgment of self-defense or the knowledge of committing outright murder. I could speculate all I liked, but I would have to wait. I knew nothing of Francisco's intent outside of his dedication of purpose.

What I did know for a certainty was that death was waiting at the end of our trail.

# CHAPTER NINE

The day we began our journey out of Santa Rosina we passed the old mission on the outskirts of the town. Francisco slowed his horse before coming to a complete halt just outside the courtyard and he blessed himself. I refrained from doing likewise since that opposed my lack of belief but allowed him his moment or two of prayer.

I had to wonder if he was asking his God for success in his venture, or was he seeking early forgiveness for what he intended to do should he find Silvano Ramos? If it was the latter I wondered if Francisco was truly convinced his prayer would do much good for the salvation of his soul. From what I recalled from my early religious teachings, only God was allowed to dole out vengeance — in His own time and place, and in His own way. But I could never rightly agree with that. If that were the case, a vicious brute like Ramos would be permitted to roam free and commit other inhuman acts until God Himself saw fit to punish him. There would also be no need for courts, jails, and hangmen. In fact, there would be damned little need for me.

No, whether or not God existed, if Francisco succeeded in finding and killing the murderer of his sister, I doubted his soul would be tarnished, just as I doubted any mortal man could truly condemn him for his action.

As for myself . . . I still struggled with the idea of a man committing outright murder, but I also could see no other way for this search to end. I would have preferred the matter be handled legally, that Ramos be brought to trial for the murder and the law enforce proper justice with a noose the outcome. I would stand forefront among the crowd waiting to hear the snap of Ramos's neck as his body swung through the trap and his black soul plunged into eternal limbo. But Francisco had spelled it all out, and his arguments were valid. Silvano Ramos would likely escape such justice for his crime and, therefore, he could not be taken alive.

From what Francisco told me, I was convinced that Ramos would continue to give full rein to his criminal tendencies — it

175

was unlikely that a man of such character would of a sudden decide to pursue an honest life — and it was inevitable that at some point the law would catch up with him and justice would then be served. But that justice would not be for the crime for which Francisco wanted to see him punished. And because that justice would be denied him, Francisco could not surrender his need to watch Ramos die under his own hand.

That was to be his privilege alone.

For myself: money, perhaps a salve on my conscience . . . and now trying to convince myself that if civilization was to prosper in the West, it needed to be rid of men like Ramos. Money and civilization were my motivation and my reasons for justifying the ride alongside Francisco into Texas.

As I stated, there wasn't much talk between Francisco and me. But one question kept gnawing at my brain. On the third night of our journey, after we had some decent miles behind us, we neared the southern bank of Río Bravo del Norte. After we set up camp come the approach of sundown, I could no longer restrain my curiosity.

"I find it interesting, Francisco, that you stopped for a blessing before we rode out of Santa Rosina," I said.

Francisco responded in a somewhat bewildered manner to my comment. He looked chilled by the night air and held his coffee cup tightly in both hands as if to warm his fingers.

"It was a prayer, *Señor,*" he explained. "I have always been a man who puts his faith in prayer."

I nodded. "Admirable, I reckon. But given what you're intending to do . . . well, it seems a mite hypocritical."

The perplexed expression on Francisco's face told me he was not familiar with the word.

"Not genuine, sincere," I defined for him. "To my way of thinking, a man who believes in prayer isn't someone who plans to commit murder."

"You see it as 'murder,' *Señor*?" Francisco asked.

"How else can you regard it?" I asked him back.

Francisco hesitated before he gave me a devious look.

"An eye for an eye," he responded.

I drew a breath. "Reckon one could interpret it that way."

"You, however . . . you do not sound convinced."

I tossed what was left of my coffee into

the fire and stretched out on my back, laying my head on my saddle and lowering the brim of my hat over my eyes. I knew Francisco had more to say, so I decided to wait. I didn't want to seem too eager and risk getting into an argument with him.

Unfortunately, it appeared I had already put the match against the flame.

Francisco spoke abruptly. "You speak also of what happened to my brother."

I remained quiet and for the next moments the only sound that met my ears was the crackling of the fire. The night air itself was still.

"Had I let him kill you, would that be preferable?" Francisco said in a harsh voice.

"Not my call to pass judgment," I said simply.

"But I ask, would you rather it be you who is dead?" Francisco repeated, his tone now solemn.

I tilted up the brim of my Stetson and lifted myself on an elbow.

"Don't rightly look at it as you were doing me a favor," I confessed. "You outright told me you needed me along with you. I'd not be of much value to you dead."

Francisco squinted as he rubbed a slow palm along his jaw. "Perhaps. Yes, that is true. But my brother would have been a much more effective partner — that is, once we meet up with Silvano Ramos."

I spoke quietly. "Sure, don't doubt it. But you profited from him in another way."

Anger flashed in Francisco's eyes. I felt a brief moment of trepidation. Maybe I was speaking a little too aggressively to a man whose intentions toward me were still unclear. He might need my skills as a seeker, but I would be sensible not to place too much confidence in that direction.

Francisco slowly calmed himself, though he said, "Now you speak with a cruel intent."

I didn't respond. Instead, I settled my gaze on the distance, where I watched the night shadows descend over the peaks of the Sierra Madre Occidental range, whose crests had earlier shone with a twilight brilliance. Now those mountains looked ominous and foreboding. I was starting to get the same feeling. Even though I wasn't looking at him, I could sense Francisco's gaze focused steadily on me, his eyes boring into me. For a long while he was very quiet, and I began to find his silence unsettling.

Finally, he spoke. His voice was low, his tone grave. "I feel no guilt for what I did to Fernando, *Señor*. Brothers, yes, but it was, how you say, inevitable that one of us would kill the other." He paused and looked to give serious consideration to what he was about to say next. Before he spoke, he rose to his feet. I was unsure of the intention behind his move and likewise started to lift myself from the ground. But I halted when I saw how he turned his back to me.

"You do not owe me your life," he said softly. Strangely, and perhaps it was only my imagining, for just at that moment, much of Francisco's thick accent seemed to have vanished. He seemed to be speaking nearly perfect English.

Was this another of those secrets I was slowly discovering about the man?

I was confused, to say the least.

"The man my brother tried to kill that day outside the cantina was not you," he went on. Then he turned to face me. Rather dramatically, he looked directly into my eyes, his gaze deep and penetrating.

"It was *me* who he had marked for death," he stated.

In that instant I felt as if I'd been hit with a load of buckshot — and while questions began to pour through my brain, I was at a loss how to respond.

"Yes, I lied to you," Francisco admitted. His gaze lowered toward the campfire, the streaking of flames flashing against his face.

"I thought that if you felt you owed me a debt, I could persuade you to accompany me on my search for Ramos. It was not planned that way — that much is true. I was hoping to find some other way to convince you. My brother appeared unexpectedly. I knew that, once he saw me, he would try to kill me. My aim was sure. His would have been, too. But I moved faster. Skill, luck, that I do not know."

Finally, I could speak, and my words were blunt with accusation. "And that was when you saw a way you could use that . . . *missed opportunity* to your advantage. To talk me into joining you."

There was no hint of apology in Francisco's reply. "Yes."

I continued. "And you gave yourself extra leverage by convincing me my life was in danger in Santa Rosina . . . with your mother holding me responsible for your sister's death."

Francisco finally spoke in his defense. "You *were* involved, *Señor,* as you know. You were the man who talked my sister into going back with you, to speak against the man she called her husband."

That much I could not argue against.

"Yes. It fit together well. Like the pieces of a puzzle," Francisco said.

181

I folded my hands and held them against my chin and sat in thought.

"Now you surely feel that I have betrayed you," Francisco presumed.

I didn't know how to answer him. *Betrayed* was not exactly the word I would have used. *Deceived* — yes. I wasn't pleased to learn I had been tricked, but oddly — for a reason I could not fully comprehend — I felt less provoked than I should have been.

Of course, come tomorrow, it might be another matter. Still, I reckoned I could understand Francisco's motive for doing what he did.

I also admit any resentment I was feeling was alleviated by a sense of relief. With Francisco confessing his true motives to me, I felt less apprehensive about the possibility of him killing me once he settled the score with Silvano Ramos.

At least in vengeance. I still wasn't quite as sure about his not wanting to leave a witness behind once the deed was done.

"So you see," Francisco concluded, "it does not disturb me that I have, as you say, 'profited' from my brother's death. Neither of us had much love for the other, even as children. We were not bound so much by blood as by family loyalty."

There still remained one question festering about in my thoughts. I debated asking Francisco why his brother had wanted to kill him. But I held the reins on my curiosity. Francisco might offer the answer himself — if not now, perhaps later.

But even with the deception he had pulled on me, I respected his wish to maybe keep this knowledge private.

# CHAPTER TEN

Before we crossed the border into Texas, I followed my usual routine. A ritual, really. I dismounted by the riverbank and, much to Francisco's curiosity, I stripped myself naked and plunged my body into the slow-running currents of Río Bravo del Norte. This was the precise location we would cross with our horses, since the river was narrow at this point and the water shallow. The animals were grateful for the respite and cropped at the plentiful vegetation in this area, which contrasted with the arid landscape through which we had just crossed.

This bathing was something I did every time I entered Mexico and, again, each time I was about to cross the border back into my own country. A type of symbolic cleansing, I suppose, though in truth I really cannot recall why I began the practice.

Francisco walked over to the water's edge

and gazed at me with a puzzled expression. I signaled for him to join me. After traveling for so long in the stifling heat of the day, the water was refreshing. I was in no hurry to rush my bathing. But Francisco, in response to my invitation, lifted his hand and waved it slowly in a "no" gesture. He noticed how I regarded him peculiarly, amazed at how anyone could refuse a dip in these cooling waters, and he looked a little sheepish. He shifted in his stance and glanced about before he called out, "I no can swim, *Señor.*"

I fountain-spat some of the river water from my mouth.

"Can't swim?" I shouted back. "The river is low. I can touch bottom with my feet."

Francisco nodded timidly. "*Sí.* You can, but possibly I cannot." He gestured our unequal height measurements with the flat of his hand.

"Well, suit yourself," I said. "But we still gotta cross the river if we're going to make it into Texas."

I heard Francisco sigh then mumble unenthusiastically, "*Sí.*"

And a short time later, very carefully, tentatively, exercising what I saw as exaggerated caution with each step of his horse, Francisco rode alongside me as we traversed

185

the ford to the opposite side of the river. It was not a great distance, and the currents were mild, barely noticeable. Thankfully for my *compañero,* his horse did not have to swim, but when Francisco was not nervously watching the movements of his mount with his two-handed grip so strong on the reins that his brown knuckles actually whitened, his eyes kept lifting from under the shadow of his *sombrero* to see how much farther we had to go until we reached the safety of dry land.

I had to admit I was both baffled and amused by Francisco's obvious fear of water. Once we had completed our crossing and started up the small rise, I decided to enjoy a little fun at his expense. I felt I was entitled to some payback after what I had learned from him last night.

"Take it you aren't much for bathing," I said.

Francisco regarded me quizzically. *"Señor?"*

"This aversion you have — to water," I said.

"I prefer to wash from a basin," he replied quickly.

"Which you just conveniently neglected to pack along with your gear," I said with a smirk.

"Too cumbersome, *Señor,*" he explained with justice.

He wasn't responding as well as I had hoped at my attempts to ride him.

Finally, I sighed and said with a straight face, "Well, just do me a favor and try to keep downwind of me. 'Specially at night."

We rode on a little farther.

"Many things I find odd about you, Francisco," I said.

He appeared more relaxed now that the river was behind us. We were both riding at a steady, easy pace across flat, even ground. He looked at me, his expression reflecting a curious frown, waiting for me to expand on my remark. But I deliberately took my time. Francisco was a patient man, and it soon appeared that he lost interest. He refocused his attention to the trail ahead.

"Yep," I said as I exhaled a breath. "You seem to have no worry going up against a man who's a known killer — someone whose capabilities you've got no way of determining . . . yet I've never seen no one look so scared of getting a dunking in less than six feet of water."

Francisco hesitated before he reflexively pulled himself upright on his mount and cleared his throat.

"If one cannot swim, water can be a

frightening thing," he presented.

A valid point.

"Reckon," I acknowledged.

"Not only can I not swim, I hold memories of the time I once watched a man drown," Francisco explained. "It was a terrifying sight. One that at times still haunts my dreams. The water appeared not to be deep, but the current must have been strong. It kept pulling him under. I saw him rise to the surface several times . . . until finally he did not come up again."

"That specific incident troubles you, when I'm sure you watched men — many men — die just as tragically when you were a soldier?" I questioned.

"Yes, many," Francisco replied, his tone distant. And then he fell silent.

We rode on a bit farther, and then I said what I had been pondering. "Yeah, funny how different people interpret courage. And cowardice."

"How do you mean?" Francisco asked.

"Just idle thinking," I replied offhandedly.

Francisco wasn't convinced.

"I think maybe there is more to what you say," he said.

"You do?"

"Perhaps it is that while *you, Señor,* do not fear the river, you fear Silvano Ramos."

"If that is so, I'd consider it a more rational fear," I countered.

"Rational?" Francisco questioned. "How do you mean?"

"Ramos is a *thinking* enemy."

"Yes," Francisco agreed. "But if one is not prepared, if one treads carelessly and unwisely, the waters of the river can kill you just as dead as an enemy of your own kind."

"And how prepared are you to face Ramos, Francisco?" I asked him.

Francisco turned his face toward me with a confident grin. "Perhaps more than you might think, *Señor.*"

"I saw your skill with a knife," I remarked. "Impressive. But I've rarely seen a blade that can outdraw a gun."

Francisco became silent as he looked to consider my words. And then he cast his gaze off into the distance and said softly, "It depends on how one chooses to play the game."

Whether Francisco had intended it or not, he had just answered a question that had weighed on my mind since the beginning of our journey. He was not intending to give his quarry a fair chance.

He would kill Silvano Ramos at his first opportunity.

# CHAPTER ELEVEN

While we still had sufficient supplies, it was debatable whether they would see us into Chesterfield City. Therefore, Francisco insisted we stop at the trading post he knew of several miles north of the Mexico/Texas border. I'd never heard of Pawnee Joe's, and once I took a look at the establishment, I could understand why. A ramshackle structure, it had been built in the middle of nowhere, surrounded by wide open country as far as the eye could see. The property itself sat on dry, sandy ground, dotted with sparse desert vegetation. Who the store could service, I really could not guess. It looked like a prospector facility, but it stood miles from any place that might even hint at holding a valuable ore deposit.

I wasn't expecting to find much by way of merchandise, and I was certain that whatever was stocked inside the store had probably grown rancid with age.

Francisco and I rode up to the place slowly; our mounts were tired and would appreciate water and a rest. There was a trough outside the building, but when I directed my horse over to it and took a gander inside its wood frame, it looked as if the little water remaining had gone stagnant. Another less than encouraging sign.

Fortunately, we had watered our horses at a little stream a few miles back. Francisco assured me there would be more watering holes ahead of us. Looking out over the arid, virtually barren landscape that seemed to stretch out for more miles than I was ready to count, I had my doubts. However, I also figured that Francisco could not afford to take chances with our transportation and, after all, he'd been correct about the trading post, so I took him at his word.

We tethered our horses to the hitching post and climbed up the creaking dry wood steps onto the porch and sauntered into the store. The place was dusty and had a peculiar smell to it, though I reckoned whatever customers the store serviced were not particularly . . . particular.

*"Buenos dias,"* Francisco greeted — to no response.

A balding, bull-necked, heavyset individual whom I assumed was *the* Pawnee Joe

191

(though there was nothing Indian about his appearance outside of his ruddy complexion and maybe the buckskin shirt he wore) and a couple of other men who were standing idly by the front counter eyed us suspiciously. The quick, wary glances that came my way soon passed but Francisco was hit full force with their glares. They stared at him as if they had never seen a Mexican before, though given the store's proximity to the border Pawnee Joe's must have done a large share of its business dealing with people of my *compañero*'s breeding.

I caught sight of a third man sitting on a barrel off to the far side of the counter. He didn't seem interested in us, as his attention was on something he was doing with his hands. Curious, I looked a little closer and noticed he was whittling a small piece of wood. The wood looked so tiny I figured the only thing he could be carving from it was toothpicks.

Within those few moments as we stood inside the store, I got an uneasy feeling — not a concern for myself so much as for Francisco. Yet at the same time, I figured that if my *compañero* knew of this trading post, he must have been here before and so could not be a stranger to the proprietor, at least.

But one could never have guessed that by the way Pawnee Joe fixed Francisco with a tight, critical — and downright suspicious stare.

Since I seemed to be of less curiosity, I decided to see if I could temper the situation before a wrong word could be said.

"Heading into Chesterfield City," I announced. "We'll be needing some provisions."

Pawnee Joe unscrewed his gaze from Francisco and gestured with his neckless head to the shelves to his left and on the far opposite wall, which, as I had predicted, were virtually empty.

"Hadda coupla pepper guts in here last week," he said miserably. "They held up the place. What they didn't take is what I got left."

With that, he sneakily shifted his gaze back to Francisco, who stood there with a troubled look on his face. Now I could pretty much understand the reason for the stares . . . as I'm sure could my *compañero*.

Francisco spoke up. "That is unfortunate." And then he said more, words that, under the circumstances, I reckon he felt were necessary to settle the tension and hopefully cast suspicion away from himself. It certainly seemed obvious Pawnee Joe held no distinction when it came to men of Francisco's color. "I have only been once in your establishment, *Señor,* and that was many months ago. Perhaps even a year."

Pawnee Joe studied him from afar, not venturing out from behind the counter, where I assumed he was in close proximity to some handy firepower.

"Maybe," he said. "But I can't know that for definite. Can't tell you no different from those other two who robbed me or any other Mexican half-breed that comes into my store. Y'all look alike with your dark skin and wearin' them wide, funny hats that makes it look like yuh got somethin' to hide."

*"Sombreros,"* Francisco corrected, adding a slight smile.

"Know damn well what they are," Pawnee Joe said with a scowl.

I wasn't the one being insulted, but I was starting to take offense at the proprietor's attitude, particularly at what he was insinuating. I understood the reason for his suspicious manner and could even understand his hostility — to a point. But neither Francisco nor I had come into his place looking for trouble — or to be unfairly judged because the men who robbed his store were Mexicans. We were there as customers, but even in that regard, we looked to be disappointed because his merchandise was very scarce.

"These shelves were stacked full just over a week ago," Pawnee Joe grumbled, his lined face wrinkled with disgust. "Then those *culeros* (and he spoke the word with a blunt emphasis that he directed at Francisco) rode in one night 'round closin' and demanded my money at gunpoint. Then, with their faces grinnin' the whole time, they cleaned out most of my stock. They'da grabbed it all, but only took what they could carry with 'em. Not only cowards but lazy, these pepper guts are, even when they're thievin'."

Another insult he directed at Francisco, who, if he was taking umbrage at these remarks, stood stoically, his expression set and solid. But from all I'd seen in the short time I had been with Francisco, I knew that just a thorn scratch beneath his passive demeanor he likely was seething. Because, as he told me, he *was* a man of two heritages — and proud of both.

I stepped in, hoping to diffuse a potentially powder-keg situation.

"As I told you, we're here just for supplies," I said again to Pawnee Joe. "We'll pay you — for whatever you've got on hand that we can use."

Once more Pawnee Joe pivoted his head around the store. "You see what I've got."

"Well, maybe you have goods stored away," I suggested. "Maybe in the back."

"My stock comes in once a month, and I don't order no surplus," he said impatiently on a heavy breath. "Whenever items get here, they go straight on the shelves." He added with a lopsided curling of his lip, "I don't do no thrivin' business out here to have the luxury to keep stuff in storage. I order just as much stock as I know I'm gonna sell, and that's why it don't come in too regular."

I turned to Francisco. He kept his eyes steadily on Pawnee Joe, but not in a threatening or intimidating manner. His expression was vacant, betraying nothing of what he might be thinking. But I saw that in his own quiet way, he was defending his honor. He was innocent of any wrongdoing, but he knew that if he dared to lower or shift his eyes, he might give Pawnee Joe and the others a right to justify their judgment of him as a cunning and disreputable Mexican.

I admired Francisco for his nerve, at the same time recognizing that among the suspicious and possibly even accusatory stares leveled at him by these men, his attempt at retaining his dignity might be construed as defiance. It could even prompt an aggressive action.

"Hate to see you take a bullet for no good reason," I muttered out the corner of my mouth as I sidled alongside my *compañero.*

Francisco responded to my remark with a look of astonishment. And when he spoke, his words were delivered in a loud, strong voice.

"This man has suffered a misfortune," he said, looking directly at me but intending his words to be heard by all. "Surely there must be, how you say, *compensation* for his loss."

I could see Francisco was headed somewhere, so I played along and wiped the expression of perplexity from my face. But his words struck me as peculiar. Was Francisco suggesting that he himself was willing to make restitution for something he did not do? Apparently this was so . . . as I watched him withdraw a handful of pesos from the pouch he carried with him and slap the silver onto the counter.

Pawnee Joe did not look impressed. But as it turned out, a gesture of generosity was not Francisco's intent. He merely wanted to show Pawnee Joe and the others that he had the money to pay for what we needed. This was his way to assure them he had come to the store in good faith.

"You will accept these coins for our purchases?" Francisco said.

Pawnee Joe picked up one of the silver pieces and inspected it.

"Yeah," he breathed out in a wheeze. "I'll take your Mexican money. But just so yuh know, whatever I got left here ain't goin' cheap. Reckon you can understand that, can't yuh — *Peedro.*"

I wasn't sure if Pawnee Joe was as bitter-mean as he seemed or was simply trying to impress his friends; maybe restore his pride, ease his humiliation at being robbed by the two Mexicans. Whatever his reason, he was riding Francisco pretty hard. I admit I was curious to see how much more abuse my *compañero* would take from him. I didn't consider it wise for the proprietor to under-estimate Francisco. I knew what the little Mexican was capable of, and despite my own earlier teasing of him for his timidity around water, I recognized that if it came to a showdown, he was no coward.

At the same time, I didn't want to see this situation get out of hand. I wasn't eager for any bloodshed. That was still ahead of us.

"Do you mind if I, how you say, peruse your shelves?" Francisco asked politely.

"Peruse all you like," Pawnee Joe responded, his tone only a little less hostile now that he understood he had a paying customer. "But what yuh see is what I got."

I let Francisco do the shopping. After all, he would be paying for our goods. Plus I thought it wise to keep a watch on his back. I still didn't completely trust this unfriendly bunch.

Francisco took his time inspecting the shelves, considering each item before deciding whether or not it was necessary. He was interested only in the essentials. I also suspected his slowness in making choices was intentional, a way of letting Pawnee Joe know that if he was going to gouge him on the prices, Francisco was not going to be hasty in selecting his purchases.

Finally, Francisco brought his few packages over to the counter. Without even calculating the price of each item, Pawnee Joe provided a cash total, an amount that he simply pulled from the air. As I suspected, it was way out of line: Twenty-five dollars for some flour, sugar, coffee, jerked beef, and a couple of slabs of bacon that had to be brought in from the smokehouse. Yet Francisco didn't flinch. He reached into his pouch to extract more silver. Personally, I felt Francisco was a fool for agreeing to pay such high prices. Pawnee Joe had been robbed and now he was robbing us. And I knew damn well the main reason was because Francisco was a Mexican.

But since Francisco didn't say anything, neither did I. And, of course, with many miles still to go, we needed the guarantee of extra provisions. And . . . because I'd made the mistake of mentioning our destination, Pawnee Joe knew it, too. Another likely reason why he could slap his own prices on his merchandise.

While Francisco slowly and deliberately counted out the coins, my eyes wandered and came upon a curtained back room open just enough to reveal what looked like a small serving area. I walked over and peered inside. A counter, a few tables, and bottles of liquor on the back bar. I decided I could use a drink right about now. At the same time, my curiosity was aroused. If Pawnee Joe had been robbed like he'd claimed, why hadn't his liquor been taken? To my way of thinking, liquor would have been the first thing those *banditos* would have grabbed.

"Think I can get a drink?" I said over my shoulder.

Pawnee Joe didn't look too pleased that I had discovered his makeshift saloon. He was probably hoping the two of us would just take our purchases and skedaddle.

He hesitated before he huffed and said, "Be with you in a minute."

I walked through the curtain and stood at the bar. I could hear some whispered conversation going on in the store, and presently I found Francisco standing next to me.

"Very expensive to shop here," was all he said.

"Thought you knew this place," I returned quietly.

Francisco frowned. "I have been here, of course. How else would I have known where to come?"

I scratched at the stubble on my face. "Our friend didn't seem to regard you as a familiar customer."

"No, that is true," Francisco agreed with a sigh. "He has always made Mexicans pay more." Then he grinned. "Perhaps that is why it was Mexicans who robbed him."

"And one of those *banditos* wouldn't happen to have been you?" I kidded him.

Francisco fixed me with an offended frown. Before he could speak, Pawnee Joe came up behind the bar.

"Awright, what d'yuh want?"

With a hearty slap of his palms atop the dull, stained wood of the counter, Francisco said, "A drink of tequila for my *amigo*."

201

I would have preferred a whiskey or even a beer, but Francisco was paying so I didn't contradict his choice. Besides, a drink of any sort would go down good.

"Nothin' for you?" Pawnee Joe asked Francisco.

"No, *Señor.* I am not particularly fond of alcohol."

"A *Mexicano* that don't drink," Pawnee Joe muttered under his breath. Then he spoke louder. "Never thought I'd see the day."

He looked pleased that he would not have to serve Francisco any of his liquor. I suspected my *compañero* also detected this, because he suddenly blurted, "On second thought, I think I, too, will have some tequila."

Pawnee Joe narrowed his eyes in displeasure and grunted. His moves deliberate, he set two small glasses on the counter and pulled a bottle from the back bar. Before he uncorked the bottle, he told us outright, "Liquor don't go no cheaper than anything else I sell in my store."

That hardly came as a surprise.

"And how much is that?" I said.

Pawnee Joe smiled snidely. "Each shot'll cost yuh two dollars."

I said nothing. Instead, I turned to look at

Francisco, curious to see whether he would permit himself to be swindled again.

But once more he surprised me.

"You will again accept pesos?" he said with a grin.

"No, it's a mite different back here. When I serve liquor I want my money in U.S. dollars," Pawnee Joe told him flatly.

Francisco remained patient and frustratingly courteous. "That, my friend, I do not have. I have the money, *sí,* but not in the dollars you request."

Pawnee Joe nudged his head toward me.

"What 'bout him?" he said, speaking past me directly to Francisco.

Before I could answer for myself, Francisco interjected swiftly. "My *compadre* is short of funds." He turned to me and gave a quick wink of his eye. It was apparent that Francisco was not looking for the easy way out.

I kept my face expressionless, not saying anything if that was the way Francisco wanted to handle it.

"Well, then, reckon the two of yuh'll have to stay dry," Pawnee Joe said curtly as he prepared to return the bottle to its place on the back bar.

"Or perhaps is it that you choose not to serve liquor to a Mexican?" Francisco conjectured.

Pawnee Joe turned back around and looked hard at my *compañero.*

"One of your breed walks in here with American dollars and I'll gladly serve him," he huffed.

Francisco considered before he smiled thinly and said with just the faintest trace of indignation, "Though I imagine that does not happen regularly. That those of my, how you put it, *breed* carry with them the good Yankee currency."

Pawnee Joe held his posture upright and gave his thick head a tilt. "Yuh got that right, *Peedro.*"

Francisco sighed resignedly and again turned to look at me. He was silent for several moments before he said, "Well, if that is how he chooses to conduct his business, perhaps we should leave."

"The hell with it," I spouted. I reached into my pocket, pulled out some silver, and slapped it on the bar. Fun was fun, but I damn well wanted a drink.

"Good Yankee currency," I said to Pawnee Joe in a sneer. "So why don't you just pop the cork offa that bottle." I added, "And since there doesn't seem to be any shortage of liquor, can't rightly see a reason for you to be overcharging."

Pawnee Joe gave me a contemptuous look and snorted. "Price is whatever I say it is."

Unless I wanted to start a ruckus that would see me and my *compañero* outnumbered and probably lying out in the street, I had no choice but to grudgingly pay this . . . "storekeeper" what he was asking. But I still wanted to reap my own satisfaction. So I said, "Find it kinda odd why those *banditos* who robbed you woulda taken your stock but left your liquor behind."

As I expected, Pawnee Joe didn't look pleased at what he assumed I was insinuating. I noticed how his features started to tense. But to my surprise, instead of responding aggressively to my comment, he offered a hasty explanation. "Shipment came in after the holdup. Otherwise there wouldn't be a bottle left standin' on the back bar."

He opened the tequila and poured both Francisco and me a shot. We raised our glasses to each another in a salute. I knew minimal Spanish, but through repetition had retained a toast I decided to recite if only to tick off Pawnee Joe.

*"Salud y tiempo, y amor, y dinero, para gastarlos."* The translation was a simple: "Here's to health, and time, and love, and money to enjoy them."

Francisco responded to my toast cheerily, and we clinked our glasses with enough enthusiasm to almost shatter them.

I then downed my drink and raised a hand to halt Pawnee Joe before he could re-cork the bottle.

Once again I spoke audaciously. "Considering all the money you took from my friend, it would be right hospitable if you poured us one on the house before we ride out." I smiled. "Nice for customer relations."

"Not for me, *Señor,*" Francisco said quickly, with a sharp lift of his hand. "One glass of tequila is sufficient."

Pawnee Joe looked incredulous at my suggestion. "You got a nerve. I don't pour *myself* a drink without payin' for it. Yuh want another, it's two dollars." He then smiled smugly. "You won't find no other place to get a drink for at least the next twenty miles."

"Reckon we can expect their prices won't be any different," I presumed.

Pawnee Joe lifted a shoulder as one corner of his mouth likewise twisted upward. "Maybe more. A lot farther to go after that. Might even have to wait till yuh get to Chesterfield City."

"All right then. How much for the bottle?" I asked.

Pawnee Joe slowly scratched at the back of his neck, trying to give the impression that he was considering a price.

But then he said, "Don't make it a point to sell liquor by the bottle."

That was a downright lie. I got the feeling Pawnee Joe would sell his own mother for the right price. But just by his making the comment, I knew he had upped the cost considerably.

"How much?" I repeated.

"Reckon . . . oh, I'd say twenty dollars will put it in your saddlebag."

I shook my head. "Don't have that much cash, 'less you bend a little and accept my friend's pesos."

"*Señor,* I have no need for —" Francisco began to object.

"Costs me plenty to get my liquor shipped here. Gotta be brung in from the city, along a two-day travel route," Pawnee Joe said by way of explanation. " 'Less I charge customers more, don't hardly make a profit. And my suppliers don't accept Mexican . . . *dinero.* U.S. dollars. Cash on the barrelhead."

He might have had a valid argument. I didn't know. In any case, I was tempted to have him pour us both another drink since buying the bottle was out of the question at what he was charging, and it would likely be a long way until we came to a saloon that served liquor at a reasonable price. But spending another two dollars on a shot seemed ridiculous and, worse, it was playing right into his money-grubbing hands. Besides, I'd had my fill of Pawnee Joe's and, since Francisco wasn't thirsty, decided it best if we just be on our way.

I turned and walked out of the "saloon" and back into the store where Francisco and I were once more greeted with stares from the two men leaning against the counter. We were again ignored by the fellow sitting on the barrel who was still whittling away on his miniature wood carving. Francisco walked out of the store behind me, carrying the few packages he had purchased. I admit I felt relief once we were outside in the fresh air heading toward our horses, though I'd feel even better once we were galloping away, even if miles of flat, open country was all we'd have to look forward to.

I was shaking my head in aggravation and Francisco noticed.

"You do not think well of Pawnee Joe," he said with mild humor.

"He didn't think well of *you*," I returned.

"No different from when I last was here," Francisco admitted. "Only much more . . . *disagreeable.*"

"You're mighty generous," I told him. "I could think of a lot stronger words to use."

*"Hijo de puta?"* Francisco offered.

I had no idea how that translated into English, but it must have had some value as Francisco looked immensely pleased with himself when he spoke those words.

As Francisco fit the packages into the Hessian cloth sack, I glanced over my shoulder, half-expecting to see either Pawnee Joe or one of his cronies standing outside on the porch checking to see if our intention truly was to ride off, or if we might live up to their suspicions and storm back into the store with shotguns loaded and ready. But after I "saluted" them with the twist of a smile, they lost interest in us — just about as quickly as I wanted to forget about them.

Still, I couldn't help thinking that the bad taste this brief stopover had left in me could be a prelude of what was to come.

It had taken Francisco a long time to ask but finally, as our day's ride neared its end and the sun began to settle deep into the horizon, he broached the question I had been waiting for.

"You know it's funny, *Señor,* but here we ride together, and I do not know your name."

I had wondered how I would respond when the time came. Not very cleverly, I admit.

"No, you don't," was my reply.

When he saw that I was not going to offer anything more, he said, "Is there a reason you no tell me?"

"Might be," I said nonchalantly.

"And you no tell me that, either? The reason."

I hesitated for a moment.

"No," I then said.

I glanced askance at Francisco and noticed with amusement that he looked slightly frustrated.

"Does not seem fair," he said, almost petulantly. "You know my name. I have no secret."

"You offered it, I didn't ask," I reminded him. And then, just to annoy him, I said very slowly, "Francisco Velasquez."

"Francisco Emilio Velasquez," he returned with emphasis.

I said with a smirk, "Well, now you're *three* up on me."

Francisco said with an exaggerated sigh,

"I suppose then that I shall go to my grave never knowing for sure who is *mi amigo.*"

I gave Francisco a disapproving stare. "Bad choice of phrasing."

We kept our ponies at an easy trot while we looked for a suitable place to camp out for the night. I was trusting Francisco to lead us to one of those watering holes he said we'd find along our trail. Eventually, he did — a clear, clean-running stream where the horses could drink their fill and Francisco and I could top up our canteens and replenish our water pouches. But I had to wonder whether Francisco truly knew of this location or if we'd just stumbled onto it through luck.

It was promising to be another cold night on the desert, and we both were eager to get a fire started and have supper. I had a hankering for some of that bacon Francisco had bought at Pawnee Joe's. I knew that even if it was prime pork, the meat wasn't worth the price my *compañero* had paid for it; I just hoped it would be digestible. I didn't relish the thought of suffering stomach distress out in the middle of nowhere.

Francisco assured me he had inspected the bacon back at the trading post and that it was of acceptable (he didn't say good) quality. I trusted his judgment since he was the one who did the cooking. He had insisted taking on that chore at the outset and I didn't object. When I had to fend for myself when out on a trail, I generally ate from a can and munched on jerky and store-bought biscuits. Once in a while I might be daring and scramble myself an egg or two.

Francisco, on the other hand, prided himself on his cooking. I had to admit he wasn't half bad. He cut off some of the bacon from the length of one of the strips and then cut that piece into two halves and gingerly laid the portions out in a pan he set over the campfire. Once I heard the welcome sizzling, and the aroma of frying bacon greeted my nostrils, I felt pretty confident that neither my taste buds nor my belly would have reason to complain.

And it was a memorable meal. We both ate heartily. The only thing that disrupted my appetite was Francisco's insistence at still trying to pry from me my name. Frankly, I didn't know why it seemed so important to him, unless he truly had it in his heart to be my *amigo.*

But I wasn't yet ready to place gambler's odds on that likelihood.

# CHAPTER TWELVE

Times were tough on the Texas frontier. As we rode, I kept ever mindful that Indians roamed these parts and that many a settler had been killed by the Comanche. I'd had surprisingly few encounters with Indians during my travels; I reckon many of the people I tracked knew what areas to avoid when seeking their places of refuge. What was unfortunate was that any peace that existed between the white man and the Indian was generally tenuous and most often short-lived.

On this particular day I caught sight of a lone mounted Comanche brave watching us from a small sandy rise not too far in the distance. I kept my head straight and only shifted my eyes to check for any aggressive movement on his part. I advised Francisco to do the same — not in any way to let the Comanche know we were aware of his presence. Unfortunately, my *compañero* either misheard or ignored me, and he turned his gaze full on the Indian. The brave then did what I had feared: He spun his horse around and galloped away.

Francisco grinned. "You see, *Señor,* he is riding off."

He didn't understand what I knew was to come.

I was faced with a difficult decision. My worry was that he could be a Comanche scout who was hurrying back to his tribe to alert them to our being there. Although I was familiar with certain parts of Texas, where we now traveled was unfamiliar territory and we could be prime targets for a Comanche attack. Francisco and I could never outfight them and possibly not even outrun them. My only option was to try and stop the rider before he could reach his camp. Without even telling Francisco of my intention I wheeled my horse, whipping him into a dead run, and set out after the brave.

I would either have to kill or disable him to give Francisco and me plenty of time to get a good distance between ourselves and any pursuing Comanche.

I heard Francisco call out after me. I allowed myself a quick look over my shoulder and saw that he was racing after me. The Comanche brave rode fast; he had a strong horse that galloped like the wind. I doubted I would catch up to him. I would have to try and shoot him off his mount. With one hand steady on the reins I lifted one of my Colt revolvers from its holster and took steady aim. But before I could pull the trigger, I noticed that the brave had half-turned in his saddle and was pointing a rifle in my direction. I had no time to waste, and hoped my shot would be accurate.

Francisco was urging me to shoot, and in the next moment I obliged him. I don't know where the bullet struck but I saw the brave jerk upright in his saddle and try to hold his balance, but with the horse still running at top speed, he toppled from the animal, his body rolling over several times before finally lying motionless.

On the open prairie the report of a gunshot has an echo that can reach across quite a distance. I couldn't chance that the shot I had fired hadn't been heard, so I wasn't going to check on the Comanche to ensure he was dead. In truth, there was no point. His horse had continued its rapid pace without its rider. Even if the brave still lived, he was no longer a threat. But this territory was another matter. We had just discovered firsthand that the Comanche roamed the land, and I had no desire for another run-in that might lead to a less favorable outcome. I urged my mount into a half-circle and raced back the way I had come, my horse galloping hell-for-leather, with Francisco following close behind.

We got lucky. We rode far and fast, but could finally settle our mounts as it looked as if we were free of pursuit.

"I see an Indian holding a rifle and I see trouble in times to come," Francisco mused.

"You might be right," I said. "But I blame the white man: the *Comanchero*. He profits by supplying guns to the Indian, all the while knowing that if war comes, it will be his own people who will be killed."

Francisco appeared momentarily thoughtful, then gave me a deliberate sideways glance.

"*Sí,*" he said. "But maybe people do many things they might not like to do . . . for, as you say, profit."

I found I couldn't respond to that remark.

Finally, after many days of travel, we neared Chesterfield City. I was of two minds as we came to the end of what was sure to be only the first part of our journey. I was glad to leave the flatlands behind and enjoy civilization again — but I also knew that the true purpose of our work was only beginning.

And the knowledge brought with it a concern that, for my own peace of mind, I needed to address.

I wanted to see for myself if Francisco was handy with a gun. He carried a small derringer on his person along with a pistol in a shoulder holster under his poncho, but I'd yet to see him draw, let alone fire the revolver. Since I could not be certain what to expect once we encountered Silvano Ramos, it was imperative I be sure that Francisco could hold his own should we find ourselves in a gunfight.

I mentioned this to Francisco late in the afternoon the day before we would ride into Chesterfield City. When I specifically asked him about his skill with a gun, Francisco did not answer me with the confidence I had hoped for.

In fact, he admitted almost sheepishly, "I have not fired a weapon since I was in the army, *Señor.*"

"Were you any good?" I asked.

"Not as handy as I am with a knife," Francisco admitted.

"That might give Ramos the advantage," I said dourly.

Francisco spoke gravely. "Oh, no, *Señor.* I would never permit Ramos the advantage. But to kill him from afar with a bullet is not

217

my desire. It is too quick, and his death would be merciful. He must not only die but be made to die in pain. As he made Felicia suffer." He paused, lowered his eyes then raised them, slowly, to bore directly into my own gaze. "He must see who has come to kill him. And I must see the light of life leave his eyes."

I felt a chill course through me — not so much at his words, since I'd become familiar, if not yet thoroughly comfortable with his intent. What affected me was the coldness of his stare. I'd seen that look before, but never quite as . . . soulless as it appeared now. If that was the look he had in mind for Silvano Ramos when they came face to face, even a beast like Ramos could not help but believe it was not a man, but death itself, that had come to claim him.

I needed a second or two to recover, though I tried not to expose my uneasiness to Francisco.

When I spoke, my voice was even. "You can't be sure exactly what we might run into. Your knife might not be enough."

"You know this naturally from your work," Francisco presumed.

I responded with a solemn nod. I had only to think back to when I found myself cornered by the murderous hill folk in the

Bodrie Hills. If I'd had only a knife to rely on, I knew definitely I would not be talking to Francisco now.

I shifted my posture in the saddle. "You spoke of how a person or a thing can kill you if you're not prepared."

"Yes, I remember."

"You were right," I declared. "I learned the hard way to keep myself ready for every eventuality. But even then there are no certainties. All you can do is use whatever you can to strengthen your odds."

"Yes," Francisco agreed slowly. "As I think about what you are saying, it is wise that I should not disadvantage myself . . . should the need arise. When dealing with a man like Ramos, one never knows what to expect. He may prove a tricky adversary."

"Then maybe it's best you show me what you can do with a gun," I suggested.

Francisco squinted against the glare of the afternoon sun and glanced about the landscape, dotted with rocks and sparse vegetation.

"Here . . . in the desert?" he said, uncertain.

I nodded. "Before we head into Chesterfield City."

Without uttering another word, Francisco halted and dismounted from his horse. I remained in the saddle and watched as he looked to scout the area. I wasn't sure what he was searching for. Finally, he lifted an arm under his poncho and pointed to a large rock maybe twenty feet in the distance.

I understood. "Is that your target?"

Francisco didn't answer. He stepped over to one of his saddlebags and sifted through the contents. He finally withdrew a can of beans.

"This might spoil our supper," he said with a grin.

"Prove to me you're any good and we'll get a steak in Chesterfield City," I told him.

Francisco nodded. He began to walk toward the rock. He halted suddenly and looked back at me with concern.

*"Señor,"* he called out, "it makes no difference whether I am good or not if that is the deal you offer." He jerked a stiff thumb at himself. "You forget I am the one who has the money."

"No, didn't forget exactly," I said casually.

Francisco frowned at me.

"Pesos," I reminded. "Which we'd better trade off for U.S. McCoy money, 'lessen we want to chance depriving ourselves of a good meal."

"What do you say, *Señor?*"

I spoke louder, "I said we don't want a

repeat of what happened with your friend Pawnee Joe."

Francisco shook his head as he muttered "Pawnee Joe," then he turned and resumed walking toward the rock.

"No, that would not be good," I heard him mumble.

Still seated atop my mount, I watched as Francisco perched the can carefully upon the surface of the rock, then he paced back to me. When he decided he had a wide enough distance between himself and his target, he flipped the side of his poncho over his shoulder with a flourish and assumed an awkward gunfighter's stance. Not a sight that filled me with encouragement.

The air was quiet and still, as if the elements were favoring him by providing the proper environment. It gave Francisco an advantage I knew he wouldn't have if we ran into gunplay with Ramos, so it was I who broke the calm.

"Go for your gun, *amigo*!" I shouted.

Francisco raised his left arm and withdrew the pistol from its holster. It was a quick, sure movement. Good.

But then he took too long as he steadied his aim. Before he could even fire off his first shot, I spoke up loudly, "You'da been killed three times over by now!"

Francisco slowly dropped the gun to his side and just as slowly turned to face me.

"I must be sure of where I am shooting," he protested.

I slid off my saddle and walked over to him, my hand lifted in a pacifying gesture. My *compañero* looked displeased at my having interrupted him.

"That's a luxury I can practically guarantee you won't have," I told him outright. "You'll be shooting like you did in the army. You probably won't even have a specific target with everyone ducking for cover. Just aim the gun in whatever direction the firing's coming from, pull the trigger, and hope to God at some point your shot hits its mark."

A strained expression etched across Francisco's features. He fell silent.

"Something wrong?" I asked him.

Francisco took his time before he struggled to raise his eyes toward me — but of a sudden couldn't, as his focus once more descended to the ground.

I had a suspicion of what was troubling him.

*"Señor,"* he finally said, his words delivered in a near-whisper. He halted, clearly reluctant to finish.

"Go on, Francisco," I urged him.

Although he still found it difficult to meet my eye, Francisco readied himself for what he was about to say. I gave my head an upward tilt to encourage him.

"*Señor,* I have told you many things," he said. "Most are true . . . but some are not."

"Yeah, so I found out."

Francisco suddenly appeared flustered. "I — I wish I knew your name. It would make it much easier for what I am about to tell you."

"Just tell me," I insisted.

"Very well. *Señor . . .* one of the things that I was not truthful about was . . . that I had served in the army."

Francisco then took a step backward, as if he feared I might take a poke at him. Since I'd already figured this was to be his confession, I showed no emotion other than a flickering of disappointment in my expression. And even that response wasn't completely genuine. What I *did* feel was a renewed and amplified uncertainty about this undertaking he'd dragged me into.

"What about all those stories you told me?" I asked him grimly.

"They . . . they were stories told to me by my mother . . . about my father. When *he* served in the army."

"So in other words, you brought us both

into something that neither one of us is equipped to handle," I rebuked him, my voice critical.

Francisco suddenly raised his gaze to me. And his dark eyes held conviction. "It is only fair now that we have reached this point in our journey that I speak honestly with you."

"Shoulda done that before we rode out of Santa Rosina," I countered.

"Then you would not have joined me," Francisco said.

"We've been down this trail before," I reminded him. "That tactic you used to get me to come along with you."

Francisco wore an expression suggesting self-reproach. "*Sí.* Yes, I know."

"That's two marks against you, *compadre,*" I said without humor. "Don't know if my personal well-being can afford to wait around for number three."

"No more — *deceits, Señor,*" Francisco said, his pledge so determined that he practically shouted the words. "On that I give you my word." He thrust out his arm. "On that I give you my bond."

He obviously remembered what I had told him earlier about the honor of a handshake.

But I never acknowledged his outstretched hand. Not even with a look toward it.

Instead, I kept my eyes focused on the little Mexican before I turned and started to walk away, just wanting to be alone for the next moments to sort out my thoughts. It didn't matter if he'd emptied clean his bag of lies. What he'd just admitted was all I needed to hear. Since the beginning of our journey, I'd ridden alongside Francisco without complete confidence — either in what he was setting out to do or what might come in its aftermath. But he had now provided me with an out, if I chose to take advantage of it. He would not see me as a coward, only as someone who had lost trust in him. And I could convince myself like-wise. I would not look upon myself as a coward if I turned away from him. Under the circumstances, it would be a sensible decision. Regardless of how strong his lust for vengeance was, he wouldn't stand a dog's chance in hell going up against a man like Silvano Ramos. He'd just proven he didn't have the skill — and that put not only him but me in a precarious position.

"Very well, *Señor,*" I heard Francisco say.

I looked behind me. His tone of voice sug-gested Francisco would understand if I chose to end our trail, and I pretty much had decided that was what I was going to do.

But then I was surprised. Not merely surprised — but *astounded.*

Francisco suddenly spun around, as if his slight body had just been manipulated by a strong gust of desert wind. He knelt to a crouch, balanced, and fired off six swift shots that blasted the can of beans into shredded tin.

I'm not sure, but I think my jaw unhinged at this display of his gunmanship.

Francisco held his position for another moment or two. Then he rose to his full height of about five-foot-four and walked in a sort of swagger toward me, twirling his pistol as he did so.

When he was just inches from me, he grinned into my face and spoke almost apologetically. "As I said, *Señor,* I am much more skilled at using a knife."

When I finally found my voice, I said, "You coulda saved me plenty of misgivings if you'd showed me this earlier."

Francisco heaved a breath. "Yes. Perhaps that too was unfair. But you proved to me that you are a dependable man, riding all this way with me . . . with you having these, as you say, misgivings."

"Mainly my motivation was the money, Francisco," I told him — with half honesty.

"Yes, the money," Francisco said, smiling

and nodding, and clearly not entirely accepting my mercenary claim.

Still I was puzzled.

"So — why did you feel it necessary to lie about serving in the army . . . when you shoot like a marksman?" I asked him.

"I just like telling the stories," Francisco replied with an impish grin.

And of course there was the inevitable question. "So — just where did you learn to shoot like that?"

"Practice, *Señor*. Beginning back when I was a young boy." Francisco paused, then eyed me furtively. "Perhaps I never learned to swim, but I have found knowing how to handle a weapon a much more useful skill."

I could not argue with him there.

Francisco then eyed me speculatively.

"Perhaps there is another talent of mine that will impress you equally," he said, adding, "In a practical way, of course."

"Practical?" I repeated, not sure of his meaning.

"*Sí*. For when we meet up with Ramos," he clarified.

I nodded my interest. Francisco fixed me with a peculiar smile, walked over to his pony, and began to rummage about in one of his saddlebags. I watched him carefully — admittedly with just that shred of mistrust I simply could not alleviate — and when he glanced over his shoulder and noticed my eyes were glued on him, he frowned and deliberately hid his action from me, giving further rise to my suspicion. Perhaps to ease my doubts, he spoke aloud while he performed whatever it was that he was doing.

"My family was wealthy," he said. "We had all the food we could eat. The very best dishes were served upon our table. But my father, *caballero* that he was, was also a wise, common man. He knew well the importance of seeking sustenance from the earth. Not just through the growing of crops, but also seeking and slaughtering one's meat. With the revolution soon to take its toll, especially among the privileged, my father took precautions. He taught my brother and me to hunt for our food, should the need arise. He also taught us that a gun is not always the best weapon. I recall him saying that to eat from a beast slain by a bullet was a violation of the meat the animal provided for food."

With those curious if revealing words, Francisco turned to me. He was brandishing a *boleadora,* or bola, a potentially deadly instrument I had heard of but had never seen outside of photographs. Watching

Francisco manipulate those three iron balls attached to cords with a practiced speed and movement sent a shiver through me. While I understood they were designed to capture an animal by entangling its legs and making it helpless for slaughter, to be struck by one of those weighted balls could have devastating results.

Francisco noticed my tentative reaction and smiled. When he spoke, it was as if he were reading my thoughts.

"A man's skull could be crushed into sand by one who wields this weapon properly," he said. And then he whipped the bola loose from his grip with precise skill. I heard the *whoosh* as the device whizzed past me, and I watched as the leafy spiked head of a yucca plant some yards away blew apart on impact, as if shattered by a shotgun blast.

A marksman-like hit.

Francisco took a moment to admire his handiwork. I had to admit it was a damn impressive demonstration; though, despite what Francisco said, I could not really define it as *practical* once one was engaged in battle. It required time to work up speed and to mark the exactness of one's aim. Hardly convenient if gunfire was erupting all around you. And it provided only a one-shot opportunity.

Francisco went to retrieve the bola. When he walked back over to me, head lowered, face shaded under the wide brim of his sombrero, he sighed and spoke contemplatively. "The question one must ask himself before he decides to use such a weapon —" and here his face lifted and he looked directly at me — "is does he intend to cripple his prey . . . or to kill it."

He was speaking rhetorically. But still I pondered the exactness of his wording.

*It . . .* or *him?*

# CHAPTER THIRTEEN

We weren't even an hour into Chesterfield City before we learned about the incidents of violence perpetrated by Silvano Ramos and his gang. The bandits primarily targeted small settlements along the western border of the state. A clever move since initially these attacks could be blamed on the Apache and Comanche raiders who were known to use the Franklin Mountains as bases for their raids upon river settlements. But it wasn't long before the true culprits were identified and a large reward was posted. Few men were foolhardy enough to attempt to claim that reward, and those who did were sure to be found slaughtered. The killers were clever in their ruthlessness: They made certain to leave the bodies where they could easily be found. Their mutilated conditions suggested a lengthy and agoniz-ing period of torture that discouraged others who might be tempted by the $2,000 bounty.

In a very short span of time the Ramos Gang had achieved a near legendary reputation. Unlike many desperados, the exploits of the Ramos raiders did not require embellishment. Not even the most imaginative dime store novelist could paint a more graphic picture than what was factually reported. The gang struck suddenly and without mercy. Homes looted, property destroyed, people killed. Committing these atrocities brazenly, without fear of reprisal from the law. Even to Francisco, this was a startling revelation. But it didn't take me long to figure out that it was not so much the savagery of their attacks that troubled my *compañero* — Francisco could expect no less from Ramos after how the man had butchered his sister, Ramos's own wife. His concern was that the man he sought now rode with a gang. No longer would it be one man against another. Francisco had assumed their confrontation would be more evenly matched, only now to discover the odds favored his enemy.

Yet his resolve remained undiminished. And even now that I knew Francisco was capable of defending himself, I feared his unyielding decision. We were hardly equipped to go against such a bloodthirsty outfit. We would be as outgunned as we were outnumbered.

We had been sitting in a saloon on the outskirts of the town refreshing ourselves with a cold drink (beer for me and a sarsaparilla for Francisco), when we overheard the gang's exploits being discussed at a table next to us, the conversation being exchanged by three excited cowboys. Both Francisco and I listened quietly but with aroused interest as we sipped our beverages. I knew Chesterfield City itself was a wild boomtown and had a reputation for prostitution, gambling, and outright lawlessness — hence its nickname the "Six Shooter Capital" — so to hear these cowboys gibber about bloodshed in other parts of Texas told me this was looked upon as big news. Mighty serious stuff.

Francisco pushed his glass aside, folded his arms on the table, and leaned forward. He spoke softly, in a conspiratorial tone; exercising caution in case there might be ears nearby ready to report back to Ramos.

"It is not his *compadres* that concern me," he said. "It is only Ramos himself I am interested in."

I provided a stern reminder. "It's not likely you'll be able to get to Ramos without having to go through his men."

Francisco's next words came easily. "Every man takes time alone. When we locate Ramos we will wait. We will watch until that time comes. If all goes well, Silvano Ramos will be dead long before his men even suspect he is missing from their camp."

The way Francisco laid out his plan, simply, it almost sounded workable. But I knew his commitment was so firm that he was prepared to combat hell's minions to get at the devil.

I, on the other hand, was not quite so dedicated.

He also might become reckless, and that possibility concerned me. I could not guess how Francisco would react once he laid his eyes on the man who killed his sister. I could not be certain he would restrain himself. He might choose that moment to act blindly, on impulse, mindless of the consequences — and thereby put us both at risk.

He'd proven adept at handling a side iron, but if we did succeed in locating the Ramos Gang, Francisco would need more than a gunfighter's skill in his arsenal.

He would have to utilize sound and sensible judgment.

■ ■ ■ ■

Neither Francisco nor I had really expected to find Ramos lying low in Chesterfield City. But now that he was running with a gang, he could be anywhere in the state. And all of a sudden our task looked to become more difficult. There was a lot of territory to cover. My first thought was that the outlaws might have taken refuge somewhere in the rugged isolation of the Franklin Mountains. Although a small mountain range, there was plenty of natural cover that would provide protection for Ramos and his cohorts. Tracking could prove difficult, since there were few trails and much of the terrain was treacherous. If the gang managed to scout out a good spot — particularly where they could keep themselves concealed yet be afforded a lookout view — they could hole up in the mountains at least until the snows came.

If that was where the bandits kept camp between raids, they likely did much of their travel through the Mesilla Valley, which was a fertile region that provided water and vegetation, sufficient both for themselves and their horses. But it was also an open trail, which meant they probably had to travel by night to avoid being spotted.

When I mentioned this theory to Francisco, he was swift to dismiss it.

"Ramos would not stay in one place for long," he said. "He is a man who must always be on the move. That is the way his brain works."

I pierced Francisco with an inquisitive look. "How can you be so certain what Ramos thinks?"

Francisco replied with a finger tap to his head. "As your part is to seek, mine is to try and think like Ramos."

"To think like a Mexican bandit?" I remarked, smiling thinly.

"Perhaps." There was no levity in his reply.

I regarded my *compañero* speculatively. "Maybe I've just learned too much, but I'm getting another of those suspicions that you're not being straight with me."

Francisco's uneasy silence seemed to provide the answer to that searing doubt.

"I thought there weren't going to be any more lies between us," I reminded him.

"No lie, *Señor,*" Francisco said.

"Then what is it you're trying *not* to tell me?"

Francisco didn't answer.

I was becoming impatient, and when I spoke my words came forcefully. "We've come a ways together. We might be nearing the end of our journey. So I'll say this, if you expect me to go any farther, I need you to tell me everything you know. That, *amigo*, is part of my being a seeker. And why you hired me."

Francisco's face took on a distant expression, as if he were trying to find the best way to broach whatever it was he had to reveal.

He said, "Perhaps it is partly guilt. Perhaps mostly it is what I choose to forget." Evasive words, and then he once more went quiet.

"I mean what I said, Francisco," I told him firmly. "Honesty . . . or I walk outta here."

It took what seemed another long while before Francisco obliged me. I waited out those minutes with a determined patience.

Yet when he next spoke, he spouted more mystery. "I did not feel it necessary that I tell you, *Señor.* It was not something I thought important for you to know. But you are clever . . . or maybe I no longer have the right to keep this to myself, knowing that you have committed to ride beside me."

"The jury's still out on that, Francisco," I said humorlessly.

"*Sí,* I understand."

I waited a little longer. Francisco finally

prefaced what he was about to say by drawing a deep breath.

"The truth, *Señor,* is that I know Silvano Ramos well," he began, this revelation giving me a bit of a start, since he'd said nothing earlier to suggest they'd shared any sort of familiarity with each other.

He resumed and spoke his piece briskly. "I know him because I grew up with him. We played together as children in our village. We were of two different upbringings. I was born of privilege, Silvano of poverty. Yet we became *amigos.* And later . . . I rode with him. Yes, I, too, stepped outside the law. My only excuse was that I was young. Restless. And Silvano was a stimulating companion. But it was a life I soon abandoned, as did Silvano — or so I thought. Otherwise I would not have agreed to speak to my sister on his behalf as she became a beautiful young lady. I saw how Felicia, even as a child, was attracted to Silvano — and how he had become attracted to her. He was my closest *compadre* and I saw no harm in the two of them sharing a courtship. He had given me his word that he was putting his dishonest past behind him. My mother and even my brother were not as trusting of Silvano. And, sadly, they were right. My mother, she forgave me for my part in

238

encouraging the romance that led to their marriage. But perhaps now you understand why my brother Fernando, a man no better than I, swore to kill me after we buried our sister."

"He blamed you?" I said.

Francisco nodded. "He waited until we had laid Felicia in the ground, and then he promised that the next grave to be dug would be mine."

"You are a man of many secrets, Francisco," was my only response to his story.

"Have you no secrets in your past, *Señor*?" Francisco asked, cocking his head. "For instance, why is it that you do not reveal to me your name?"

I was not about to favor him with an answer. I remained adamant on that point. My identity was mine alone. Besides, it wasn't me who had anything to answer for.

I suppose Francisco came to recognize that, because he let the subject drop.

"So you see, I know much about Silvano Ramos," he concluded. "Especially how he thinks. Which is why, together, we will have success in finding him."

"And *you* will find pleasure in killing him," I said, phrasing my words not as a question but rather a statement of fact.

Francisco spoke his next words totally

devoid of emotion. There was no hesitation. No regret.

"Yes. Because he betrayed me," he replied. "To kill my boyhood friend will give me much pleasure."

# CHAPTER FOURTEEN

Mexicans were plentiful in Chesterfield City so Francisco's dark-skinned, *sombrero*-wearing presence did not attract unwanted attention as our horses trotted through the muddy streets toward the sheriff's office. We needed a lead, and I hoped the sheriff would be obliging. The problem was I wasn't sure how I was going to explain the reason for our inquiry; we certainly could not be forthright in our intent. Could damn likely get the two of us run out of town before we learned anything — if not outright jailed.

Francisco had obviously done his homework. He surprised me with his knowledge of the sheriff and his accomplishments, the most noteworthy of which was his capture of a particularly nasty desperado named Jim Weaver — known as the "Terror of the Rockies." His crimes equalled those of Silvano Ramos and his crew of murderers. Weaver was credited with committing at least twenty-five killings, but his bloody trail ended when Sheriff Austin Briggs and his one-man posse, consisting of his deputy at the time, engaged the outlaw and his bunch in a gunfight as the gang fled toward Mexico. By the time the gun smoke had cleared, Weaver and his bandits were dead, their bodies blasted to bits.

I firmly believed that Sheriff Briggs would be a valuable man to have ride alongside us. But Francisco would not hear of it. He didn't want there to be even the remotest chance for Silvano Ramos to be taken alive. Surely he would be hanged for his recent crimes, but to Francisco there was only one crime for which Ramos must be punished. And that punishment must be at his hand.

Francisco suddenly brought his horse to a halt. He pointed to a two-story, wood-framed building across the street.

"*Señor,* look," he said. I followed his pointing finger and noticed the words *Chesterfield City Chronicle* etched across the wide front window.

"This might be a better place for us to start," he suggested eagerly.

He had a point. I also understood his reasoning. He thought it less conspicuous to try to collect information from a source other than the local law. I had to agree; a newspaperman might not get the itch to ask the probing questions a sheriff would. Might not regard us with the same suspicions, either.

I nodded and we directed our mounts toward the office. We tethered our animals to the hitching rail, then stepped up onto the boardwalk and walked into the building. Some fellow who either didn't hear us over the noise of the press or chose to ignore our presence seemed to be the only person in the building, which was redolent of printer's ink. After all the fresh air Francisco and I had been breathing along our trail, this was a particularly cloying smell. I glanced around the place and noticed a far office with its door closed. The name of the paper's publisher, J.C. MONTGOMERY, was neatly and prominently printed in bold black lettering on the blue frosted glass. I nudged Francisco, and we stepped away from the oblivious press operator to the office door.

Just as I was about to rap at the glass, Francisco took me by the elbow.

"Have you decided what you are going to tell him, *Señor*?" he asked. "The reason for our call?"

"I don't suppose you have," I returned.

Francisco shrugged his shoulders and

tried to hide his awkwardness with a feeble grin.

And then the office door opened and an attractive young lady, very properly and professionally attired, started to step outside. Seeing the two of us dusty and unwashed cowboys standing a couple of feet from her gave her an immediate and certainly understandable start.

She clasped a hand against her chest.

"Oh, my goodness," she gasped.

I quickly removed my Stetson and gave Francisco a poke in the ribs with my elbow to get him to doff his *sombrero.*

"I apologize, ma'am," I said in as sincere a tone as I could muster.

Francisco, *sombrero* tightly clutched in both hands, offered a grin and a bow.

"I was just about to knock when you came out," I assured her.

Recovering, the lady responded in a rather stiff manner.

"And what business would you have with me?" she inquired.

"Uh, no, ma'am," I said, fiddling with the brim of my Stetson. "Actually, my partner and I would like to speak to Mr. Montgomery."

I noticed a very faint smile start to slide across her lips.

"*Mister* Montgomery?" she said with a slight tilt of her head.

"Yes, ma'am."

Her peculiar smile widened a bit more.

"Ma'am?" I said, curious. I noticed that my hand manipulations with my hat were becoming a little more energetic, starting to crease the fabric, and I steadied my fingers before she could notice.

"There hasn't been a 'Mister Montgomery' in this office for the past three years," she explained.

"The name on the door —" I started to say.

She pointed a long, slender finger at the lettering.

"J.C. Montgomery, Publisher," she read aloud, pronouncing each word deliberately, as if she were a schoolmarm instructing children in a classroom. "As you'll notice, it says nothing about a 'mister'."

I felt a tad embarrassed as I understood. My *compañero,* on the other hand, still looked baffled.

I cleared my throat. "You'll have to accept my pardon, ma'am. I naturally thought —"

"I do," she interjected indulgently. She allowed herself a more friendly smile. "Believe me, it's not the first time."

Trying not to appear obvious, as this lady

was the first female I'd seen since leaving
Santa Rosina, I thought to myself there was
no way anyone could mistake J.C. Montgomery for a man. Although she was for-
mally attired, she was mighty pleasing on
the eye. She was likely in her late twenties
with smooth, fair-complexioned skin and
light sandy hair that could have hung softly
curled against her cheeks. But she wore her
hair piled high atop her head, which I
decided was intended to give her a professional appearance since, after all, she was a
businesswoman. On the more feminine side,
she had full, puckered lips and soft blue eyes
framed by long, curving lashes that I imagined could express great joy or show deep
irritation in equal proportion — depending
on the circumstance.

And I dare say she fulfilled every fantasy
I'd entertained during those dull, hot days
riding with Francisco.

*Miss* J.C. Montgomery invited us into her
office where we could speak away from the
clanking din of the printing press. I noticed
how she wrinkled her nose in our presence,
which was not surprising since the two of
us certainly could use a wash-up if not a
bath. But we could tend to that later. The
room was small and sparsely furnished, with
only a paper-laden desk and bureau and two

bare wood-backed chairs positioned in front of the desk. Francisco and I each took a chair while Miss Montgomery seated herself behind the desk. She immediately apologized for the disarray laid out before her, explaining that it had been a busy week, what with the manhunt on for the Ramos Gang.

Francisco and I tried not to appear obvious as our gazes veered to each other. But the truth was, we could not have hoped for a more opportune opening.

It was my *compañero* who spoke first.

"Yes, we have heard of this . . . Ramos Gang," he said, voicing his words in a deliberately detached manner.

I didn't speak, just nodded.

"They're murdering thieves," Miss Montgomery said, delivering her words with a surprising and unexpected rancor. "It's a tragic story."

Both Francisco and I hoped for her to tell us more. But neither of us wanted to come across as too eager. We waited to see if she might resume of her own accord. Fortunately, she did, expressing the same heated emotion.

"Ramos escaped justice and started this campaign of terror," she said. And then, noticing how both Francisco and I sat still

247

and intrigued by her comment, she halted her angry outburst and composed herself. She offered another cordial smile. "But I'm sure that's not why you've come to see me."

Once again Francisco and I exchanged a glance. My *compañero* looked a mite uncomfortable, as it seemed the lady publisher knew more of the back story than he had expected to hear. Actually, I became a little ill at ease myself. The history behind what Silvano Ramos had become was not a point of pride for either of us.

On the other hand, the door had been opened, and it might be wise for us to take advantage of it. I could see Francisco realized that, as well. He turned to me with a look that suggested I do the talking. I reckon he figured I was better equipped to keep a rein on my emotions.

"Actually, Miss Montgomery, that is precisely the reason we've come here," I began.

I wasn't completely straightforward with her. I thought it better not to tell her about our quest, and especially Francisco's desire for revenge. That might put a halt to her telling us anything that could prove to be to our benefit. She'd likely think us bounty hunters. In my experience, there was little love for that breed of mercenary. But with

Francisco's nodding consent, I did tell her that Francisco was the brother of the woman he had killed after first escaping justice. At first Miss Montgomery looked astonished. But once she resumed her professional deportment, she searched about her cluttered desk, finally retrieving a piece of notepaper. She was a newswoman and wanted to hear Francisco's story.

She focused her attention directly on Francisco. "So you know Ramos. What can you tell me about him?"

My *compañero* appeared distressed.

"No, no," he objected as he thrust himself forward in his chair. "This I do not want."

Miss Montgomery's hand halted just as she settled her quill pen against the paper. Her expression was perplexed. "I don't understand. Isn't that why you came to see me?"

I shook my head firmly, shifting my eyes to watch as Francisco's brown fingers nervously knitted the wide brim of his *sombrero.*

"I'd be willing to pay you for your story," Miss Montgomery offered.

That was absolutely the wrong thing to say. Francisco not only looked offended at the proposition, he appeared ready to lose his temper.

It was left to me to try and smooth over this potentially volatile situation.

"Please understand," I said in a conciliatory tone. "My friend has no interest in having his story told, nor does he wish to profit from what happened to his sister."

Miss Montgomery's eyes took on a sympathetic look as she studied Francisco, who had settled back into his chair looking morose. Graciously, she laid aside both the pen and notepaper.

"I apologize," she said. "I suppose that was a rather callous assumption."

I offered her a reassuring smile. Francisco kept silent.

She exhaled delicately. "But I still don't understand why you —"

"Silvano Ramos murdered my friend's sister," I said, speaking simply, solemnly. "There are a lot of unanswered questions. I think you can appreciate he wants to find out whatever he can about the man . . . for his own piece of mind."

Francisco twisted his head toward me and creased his lips in a faint, appreciative smile.

"Yes, I can understand that," Miss Montgomery said with a nod of her head. "But you must appreciate that I can only tell you what's been reported. There have been few witnesses left alive following one of his gang's raids and, understandably, they haven't wanted to say much because they're afraid. Ramos and his men created nightmares that will last a lifetime for those people." She paused for a moment, her expression thoughtful. "My best suggestion would be for you to speak to our sheriff. If anyone might be able to help you, it would be him."

I drew a sigh. "Yeah, but most times a lawman can be pretty closemouthed. 'Specially to snooping strangers." I then brought myself to ask, "By the way, this sheriff, has he been tracking Ramos?"

Miss Montgomery shook her head. "It's gone beyond local jurisdiction. The Rangers have pretty much taken over the manhunt. They've been combing the countryside since two of their men were caught and strung up by the Ramos Gang."

"Heard something about that," I said idly. And then with a bit more emphasis, "So the sheriff isn't in any way involved in the search?"

"There was a time when he'd have been leading a posse," Miss Montgomery said. "But Sheriff Briggs is getting close to hanging up his badge. Suffers from rheumatism, among other constraints from age."

I nodded half-heartedly.

Miss Montgomery again looked thoughtful. "I'm sorry I can't give you more, but —"

Francisco finally spoke up. "Miss Newspaper Lady, my *amigo* and I have yet to eat, and we've ridden a long trail. All the way from Santa Rosina, in fact. Would you mind maybe if we all had a meal, in a nice atmosphere, and there we could maybe talk further?"

I hadn't expected this gesture. But I wasn't about to argue with my *compañero*'s suggestion, especially since I'd begun to feel my own belly rumbling. I absolutely did not want to embarrass myself with gut grunts and growls in front of this fine lady.

Before Miss Montgomery could answer, Francisco added, "Besides, my *amigo* and I do not know of a good place to eat in Chesterfield City."

I confess it was difficult to halt the smile I felt creeping across my lips. I couldn't think of more appealing company to share dinner with.

After only a few seconds of indecision Miss Montgomery said, "Well, I suppose —"

Francisco wouldn't even let her finish her sentence. He said abruptly, "Very fine. You will join us then."

Miss Montgomery smiled another pleasant smile. Then she stood up and walked over to the bureau. She slid open one of the top drawers and removed a metal box. She opened the lock with the key she had on her person, and both Francisco and I noticed that she withdrew some cash.

"Oh, no, Miss Newspaper Lady, I insist," Francisco objected emphatically. "You must let me pay for our meal."

"I don't expect you to —"

"But you see, it was my invitation," Francisco interjected. "It will be my privilege."

Miss Montgomery sighed before she accepted gratefully, and then excused herself to go upstairs to where, she explained, she had living quarters to prepare herself. I halted her and somewhat timidly mentioned that it might not be a bad idea if Francisco and I could be recommended a bath house where we could wash away our days of trail dirt. She was keen to the idea and told us a place where we could go. Just down the street. We then arranged to meet within the hour.

Once she was gone I turned to my *compañero* and said quietly, as a reminder, "You plan to settle our bill with pesos?"

Francisco wore a troubled frown. "*Ay Chingao!* I forgot."

"I approve of the invitation," I told him. "But I don't want our dinner to end on a note that won't look good for either of us."

Francisco's face scrunched in thought. "*Sí.* No, I mean that would not be good."

We met with Miss Montgomery after Francisco and I had both took a hot, soapy bath that cost us twenty-five cents apiece. Francisco naturally was opposed to paying for the privilege of dunking himself into a tub of water but I persuaded him with the reminder that our horses likely smelled better than we did. Unfortunately, we weren't able to do much with our clothing and so I'm sure an odor still accompanied us.

Miss Montgomery had changed from the formal clothing she'd had on into a fresh periwinkle blue dress and was wearing a waist-length silk town jacket as comfort against the later chill of the evening. But what most caught my eye was that she had loosed her hair and her long locks flowed fetchingly over her shoulders and down her back. Even my *compañero* looked on approvingly. Too approvingly, as I had to deliver him an elbow nudge to not appear so obvious.

I regretted having to spoil the moment with a practical concern, but I tactfully explained our money situation to spare us possible humiliation later on. Miss Montgomery smiled understandingly and told us that the town bank should be able to exchange Francisco's pesos for U.S. currency. The bank manager knew her well, so she volunteered to come along with us in case there was any argument.

Fortunately, the transaction went smoothly. Soon the three of us found ourselves comfortably seated in the restaurant of The Benedict Hotel.

One thing I did notice: Francisco did not exchange all of his pesos. He carefully and precisely counted each coin from his pouch, but there was still a lot of silver jangling around inside the leather. I had the distinct feeling he didn't want me to know how much money he carried with him. What I assumed was that my fee was to come from that pouch, and I suspected Francisco did not want to be any more generous in paying me than he had to be.

After a most enjoyable beefsteak dinner (which Francisco ordered with a side order of beans and Mexican flatbread; Miss Montgomery and I garnished our plates with carrots and slices of ripe tomato) we each relaxed with a liqueur. Even Francisco indulged himself to a glass, though I'm sure it was merely for the sake of appearance. He never once lifted the drink to his lips.

Miss Montgomery certainly wasn't a shy companion, and I found that refreshing. She told us plenty about herself. How she had gone from being a rural schoolteacher in Oregon to traveling to Chesterfield City to find work with a newspaper, boldly assuming that in the rugged territories of the south a woman's views would be solely lacking when it came to newsprint contributions. As with me, she was fond of books and reading, and she confessed her goal was to become a novelist. She said she had an idea for a book she wanted to write. Working on a newspaper, she figured, was also a good way for her to develop her writing skills. Unfortunately, she never got her opportunity to write stories for the paper as her boss, J.C. Montgomery, put her on as his editor, making sure that spelling and punctuation was proper. Reporting stories in Chesterfield City could be a dangerous occupation, especially for a woman, Montgomery had explained to her. He claimed that he had already lost two good men to brutes unhappy with the way they were represented in the press. After he himself was threatened with physical violence, Montgomery became very particular about what the *Chronicle* printed.

Miss Montgomery was discouraged, but she patiently bided her time. After the publisher died and she was handed control of the paper, she let loose with both barrels. In particular, the recent exploits of the Ramos Gang could not be ignored. People were clamoring for news, and the paper, under Miss Montgomery's leadership, was happy to oblige. Miss Montgomery was not timid in either her reporting or the wording of her headlines.

"Doesn't it worry you they might not be too flattered by what's been written about 'em? Maybe 'encourage' the gang to pay your office a visit," I inquired of Miss Montgomery.

She answered firmly — and heatedly, "They're killers, but more than that, they're cowards. They wouldn't dare risk riding into Chesterfield City. Homesteaders, river settlements, that's more their style. Where there's maybe a single man protecting his family and property against all their guns."

Miss Montgomery was definitely a woman with backbone, I had to say that for her. An admirable quality, even though I could see she also had some venom in her veins — at least when it came to the Ramos Gang.

She caught herself beginning to lose

control of her emotions and suppressed a blush of embarrassment.

There was a short silence at the table, and Miss Montgomery sipped at her liqueur before she set down her glass. I decided to lighten the mood by pursuing what we were discussing before the conversation shifted toward the unsavory topic of Silvano Ramos.

"I'm still curious about you being J.C. Montgomery," I said.

"I suppose it does seem a bit peculiar," she admitted. "Actually, it was a request from Mr. Montgomery before he passed on that I keep the paper running under his name. So to honor his request and keep things simple — and to give our readers the satisfaction of thinking J.C. Montgomery was still the trusted name behind the newspaper — I adopted the name for myself when I took over as publisher."

"So — that's who you are: J.C. Montgomery?"

"In name," she answered. "If I ever get around to writing my novel that will probably be the pseudonym I'll use. Does have a literary ring to it."

"Does indeed," I agreed.

Francisco halted his forkful of beans before it entered his mouth. His eyes creased questioningly.

*"Pseudo . . ."* He was unfamiliar with the word.

"Pen name," I explained. "When the writer doesn't want a reader to know who he or she really is."

Francisco frowned. "Write a book. Don't want no one to know you wrote it. Tell me, why would that be?"

I breathed out my answer with a sideways glance at Miss Montgomery. "Well, might be the book's not very good."

Miss Montgomery cast me a disapproving look. I winked at her to let her know I was teasing. She responded with what I hoped was a playful frown. And then she gave her own explanation as to why she was considering a pseudonym.

"Some names just look better printed on a book," she said. "I think J.C. Montgomery has that quality."

"Then . . . who are you really?" I asked her delicately.

She offered a mild smile. "My real name. It's Berry Dale."

I could feel Francisco's eyes sliding toward me. I wouldn't acknowledge his look or the subtle but telling lift of his eyebrows. I feared if I did, our joint amusement over her name might inadvertently cause a wide grin to spread across my face — or worse, that I might sputter a laugh and risk offending our guest.

*Berry Dale.* It downright sounded like a dessert.

Instead, to steady both myself and the potential embarrassment of the moment, I pretended to surrender to a brief coughing spasm. I hoped convincingly.

Francisco smiled knowingly. Miss Montgomery wore a look of concern.

"Are you all right?" she asked.

I pulled myself out of my act, took a few extra minutes to "recover."

"S-something I musta swallowed," I explained, deliberately avoiding Francisco's gaze. "I'll be all right."

Another couple of moments went by before I felt composed enough to go on. I noticed the looks I got from other diners. I smiled self-consciously, then apologized directly to Miss Montgomery.

Managing to keep my humor in check, I asked her, "So do I call you Miss Montgomery or Miss Dale?"

She lifted a shoulder. "Makes no never mind. You can choose, between J.C. or Berry."

I felt amusement start to rise up in me again, so I forced myself to tighten my expression, as if seriously considering the two options. "Tough choice," I said.

"And come to think of it," she said, "neither of you gentlemen has properly introduced yourself."

That was true, we hadn't. I hadn't deliberately. My *compañero* obviously had just not thought to do so. My eyes shifted over to Francisco, who looked at me expectantly. I responded with a smirk.

"My friend's name is Francisco," I said. "Me . . . I'll answer to just about anything."

Miss Montgomery looked understandably puzzled. "Would hardly call that a name."

"Maybe later."

Miss Montgomery held her gaze on me for a long time before she finally looked to accept my disinclination to reveal my name.

The levity had already lifted from my *compañero*. A quick glance at Francisco told me he was beginning to get impatient with this discussion, and it was time for us to get back to business.

I only hoped that returning to the topic of Silvano Ramos would not upset Miss Montgomery. It was made clear she harbored a hatred toward the outlaw almost as deep-rooted as Francisco's.

And as it turned out she had reason to feel the contempt she did. She told us that one of the first friends she had made upon coming to Chesterfield City was a woman named Rose Claremont. Rose and her husband Zeke owned a small store, but soon decided to sell their business, which had proven unprofitable, and join a settlement many miles north where they could work the land. En route to the settlement, Rose and her husband were apparently waylaid by the Ramos bunch. Zeke was killed instantly with a bullet to the brain, but the gang was not as merciful with Rose. She was a woman, and there were other uses for her before her ravaged body had served its purpose and could be disposed of with as much respect as if it were an old dish rag. Although there were no witnesses to the crime and it could not be proven conclusively that Ramos and his "tribe" were the guilty parties, the brutality of the murders left little doubt as to who was responsible. And after hearing this story there was no question in Francisco's mind.

His tension was reflected by a tightening of his expression.

"Yes. The mark of Silvano Ramos." He spoke his words through gritted teeth.

Miss Montgomery gave Francisco a peculiar look. What she said next was another disturbing revelation concerning the outlaw gang's handiwork.

"Strange you should say that: the mark of Ramos," she said. "When one comes upon a scene where an ambush has taken place, one can always determine Ramos's first kill. He carves a deep mark into the forehead. No one knows what it is exactly, but some have said it resembles a bolt of lightning."

"Then from what you tell us, there certainly is no doubt," Francisco said.

"Except that in the instance of my friend and her husband, there was no such marking," Miss Montgomery said.

Francisco's eyes narrowed. "Which proves nothing. The kills still belong to Ramos."

Miss Montgomery gave a slight nod and then our table fell silent.

I'd eaten my meal with relative enjoyment, but now, after listening to what our dinner guest told us, I questioned my digestion. Yet with each story I heard about the exploits of Silvano Ramos and his band of cutthroats, my resolve to assist Francisco in his commitment to end Ramos's reign of terror became nearly as determined as his own. Perhaps we were still proceeding on a fool's march, but I recognized the job must be done or many more people would be tortured and killed as the gang continued its rampage. I knew that, until that happened, their crimes would not cease, and in fact would escalate.

It was Francisco's contention that the two of us, on our own, had a much better chance of locating the Ramos Gang than the Rangers. If Ramos had scouts keeping an eye out for trackers, the two of us riding alone would likely not be of much concern to them. We would certainly not be viewed as a threat. Francisco in particular looked like a peasant and, as such, would not only *not* be of matter to the gang's safety but likely would not even be considered a target since he looked like a man possessed of little means.

When I had earlier mentioned to Francisco that it was not enough just to kill Ramos, that his gang must also be killed or captured, he said, "When you cut the head off a snake, the body withers and dies."

"They're as guilty of these crimes as Ramos," I argued. "They can't be allowed to go free."

Francisco spoke confidently. "They will not. Ramos holds them together. I've seen it before with *banditos.* Once their leader is gone, the men scatter. They cannot, how you say, function alone. Some may try to continue with their criminal ways but inevitably they are caught — or killed. The others will become like dust in the wind."

These words settled into my brain as I sat mulling over concerns in my own silence, absorbing the story told by our attractive dinner companion. I also wondered how many others in the community had suffered similar losses. How many murdered and mutilated bodies had yet to be discovered?

I said to Miss Montgomery, "You mentioned earlier that there have been survivors to Ramos's attacks. Do any live here in Chesterfield City that you know of?"

She wrinkled her forehead in thought. "There is one. A young boy, maybe about eleven or twelve years of age. He, too, saw his family massacred and was himself left for dead. The Rangers found him. But the boy has never recovered from what he saw or from what he himself experienced. A church family here in town took him in. A kind gesture, but he belongs in a proper facility. His mind is damaged. He will never be the same."

I gave my head a sympathetic nod.

"Were there any others?" I then asked.

"One — an elderly lady who, for some reason, Ramos spared after he and his murderers killed her husband and son. But she died just over a month ago. She was left in a state similar to the boy's. I don't think from the time the incident happened till the day she passed away that she ever spoke a word. Just sat all day in her rocker, numb to everything around her — either remembering or trying to forget."

And then Miss Montgomery asked outright the question we should have expected:

"Are you two planning on going after Ramos?"

I could neither be hesitant with my answer nor be dishonest with her.

"Yes," I said.

Francisco twisted his head toward me, eyeing me with disapproval.

I turned to him and said, "We can't go this alone."

Against Francisco's wishes, we decided to take the advice of our new friend and have a talk with the town sheriff. It was clear we would obtain no leads from anyone else in Chesterfield City. The young boy who had survived the slaughter of his family remained traumatized by what had happened and would never be able to tell us anything of value. Besides, it wasn't our intention to stir up troubling memories in a child who likely would never live to see his teen years.

Both Francisco and I were tired from our journey and the indulgence of a satisfying meal. We would talk to the sheriff in the morning after a good rest. We decided to enjoy a night of warmth and comfort after the many nights we had slept outdoors and secure a hotel room. I suggested we each get a room but Francisco argued that wasn't necessary. Why spend the extra money, he said, when he was perfectly fine sleeping on the floor?

Once we registered with the desk clerk, the two of us walked Miss Montgomery back to the newspaper office and her home.

After a gentle handshake, a goodnight from me, and a sturdy *buenas noches* from Francisco, the two of us started back to the hotel. The night breeze was crisp, and the clear sky alive with stars. There was a good feel in the air.

And I was feeling pretty damn good . . . my brain finally enjoying a respite from the uncertainty of the days ahead. My thoughts focused on the pleasurable couple of hours I had just spent with companionship more to my desire than Francisco's. It had been too long since I had entertained and been entertained by a woman. It was an extra dividend to discover we shared several of the same interests.

And then my *compañero* spoke, and his incisive words disrupted my reverie.

"I think you are becoming attracted to this *señorita* at a very inopportune time, *Señor*," he said.

I was instantly taken aback and responded to his remark with a quick, critical stare. Before I could even think to answer, Francisco had more to say.

"Oh, you cannot fool Francisco," he said. "I've seen that look before."

"What look?"

"The look you gave to Miss Newspaper Lady all during our meal." He paused before adding craftily, "And the look she gave back to you."

I tried to be dismissive in my attitude. "Really?"

"Oh yes, *Señor.* The eyes . . . they do not lie."

I responded with an inconsequential hum, though I confess I was impressed by Francisco's perceptiveness.

We walked on a little farther.

Francisco then blurted, "And she took down her hair for you." He slapped the palm of his hand against his forehead. "*Ay caramba,* the signs could not be more clear if they were pasted in the heavens." He shook his head and repeated, "And at such a time."

Despite my attempt not to acknowledge

Francisco's observation, I found myself overcome by a rush of giddiness. I restored my restraint by clearing my throat and expressing myself sternly. "Well . . . I think you're mistaken. And by the way, her name is not *Miss Newspaper Lady* . . . it's —"

"What have you decided to call her, *Señor*?" Francisco interrupted with a mischievous smile.

I gave my *compañero* a mystified look.

Hell. Damned if I knew . . .

Yes, I reckon one might say it was an unexpected development. One that concerned Francisco as he considered the mutual attraction he'd detected as an . . . "inconvenience." A turn of events that, to his mind, could conceivably conflict with our task. I determined to prevent his worry right off the cuff and tried to reassure him in a way he could understand and respect. I halted my gait and extended my hand. He gazed at it for several seconds, lifting his dark eyes toward me, and then his hand grasped mine, solidifying the bond we'd made with a handshake.

Not that I would be forgetting the girl whose choice of names I had yet to decide on. I intended to see her before Francisco and I rode out in the next day or so. And if

I should return safely from our journey, I
hoped to see her a whole lot more.

# CHAPTER FIFTEEN

The sheriff spoke while he eased back into his chair, his long legs stretched out, boots propped up on his desk. He looked to be trying to hold the reins on his enthusiasm but, to my eye at least, not succeeding very well.

"Town ain't been too rowdy for a spell," he said. " 'Sides that, got two able deputies who can keep a watch on things."

Francisco and I stood inside Sheriff Austin Briggs's office. He surprised the two of us by what he was suggesting, which he presented while attentively rolling a cigarette between fingers stained with tobacco.

We had come to see the sheriff only for information, explaining our interest to him as we had with J.C. Montgomery, but determined in this instance not to reveal our intent. Francisco's sister had been murdered by Silvano Ramos. Was there anything the lawman could tell us about the latest developments in the manhunt? Perhaps because of the reason for our inquiry, Sheriff Briggs did not regard us with suspicion. He seemed to accept our story that we had come merely out of a personal need for information. Unfortunately, there was nothing he could tell us that we hadn't already heard from Miss Montgomery.

Sheriff Briggs looked to be about sixty, but he appeared fit. I recalled that we had been told he was suffering from rheumatism, yet initially to look at the man who sat at his desk in a confident yet comfortable pose, neither rheumatism nor or any other debilitating ailment was easy to detect.

"Been at this game for nearly forty years," Briggs said as he got up from behind his desk to pour some coffee. It was then that I noticed a slight stiffness in his walk. He held up the pot brewing atop the belly stove to offer Francisco and me a cup. I accepted. Francisco declined.

"Plan to be retiring soon," he added. "Reckon that time comes to every man, whether it's what he wants or not."

I walked over to the stove and took my coffee. The sheriff went back to his desk and seated himself, exhaling a labored breath as he did so.

"Pains and aches," he said miserably.

"Reckon the payback of too many years ridin' the trail."

We both sipped our coffee while Francisco's gaze wandered about the office. He stepped over to the far wall on which was affixed a glass-encased newspaper front page. From where I was standing I could read the big, bold headline that proclaimed Sheriff Briggs's capture of Jim Weaver: the "Terror of the Rockies."

"Nice souvenir, ain't it?" the sheriff commented. He then chuckled as he watched Francisco read the *Chronicle* story and rock his head in admiration.

"But that's 'bout all it is," Briggs added modestly — or maybe wistfully. "Was a long time ago."

"Yet a most admirable accomplishment," Francisco remarked.

Sheriff Briggs nodded wistfully, then took a slow sip of coffee.

He said with a frown, "And now there's another scourge of the West: Silvano Ramos and his killers. Would consider it a privilege to bookend my career by bringin' that scum to justice. And maybe not bein' too particular 'bout how I did it."

Neither Francisco nor I spoke. Briggs had voiced his yearning for that final triumph. And I detected it was not so much for the

273

glory as the achievement. And I further recognized that he was a man most capable of doing the job — at one time.

He settled back in his creaking swivel chair and took a long look at Francisco. Then his gaze veered toward me.

"Man can't do the job alone," he said.

Then he surprised the two of us when he spoke of how his deputies could handle the matters of the town. A not so subtle hint of what he likely had determined about my *compañero* and me.

He said directly to Francisco, "I don't figger you'd be ridin' in all the way from Mexico just to collect information for your poke. No sir, I suspect you have somethin' more specific in mind."

I looked at Francisco. He looked back at me.

Sheriff Briggs turned his attention toward me. "Like takin' it upon yourselves to deal with this varmint."

Neither Francisco nor I responded, but I'm sure my *compañero* thought as I did: The sheriff was a clever man, not one to be easily fooled.

The sheriff began scratching the back of a hand blemished with dark spots. "Y'gotta be careful ridin' with a man who has hate in his heart. But if handled right, he can be

274

useful, too. 'Cause it means he's determined and won't quit."

Briggs hadn't yet come out and spoke the words he was leading to, but it could not have been any more obvious. At least to me. It was hard to tell with Francisco. The sheriff was telling us he couldn't manage it alone; for whatever reason he didn't think his deputies were up to the task. But he saw an opportunity to wrap up his career with a victory by partnering with us to seek the most wanted outlaw in the state of Texas.

"Either of you boys experienced trackers?" he asked.

I started to shake my head but then Francisco cut in: "My *amigo* is a 'secker,' *Señor* Sheriff."

Briggs furrowed his brow, deepening the lines that creased his forehead like the driest desert arroyos. "Seeker?" he said.

*"Sí."*

The sheriff then gave mc a puzzled look and admitted, "Ain't familiar with that term."

Since the cat was out of the bag, I detailed my work to the sheriff. At the end, he looked impressed.

"No," he said. "Been a lawman for a good many years and can't say I ever heard of a 'witness seeker.' Reckon I can see the need, though. Dangerous?"

"Can be."

The sheriff narrowed an eye. "Enough to make yuh qualified to be chasin' Silvano Ramos?"

That was a peculiar and relatively insulting question to ask. Especially under the circumstances. It was as if the sheriff was interviewing me to see if I could handle the task ahead. As if he had already taken it upon himself not merely to join our hunt for the outlaws, but also to take the lead.

Francisco appeared a little distressed. He signaled for me to go with him outside the office. I excused myself to Sheriff Briggs, who nodded absently.

Out on the boardwalk Francisco spoke in a hurried voice. "The lawman seems quite determined. This is not what I want, yet I think that if we do not agree to what he is suggesting, he might find a way to halt what we have planned."

"Yeah, got the same feeling," I admitted.

"He might even find a reason to put us in jail," Francisco added. "To stop us."

"Reckon it's possible."

"So what do we do, *Señor*?" Francisco said, flustered.

"We have two choices," I answered. "We either let him ride along, if that's what he's after, or we just take our chances on our own."

"Not very good choices," Francisco grumbled. And then his resentment suddenly sparked. "My plan is not to bring Silvano back alive. He must die, and I must be the one who is allowed that privilege."

After all I'd learned I no longer felt any moral ambiguity regarding Francisco's intention to kill Ramos. The outlaw was a mad dog who must be exterminated just like any other rabid animal. Whether Francisco would be successful in his task was debatable. In fact, there was no guarantee either of us would come out alive. So, I considered that having the sheriff along would improve our odds. Physically, he wasn't a prime candidate but he likewise felt compelled by a duty, and his determination could prove a valuable ally. The problem as I saw it was that as a lawman, he would certainly take it upon himself to dictate the orders . . . and while he didn't seem to care how we brought Ramos in, it was doubtful he would condone outright murder.

Francisco and I stepped back inside the office. The sheriff lifted his eyes and leaned back in his swivel chair, arms clasped behind his neck, looking very certain of himself.

"Let's stop chasin' each other 'round the barn, boys," he said. "You got a score to settle with Silvano Ramos, and that's all there is to it."

It was apparent Francisco and I had not been too successful in blanketing our true motivation. First with Miss Montgomery and now with Sheriff Briggs.

"Supposing it is?" I asked directly.

"Then you're two of the durndest fools I ever come across," the sheriff barked. "Ramos heads up a gang that at last count numbers 'bout a dozen, and each one is a merciless killer. 'Sides that, even the Rangers ain't had much luck in their tracking. Fact, as you might know, they lost a coupla men. From what I heard, wasn't a pretty sight. Evidently Ramos don't take too kindly to bein' hunted."

"We heard," I said impassively.

Sheriff Briggs edged forward in his chair. "So tell me, what chance do yuh think the two of you have?" Here he added bluntly with an eye to both of us, "Someone who calls himself a witness seeker . . . and a sawed-off Mexican."

I didn't take offense to the sheriff's words, but I waited a mite uneasily for my *compañero*'s reaction.

Fortunately, he maintained his composure just as he had when he was insulted by Pawnee Joe.

"Against Ramos, I have a very good chance," Francisco said. He spoke with uncompromising resolve.

It appeared that his words had an effect on the sheriff, who became silent. He kept his gaze focused on my *compañero* for a long while, studying him — perhaps trying to determine whether the unimposing "sawed-off Mexican" had the fortitude and physical strength for such an undertaking. Or maybe the sheriff was attempting to penetrate Francisco's unbending will by stating the reality from a lawman's perspective of what we were up against. But that would have been futile.

Francisco met the lawman's eye and maintained an inflexible posture.

The sheriff finally unfastened his stare. He stood up and walked across the room to the framed page of newspaper hanging on the wall. He spoke very softly and pensively. "This here is the summation of my reputation in Chesterfield City. The highlight of my years as a peace officer. But that was the past and people have short memories. What now occupies their thoughts is Silvano Ramos. A lot of the folks here, 'specially the young'uns, they don't remember that their sheriff practically single-handedly brought down Jim Weaver and his gang when they was shootin' up these parts. What they know today is that I wear a badge but haven't done my part to bring Silvano Ramos to justice. I see the looks I get from some of 'em. Hear some of the comments, too. Don't reflect well on me or my obligation, sittin' here while blood has been spilled throughout all parts of the state." He turned to look at the two of us. "I know what you boys are aimin' to do, and whether or not it's an attempt that'll see yuh sharin' soil on Boot Hill . . . well, I feel the need to ride alongside you."

I considered his words. And then I thought over the situation. Francisco seeking revenge. Sheriff Briggs looking to restore a faded reputation. Each man had a personal motive for going after Silvano Ramos, and I had to wonder if these reasons would help or hinder our quest.

I took some time away from Francisco and Sheriff Briggs to pay a visit to Miss J.C. Montgomery (after some seesawing, I'd finally decided to call her by her "adopted" initials). She agreed to join me for a cup of coffee at the restaurant down the street.

Once seated at a table off to the side where I hoped our conversation would not be overheard, I told her about the sheriff wanting to join us in our hunt for Silvano Ramos.

J.C.'s expression was incredulous.

"I don't think Sheriff Briggs has left his office in two years," she said in a low voice.

I looked at her with a frown.

"Whenever trouble heats up he sends out his deputies," she offered. "Generally he gets the credit, but to my knowledge, all he does is lock the door to the cell and handle the paperwork."

*"Hmmm,"* I murmured, rocking my head. "Seems right determined to ride along with us."

"Can't imagine why," J.C. said, considering. "He's not in the best of health, and he's got a pension and a comfortable retirement coming up. Why take such a risk at this point?"

"Near as I figure, he needs this last one under his belt," I said.

"But why?" J.C. said again. "He has nothing to prove."

"Maybe to himself he does," I suggested.

J.C. looked at me questioningly.

"Might be he figures his best days are behind him," I said, although I knew it was more than a mere assumption. "Finds it hard to come to grips with that. A man with his reputation . . ."

And then I halted. It was queer but in that instant my mind flashed back to my mentor Colonel Calvin. It had never occurred to me before; I'd had no reason to consider it . . . but I saw the reason I had just given to explain Sheriff Briggs could also have been my old friend's motivation. Later in life, when he didn't need to, he had chosen to become a witness seeker. There was a personal need to show your life had amounted to something. Maybe advancing age had nothing to do with one's ability. No, Briggs maybe had nothing to prove. He'd accomplished admirable achievements during his career as a lawman. But before he gracefully accepted his retirement and possibly surrendered wholly to the physical ailments that might send him to a rocking chair on some shaded porch, he believed he had that final obligation to the citizens . . . and to himself — one provided by the butcher named Silvano Ramos.

All in all, I reckoned, it boiled down to a man's pride.

Oftentimes his *stubborn* pride.

J.C. gave a subtle nod of acknowledgment to my explanation. She sipped at her tea quietly. Then she lowered her cup onto the

282

saucer with both hands and slowly lifted her long lashes at me.

She rather surprised me with what she next said.

"I only wish you weren't so set on going," she murmured.

I managed to keep my expression fixed and proper, but I didn't know what to say in response.

"I — don't suppose there's anything that I can say that . . ." Her words drifted off.

I had no idea she felt this way. Well, not to this extent. Son of a gun, Francisco had been right after all. And . . . now, hearing it from J.C.'s own lips, I could well understand why Francisco did not welcome the attraction between us. A woman's influence could be strong and weaken a man's resolve. I could already feel that effect on me, after just hearing the few words she'd spoken. And for better or for worse, I had to exercise strength of will to resist, espccially against those strands of uncertainty I still harbored about tackling what lay ahead.

All I could bring myself to tell her was, "Ramos has to be stopped."

"Yes, I know. But why does it have to be you? You're not a lawman or a bounty hunter — and neither is your friend," J.C. argued. "The Rangers are sure to catch up with Ramos."

"They haven't so far," I said. I refrained from correcting myself. Two Rangers *had* caught up with the bunch (or perhaps it was the other way around), and both had met grisly fates.

I didn't have to mention the fact. I could tell instantly by J.C.'s expression that she was familiar with the method of their deaths.

I had to speak honestly. I could not know if she would understand, but maybe her own hatred for Ramos would permit J.C. to see that we could not turn back . . . that *I* could not turn back because of the part I had played in the unspeakable evil Silvano Ramos had become. A murderous beast. I told J.C. how as a witness seeker I had found his wife, Felicia, and persuaded her to testify against her husband. How she'd refused to turn against him on the stand, but how he still believed she had betrayed him and took his terrible revenge on her.

And then I said with even stronger conviction, "That is why it also has to be me, along with Francisco. Both of us hold a responsibility for what's happened."

I wasn't sure if I convinced her, but J.C. tried to ease my guilt.

"You were just doing your job," she said adamantly, yet with tenderness. "You couldn't know what that girl was going to do once she got into court. Or that Ramos would go after her."

I appreciated her support, but I'd had a lot of time to think since learning what I had from Francisco.

"I've tried to tell myself that," I admitted. "But if I hadn't found her and things hadn't turned out as they did, maybe Ramos wouldn't have become a killer. Maybe a lot of the suffering and death he's brought to others wouldn't have happened. He might just have . . . gone away. Never to be heard from again."

"You don't know that."

I shrugged.

"It's wrong to blame yourself," J.C. said softly.

I let out a breath and gazed into my empty coffee cup. "I don't know. Once Ramos became a murderer, there was no other path he could have followed."

"A man like Ramos was destined to become a murderer, no matter what," J.C. said definitely.

I smiled wanly. "I just helped to speed up the process."

Francisco met me on the boardwalk after I walked J.C. back to her office. He looked glum. I suspected the reason.

"There is no talking him out of it," Francisco said. "The sheriff insists on riding with us."

"I figured."

Francisco lifted a shoulder. "What can we do?"

I looked straight at my *compañero*. "Let him come."

"Let him come?" Francisco echoed.

"You're paying me for what I do," I told him. "Briggs is experienced as a tracker. You need a tracker, and you won't be paying him a cent. He'll work for free."

"So . . . then why do I need you, *Señor*?" Francisco then asked with a subtle yet curious inflection.

I couldn't tell if he was serious or not. But that was almost the wrong thing to say to me at the time.

Still, I owed him an answer he would accept, though my tone was morose. "Because you spent a lot of time convincing me of your purpose."

Francisco smiled brightly. *"Sí.* I did, did I not, *Señor?"*

The three of us saddled up later that day: Francisco, Sheriff Briggs, and me. We'd ride in a northerly direction until sundown. Then we would set up camp and get an early start come sunrise and head toward the river valley. The problem was we had no leads to go on. Our best chance would be if we could gather information from a settlement that we might come to along the way. While some had been wiped out by Ramos and his bunch, there might be small encampments the gang had bypassed but whose people might have caught sight of them somewhere along the trail. They might give us a direction to head. Of course, these camps might already have been visited by the Rangers to guide them in their own search for the outlaws, but we had to start somewhere.

As we were readying ourselves, I took furtive glances at Sheriff Briggs and noticed how he seemed to have difficulty getting his sorrel saddled. I think Francisco saw that, too, as he had his lips pursed, his eyes narrowed, and overall didn't look too pleased.

The sheriff finally finished his preliminaries and he fitted his Colt slide-action rifle into the scabbard. He then turned to us. His face wore an inquisitive expression.

"You boys don't carry a long-range?" he asked.

"Haven't used a rifle in years," I told him. "Don't cotton to it. 'Sides, in my line of work I never had the need. Kinda cumbersome. Plus, someone already a little stricken with nerves watching a stranger walk up holding a rifle . . . well, it might put that person on the defensive. Prefer just to carry a side iron. Not so intimidating."

Sheriff Briggs gave me a squinty stare. "Never had to shoot nobody?"

I hesitated.

"Not with a rifle," I then answered.

"Like my *amigo, Señor* Sheriff, I too prefer the six-shooter," Francisco offered. And with that, he leaped into play, treating the sheriff to a fancy acrobatic display with the handgun he swiftly withdrew from under his poncho, twirling and flipping the pistol with speed and precision that could have made him a featured attraction in a wild west show.

By the time my *compañero* finished, Sheriff Briggs seemed unimpressed. In fact, he looked downright displeased.

"You're both aware who we're goin' after?" Briggs said. "Ain't likely we're gonna be able to walk right up to 'em and slap on the cuffs. No, more likely we'll fight 'em from a distance. Beyond forty yards a handgun is nothin' more than cold metal in your grip. *Banditos* ain't known for close contact when it comes to gunplay. They'll hide themselves up in the rocks or someplace and start pickin' us off like we was rabbits."

Francisco wore a smile only I could interpret. The sheriff's words of caution did not interest him. The other gang members were merely a nuisance that would be dealt with as necessity allowed. He was interested only in Silvano Ramos — whom he planned to kill face-to-face. And not with the quick convenience of a gun, if he could help it.

"I got a coupla Winchesters in the office," Briggs said. "Let me go fetch 'em. Feel a mite better if'n you two carried along a rifle."

Neither of us argued with him. It wouldn't do any good in any case; the sheriff was a stubborn cuss. Besides, as far as I was concerned, he had brought up a valid point. Some extra firepower couldn't hurt, although if Ramos and his bunch were perched among some high ridge rocks and spotted us first, it was doubtful even a long-range would do any of us much good.

Not three dead men.

Shortly the sheriff brought out the two rifles and a couple of boxes of .44-40 shells, one of which he handed to each of us, fairly slapping the boxes into our palms. We were set, and we prepared to mount our horses. I happened to glance at Francisco, who gazed past me with a peculiar expression, and he gave a slight tilt of his head to tell me to look in his direction.

"*Señor,*" he said quietly.

I looked over my shoulder and saw J.C. standing outside her office. The first thing I noticed was that while she was dressed in her stiff, proper work clothing, she had her hair down in the fashion I preferred, soft and cascading in curls over her shoulders.

I hadn't given her a proper goodbye, which I admit was perhaps intentional since it would be difficult, parting with our outcome so in doubt. She looked to be smiling sadly.

I shifted my eyes toward Francisco, who surprised me when he urged me to go to her with a swift rocking of his head. Then he turned to the sheriff, already mounted atop his sorrel.

I heard my *compañero* say in nearly perfect English, "Indulge my friend just for a minute, *Señor* Sheriff."

And Briggs replied with a grunt.

I walked across the boardwalk and saw the troubled look on J.C.'s face. As I got nearer, she reached out both her hands and I took them in my own. Her fingers were smooth, soft, and delicate.

"Never figured on this happening," I told

her honestly.

J.C. gave me a look that suggested she was not sure what I meant. But I wasn't fooled; I know she did. Maybe at that moment she was just too afraid to admit it. In truth, I couldn't blame her.

But her lips then parted in a less forlorn smile.

"I know," she said. "Neither did I."

"Reckon it was bad timing," I said with a sigh.

J.C. didn't answer. She lowered her gaze to the boardwalk planking.

I had to speak with confidence. "I'll be back."

I took her gently by the chin and raised her face so that her eyes met mine.

"I *will* be back," I said again.

"You might not even find him," she said suddenly, and I detected a note of hopefulness in her voice.

I simply gave a nod. I didn't want to tell her it was unlikely we'd be returning to Chesterfield City until we could ride in with Silvano Ramos's body draped over a horse. Or . . . to put it more bluntly, Francisco would not be coming back until either he or Ramos was dead. And if it was the latter, then the effort didn't look promising for any of us.

I had to get moving. My partners were waiting. I was grateful for their patience, though I could tell they were eager to set out. J.C. and I gazed into each other's eyes, not saying anything with words, but simply sharing what we felt in our hearts. We still held each other's hands, tightly, and I wanted just to pull her forward and kiss her passionately. Yet I resisted. Deliberately. I knew that if I were to hold her close, it might be impossible for me to let her go. I had to content myself in knowing that when I came back after our work was done, J.C. would be waiting. Then there would be nothing to prevent me from expressing what I now knew was more than mere affection for this lady.

I smiled at her and started to turn away. That was when she halted me, lifted herself on her toes, and kissed me on the cheek. I responded by giving her another smile and gently touching my fingers against the softness of her own cheek. I wanted her to understand why I was being guarded with my emotions.

"I still don't know your name," she called after me.

"When I get back," I said.

Once I walked toward the sheriff's office I noticed the odd way Francisco looked at me. I could guess what was going through his mind, so before he could say anything, I said simply as I mounted my horse, "Let's hit the trail."

Francisco peered past me toward the girl still standing on the boardwalk.

He drew a breath before he said with utter honesty, "I envy you, *Señor.*" His tone darkened. "And yet I do not."

He did not have to explain. I understood what he meant. He might just as well have asked me outright if I was having second thoughts about venturing forward with him and the sheriff. To which I would have answered that I wouldn't permit myself to have such doubts. Because even though I was fighting the urge to dismount and rush back to J.C., I had to sweep such a desire from my brain. To consider the matter even a moment longer would drive a deep and maybe lasting pain into me. I could not go on and be effective with the men I would travel beside with such a hurt penetrating my heart.

I realized it was no longer only the prospect of dying that made me apprehensive. While naturally that was not a pleasant consideration, more hurtful was the thought of leaving J.C. behind . . . and never having the opportunity to tell her how I felt about her.

Just before we rode off, Sheriff Briggs reached into the breast pocket of his shirt under his unbuttoned leather vest and withdrew a cigar. He bit off the end and spat it out the side of his mouth. Then he tucked the cigar between his lips, puckered his mouth, and struck a match to the rough of his saddle to light it. He took a few short puffs then spoke over his stogie.

"Ain't normally a ceegar smoker," he admitted. "But call it superstitious; hell, maybe it's just coincidence, but back in the day, every time I set out on the trail after a lawbreaker, if I started out with a ceegar I always seemed to have luck."

"That what happened with the Weaver Gang?" I asked.

Briggs nodded. He took the cigar from his mouth and slowly rolled it between his fingers.

"Yup. 'Fact that's how it began — with the Weaver bunch," he said.

I turned to Francisco, then looked back at the sheriff.

"Maybe you'd better give us one of those," I suggested.

# CHAPTER SIXTEEN

Our first days' travels north and proceeding west through the Mesilla Valley were more tolerable than the dusty and monotonous trail Francisco and I had taken into Chesterfield City through the Chihuahuan Desert. The vegetation was quite plentiful, since the land itself was fertile with sprouting bosque and tamarisk, and we could even enjoy the welcoming shade of cottonwood trees under which we could cool ourselves when the midday sun became too hot. Off in the distance, stretching across the southwest region of neighboring New Mexico Territory, stood the towering Organ Mountains. Miles away from those rugged ridges we could end our day next to a campfire, absorbing a magnificent sunset.

On the night of our first campout, I was curious to see if the three of us might fall into conversation. We didn't. Strangely, we did not even sit close to one another, though

I don't think our individual seating arrangements were intentional. Then — maybe they were. Reckon each of us had his own thoughts.

I sipped on a cup of coffee and settled my gaze on my two companions. Sheriff Briggs sat close to the campfire, intently scribbling something in a little notebook he'd brought along with him. I wasn't ready to question its purpose, but I assumed it was likely a journal, in which he jotted down the events of the day — which up to this point must have been pretty damn dull reading.

Francisco was also in his own world, his face screwed into a frown as he slowly and methodically fed shells into the Winchester the sheriff had provided. I could tell it was simply an idle task, a way to keep himself occupied until he could fall in to slumber. Francisco saw about as much purpose in firing a rifle against Ramos as the defenders of the Alamo might have seen in fighting off Santa Ana's army with a Bowie knife.

Throughout each day's ride, and particularly when we decided to rest our horses and ourselves and camp out for the night, I kept a careful if not too obvious watch on Sheriff Briggs. Although he tried to exhibit the same tough stamina as Francisco and me, the pain and discomfort he frequently experienced was not difficult for either of us to perceive. If he happened to notice either of us catching him in one of these moments, he'd glower and struggle all the harder against his hurting to complete whatever his task, which could be as simple as unsaddling his horse for the night.

As for myself, I was feeling a little discouraged. As a seeker, I wasn't having much luck. I'd have been of much more use had I been skilled as a tracker, proficient in reading signs along the trail like redskins seemed born to do. But possibly even a tracker might have encountered the same difficulty, because after a bloody run, it seemed as if the Ramos Gang simply vanished, leaving no clues as to their whereabouts. One settlement we rode into was eerily deserted. It seemed as if all of its occupants had suddenly just up and vamoosed, since a week's old supper still sat cold and uneaten in a pot over an outdoor fire that had burned out into ash. A small encampment we later came upon provided us with nothing of value. The small group of settlers had not even heard of Silvano Ramos or the terrible crimes for which he and his band were responsible. I took note of how the camp was very isolated and virtually unprotected. Its people still lived in makeshift tents, and by all rights, should have been a ripe target for the marauders. Luckily for those few souls, they had been spared a Ramos raid. Of course, one could never be sure if the gang might come back.

Then — our first break, one we came upon as another day's ride was nearing completion, and the colorful hues of sunset painted sweeping brushstrokes across the deepening skies. Off to the western edge, deep within a thick growth of trees and dense shrubbery, the eagle eye of Francisco detected a slowly lifting cloud of gray smoke that dispersed against the horizon.

Our immediate thought was that it might be originating from a campfire, but the smoke buildup was scattering too widely. Sheriff Briggs pulled his Winchester from its scabbard and rode with one hand on the reins. Neither Francisco nor I followed suit, as far as reaching for our rifles was concerned. We could reach for our handguns pretty quickly if necessary. We carefully guided our mounts through a narrow tree-bordered path that looked to have been cut and cleared by hand, frequently shielding our faces with our forearms against the twisting, low-hanging branches that were plentiful and stretched out high above the pathway.

We soon came to what remained of a small homestead that had been built in a clearing, near the slow-running waters of a creek. A homestead . . . that had been burned to the ground. Smoke plumes and fumes were still heavy, indicating that whatever had gone on at this site had occurred not long before. Four sturdy-looking but clearly agitated horses blew and paced about a makeshift corral, but at first sight we noticed no person either living or dead — until we heard a faint, frightened whimpering.

Sheriff Briggs drew rein, bringing his horse to an abrupt halt upon hearing this distressing sound. Francisco and I did likewise. We all dismounted and followed the cry to its source. My Colt remained holstered, though I kept my hand close enough to it for a fast draw if need be. Francisco had his revolver out, poised and ready. The sheriff walked holding his rifle upright in his grip.

A young, dishevelled girl, most likely in her early teens, knelt amid the smoldering rubble of what once had been a small cabin. Her face and her clothing were covered in dirt and soot and a pocket of blood had congealed around the swelling of her lower lip, as if she had been struck in the face. She clutched a rag doll and sobbed. She seemed oblivious to our presence as we stepped slowly toward her, carefully maneuvering through the wreckage and the still-glowing embers.

As I walked in a little closer, I discovered why she was not concentrating on us. Her focus was directed on a hand outstretched under a pile of debris. The hand was badly burned, the fingers curled grotesquely, but when I saw what looked like a slender band on the charred remains of the ring finger, I knew immediately that the body was that of a female . . . perhaps the girl's mother. I never considered pushing aside the debris to reveal what lay underneath. The girl was in shock and didn't need to see more. Instead, I took her lightly by the shoulders and gingerly lifted her to her feet to urge her away from the terrible sight. She didn't resist.

And then: "Let the girl be or I'll shoot yuh dead where yuh stand."

I turned slowly toward the voice. Francisco and Sheriff Briggs did the same.

A skinny, pallid-faced, nervous-looking man stood just several yards from us, brandishing a double-barrel shotgun. With all of us in close proximity to the scatter of buckshot, no one made a move.

"Yuh come back for me — or for her?"

the man said with contempt. "Ain't figgerin' yuh done 'nuff to that poor girl?"

Sheriff Briggs spoke, after flipping open the flap of his vest to reveal his lawman's badge.

"You can put that shotgun down," he said in a commanding voice. "We ain't here to hurt yuh."

The man squinted warily, started to lower his weapon, hesitated, and again levelled it at us.

"Badge don't tell me nothin'," he said. "Coulda easily got it off someone yuh murdered."

"Don't be a durned idiot," the sheriff growled. "We know who done this. And maybe if'n you'd wise up and drop that damn gun, you can help us get a lead on 'em."

"I ain't trustin' no one," the man said firmly.

I kept my arm wrapped around the girl, who just stood numbly next to me and felt so feeble in my grip that if I were to loosen my hold, she would slide to the ground as limply as the rag doll she continued to clutch. Sadly, she would be of no help. As with the other victims who had survived a Ramos rampage, as described to me by J.C., this girl would likely be marked by scars that would follow her to the grave.

For an instant I had to consider: Who was luckier, the girl or the woman who lay dead on the ground?

Francisco stared at her, his jaw clenched. When our eyes met I gave my head a slow, stiff nod, the meaning of which he understood.

"Prefer knowin' *who* it is I'm talkin' to, rather than speakin' to the barrel of a gun," the sheriff said in a steady, authoritative voice.

The man seemed to take a firm, more defensive hold of his weapon before saying, "Name's Henry."

The sheriff gave a satisfied nod.

"I'm the girl's uncle," Henry offered further. He regarded her sadly. "Her name is Lorraine."

"Okay, Henry, I'm gonna ask yuh some questions and I'd 'preciate it if'n you'd give some straight answers."

Henry nodded his head. "Just don't try nothin' funny, I'm warnin' yuh."

"What went on here, and how long ago did it happen?"

I had to give credit to the sheriff. He was determined, yet maintained careful control. He wasn't going to be intimidated or stalled by someone nervously brandishing a shot-gun.

The tension marking Henry's face began to ease.

He spoke his words carefully. "So . . . you tellin' me you ain't part of that bunch . . . come back to finish what yuh started?"

Briggs jabbed a hard, stiff finger at his badge. The no-nonsense intent behind that gesture provided his answer.

Henry still seemed slow to free the weapon from his hands, though he did loosen his grip sufficiently for the double barrels to slide downward slightly, aiming more to-ward the ground than at us. But it was evident he was ready to raise the shotgun and discharge its contents at the slightest provocation.

"Maybe 'bout two hours ago they rode out," he said, though he looked a mite uncertain. "That was after a good coupla hours of 'em —" He stopped abruptly and didn't finish. He didn't have to. The evi-dence of the Ramos Gang's handiwork sur-rounded us.

"How many were there?" the sheriff asked.

" 'Nuff to do this," Henry said, gesturing with a swivel of his head to the destruction around him.

"That ain't no answer."

Henry hesitated. Then he lifted a shoulder. "Half a dozen. Maybe more. Sure 'nuff wasn't takin' count while all this was goin' on."

"Just you and the girl left alive?" I asked him.

Henry got a strange look to him. It appeared as if he was going to say something, but then he held himself back.

The sheriff pressed forward. He gestured toward the burned-out structure of what once had been a cabin. "Any others 'sides that woman and you two?"

"That *woman,* as you call her . . . she was my sister." Henry's voice went weak. "What's left of her . . ."

"Anyone else?"

"Her husband. Their two sons."

"Where are they?"

Henry pointed a finger without even knowing where he was directing it. "Check out by the trees yonder."

"Dead, I take it," the sheriff said.

"Are now," was Henry's response.

"Would help if'n you'd talk sense," Briggs said gruffly.

"Didn't die easy," Henry said angrily. "They was tortured first. Then they was executed."

Each of us levelled our eyes on Henry. All

304

except the girl who, perhaps luckily, didn't appear to be absorbing any of what was being said.

"How do yuh mean *executed*?" Briggs asked.

"I heard the screams," he said with a tremor in his voice. "Then . . . gunshots. Seemed like the shootin' was never gonna stop."

Francisco stepped away from us and wandered in the approximate direction where Henry said the bodies were. When he came back several minutes later, his features were rigid. He said nothing, just nodded gravely at us.

Briggs said, "We'll come back for 'em . . . or send someone out. See that they're buried proper."

"Yeah, reckon that's somethin'," Henry muttered bitterly.

"How is it that you and the girl . . . ?" I started to ask.

"Why ain't we dead?" Henry finished, a defensive edge to his voice.

"Yeah."

Henry seemed reluctant to respond. Maybe "unwilling" was the proper word. I could detect by the awkward shifting of his body that he might be trying to conceal a shame. I was prepared to wager a guess what that might be. Somehow, either through plain luck or spinelessness, he'd managed to keep himself "protected" during the carnage.

As for how and why the girl was still breathing . . . that answer eluded me. She'd been beaten, that much was evident. But from all we had learned about the Ramos Gang, the girls they encountered during their trails of terror often served another purpose before they were murdered. I was grateful Lorraine had been spared. It just didn't make any sense to me.

Francisco, too, had reached the same conclusion regarding the man Henry. I took note of how his features heated with rage.

"You let those around you die while you saved your own skin," he said in outright accusation.

The sheriff turned his head toward Francisco.

Henry appeared anxious and he spoke up frantically. "No! No, I wasn't here when they came. I was washing down at the creek and by the time I got here and saw what was happening . . . why, there wasn't nothin' that I could do. There were too many. And I — I didn't have my gun."

Francisco cast his gaze toward the shotgun Henry still held in trembling hands.

"So you cowered?" Francisco presumed.

"Like I told yuh, I didn't have my shotgun. It was inside the cabin. There was no way I could get to it with those bandits all over the place. With no gun, tell me, what chance would I have had?"

"The cabin was burned to the ground," Francisco said, gesturing to the smoldering ruins. "How is it that your gun does not appear damaged by the fire?"

Henry opened his mouth, but no sound came out. He could not provide an answer, which in itself told us plenty. He just stood there looking more panicky by the second. Trapped by his lie; disgraced by his cowardice.

"Okay, enough," Sheriff Briggs ordered. "This ain't gettin' us nowhere, and it ain't of no matter now anyhow. What's done is done. This fella ain't guilty of nothin'." Here he regarded Henry with a glowering look. "If he coulda helped and didn't . . . well, that's somethin' he's gotta live with, and I don't envy him his conscience. But we got another, more urgent, matter to deal with."

I agreed with the sheriff. I looked at the girl I held in my arms and said solemnly, "Maybe two."

The sheriff brushed his wide Stetson over his brow and grunted.

"Can't leave her here," he said. "And sure 'nuff don't see how we can bring her with us."

We all turned to look at Henry. None of us could know for sure what had happened, other than reaching the shared conclusion that Henry had saved himself while watching his sister and the others be slaughtered. But if that was the case, he had a chance to redeem himself — if slightly — by taking charge of the girl. We told him about the encampment we had passed the day before, untouched by the bloody hand of the Ramos Gang, where she might be safe until she could be moved to Chesterfield City. Henry said he was eager to help, and he guaranteed he would get her there safely.

*Too* eager, it seemed to Francisco.

My *compañero* had a dour and distrustful look on his face. He wasn't confident of Henry's sincerity. I reckon that, with what we had discerned about the man's character, I couldn't rightly blame him.

"And if they should encounter Ramos," he said with disgust. "Do you not think he will run off and leave the girl? Perhaps even sacrifice her to save his own skin?"

"No, that won't happen. They — they headed north," Henry was quick to point out. "Th-they'd have no reason to double back. There's nothin' more for them here, you can see that."

Francisco smiled craftily at Henry. "How would you know which way they were going? You would have had to follow them out to the clearing. I am sure you did not do that. They travel on horseback. Your horses are still in the corral."

There was nothing Henry could say to that.

I appreciated Francisco's cleverness, as did the sheriff, who nodded approvingly. Still, under the circumstances, what choice did we have? We couldn't take the girl back to the settlement ourselves and lose valuable time and possibly fail to pick up Ramos's trail. Not when it seemed we were as close to the outfit as we'd yet gotten.

Francisco's face twisted in a grimace and he fairly spat out his next words. "I would not trust this *hombre* to escort the *señorita* to safety if she was Silvano's own sister."

I knew what my *compañero* was leading to. Judging by the unpleasant look on Sheriff Briggs's face, he had guessed it, too.

Before either of us could speak up in protest, Francisco raised both hands to halt us. He looked at the sheriff, and then at me.

"What else can we do, *amigos*?" he said.

"She must come with us." As if to add weight to his argument, he added, "And she will ride with me. I will care for her."

It was absolutely the wrong decision. We would be heading into unknown territory, riding into a precarious situation with a girl who could barely hold herself upright in the saddle. The last thing we needed was someone who would prove a hindrance.

I shifted my gaze toward Henry. I couldn't say I was surprised to see no objection coming from him. Not after he had just been afforded a convenient way out for himself. I tried to be generous, but to my way of thinking there was a distinct difference between being frightened and showing yourself with a yellow streak. There was no doubt in any of our minds that he'd had the shotgun with him at the time of the raid and simply didn't have the guts to use it.

I was startled when I heard the sheriff himself shout to the man, "Ride yourself outta here." The command made it clear Briggs had decided the girl should come with us. Not a decision I favored, but given the situation, there really was no other answer. Each of us would ride with troubled thoughts of what might become of the girl if we entrusted her well-being to her so-called uncle and that was an extra burden we could do without. The other consideration was that we were just wasting time.

It didn't seem there was anything else Henry could tell us. The damn fool quivered, either from true fear or from what we'd exposed about him, baring him buck naked as if we'd ripped his clothes clean off his body.

But there was something else the sheriff seemed to detect in Henry's unease when of a sudden he halted Henry before he could reach the corral to fetch his horse.

Henry slowly turned at the call. The sheriff took a few short steps over to him.

"What more do yuh know?" Briggs asked him with a deliberate cocking of his head. "What is it that yuh ain't tellin' us?"

"There ain't nothin' —" Henry started to protest.

"You know somethin' else," the sheriff said with an intriguing certainty.

The look on Henry's face became one of incomprehension — a convincing display — but apparently not fooling the sheriff.

"You ain't leavin' here till you spill all of it," he assured Henry.

Henry's face grew fearful as his eyes shifted nervously to each of us.

He then spoke abruptly, as if he just wanted to say his words and be done. What he said made me despise the man even more. Francisco looked as if he were prepared to strangle the life from him.

"There was another child," Henry sputtered. "They . . . they took her with them. Lorraine's little sister."

Lorraine's eyes flickered slightly and she whispered "Bethany" before she fell back into her benumbed silence.

Sheriff Briggs's eyes shot daggers at Henry.

"Why didn't yuh tell us this before?" he demanded.

Henry was almost in tears. "Because I . . . I couldn't."

*"Why?"*

"I don't want to think about why they would have taken the child," Henry confessed. "What they . . . would do to her."

The intense expression that twisted across Francisco's face suggested he had a suspicion of their purpose.

As did Sheriff Briggs, who cursed.

"Goddamn! Son of a bitch!"

"My God," I gasped, as I finally understood. But I did not want to consider the horror that had taken root in my brain. I could not conceive that their atrocities could be worsened, yet without anything having to be spelled out, I recognized once more that there was no boundary to their evil. The Ramos Gang knew they were being hunted with a great urgency and intensity and that, with the law closing in, they would have to lie low and survive for however long off the food and supplies they had stolen until they were once again free to do their plundering.

The most critical question was, how long might it be until they were able to replenish their food stock?

"How much grub did they take from here?" the sheriff asked Henry.

Henry swallowed. "Very little. We — didn't have much. Some fish . . . a little pork —"

I didn't give a damn to hear him list his foodstuffs. I spun around to Francisco.

"You know Ramos," I said. "Could — that be true?"

"With Silvano himself, I cannot say," Francisco replied. "But for those he rides with . . . they most surely are peasants. Peasants who might not be so choosy as to what they will need to keep up their strength."

There was not much I hadn't seen during my professional years, climaxing thus far with the slaughter at Bodrie Hills, but with what Francisco was implying, I could barely hold back the clutch in my throat.

"Go on, git," Sheriff Briggs ordered Henry.

Henry walked hastily to the corral. He mounted one of the horses without bothering to saddle the animal and rode off. He rode with speed, to a destination unknown — and none of us cared. As the sheriff had said, he would have to live with his guilt and the knowledge that he might have been able to do something to rescue those who had fallen victim to the Ramos Gang. Including the child, the possible fate of whom was too grisly to contemplate.

As we rode away from the wreckage of the homestead, I caught the occasional furtive glance coming my way from Francisco. I finally turned to face him directly. I noticed how he had to frequently lift Lorraine's arms to wrap around his waist so she would not slide off the horse. She still clutched the doll in the crook of an arm. It occurred to me that she was too old to be attached to such a toy. As I saw it, the doll either belonged to her little sister . . . or perhaps in Lorraine's mind represented the child. And by not releasing the doll, she was in her own way keeping her sister safe.

"That man was a coward," Francisco said with unhindered distaste. And then he spoke more thoughtfully. "But what I must ask myself is, would any man become a coward should such a situation arise?"

I had the distinct impression Francisco's words were directed specifically at me. I questioned what had prompted his remark. It didn't take me long to reach the conclusion that somewhere along the way he might have determined some weakness in me, a chink in my armor, as it were. Perhaps it started with my attraction to J.C. Yes, that was possible. Even I could admit it was not the best time to entertain a romance. But in Francisco's view, maybe he figured that if a man's heart was softened by love, he was compromising his capacity for violence, thus making him a less effective partner when the time came for him to prove his worth. Maybe he also thought I had not truly realized the seriousness of our quest — as it was just now that we had been faced with the stark reality of our purpose.

"I didn't expect to come upon what we just did," I admitted to Francisco.

He fixed me with his dark brown eyes and said, "Yes. Now you have seen firsthand the nature of Ramos."

I asked him sturdily, "You have doubts about me, after we have come this far?"

"Perhaps." Francisco spoke thoughtfully. "It can weaken a man's spirit to be witness to such violence."

"I'm not unaccustomed to violence," I told him flatly. I had only to remember the bloodshed in the Bodrie Hills. But I was not about to share that experience with Francisco. I didn't believe I had to prove myself.

At the same time, I wanted him to understand that, despite any doubts he might have, I had misgivings of my own.

"I'm still not convinced you don't have it in mind to kill me once this is over," I told him outright.

"I would not concern myself with that, now that there are three of us," he returned, almost too offhandedly.

"Four," I corrected.

"No *amigo — three,*" Francisco repeated with the slight twist of a smile.

I looked at the girl limply hanging on behind Francisco. He was right, of course. *Three* — not *four* — of us. There was not much we could expect from this child in any desperate situation that may come up.

"And I certainly would not have such a worry with a lawman riding with us," Francisco added, jutting his jaw toward the sheriff as a reminder.

Sheriff Briggs was pacing his horse a good distance at our head, so I could speak without being overheard.

"Even with everything you admitted to me, the lies you 'fessed up to, I still can't say I trust you fully," I said. " 'Fact, because you came clean, it might give me more reason to keep hold of my doubts."

Francisco regarded me with an ambiguous expression.

"And of course there's that matter that you might still hold me to blame for what happened to your sister," I added.

"I thought we had settled that," Francisco said.

"I don't know if anything between us has been settled," I told him frankly.

"And yet even with your doubts you continue to ride alongside me," Francisco said.

I drew a breath. But I decided not to answer.

Instead, Francisco answered for himself. "Yes, as I suspected from the outset, you are a man who does not sway once he makes a commitment."

Again I said nothing. But he would not be pleased to know that within a short time, his confidence in me would not be as precise as he thought.

The lengthening shadows stretched over the

landscape as night approached. It would probably be to our advantage to ride through the darkness. For the sake of the child snatched by Ramos and his murderers, I thought we should proceed in that direction. Therefore I was disappointed when Sheriff Briggs called a halt to our travel for the day.

It was then that he said something quite unexpected. He spoke his words as if he were making an announcement. "Someone will have to stay here with the girl. Two of us can carry on."

"No, no," Francisco protested. Then he lifted a leg over his saddle and flung himself from his mount, pulling the girl down with him in a none-too-gentle maneuver. He took her by the shoulders with both hands and spoke directly in her face.

The roughness in his manner was unexpected — and startling.

"We have no choice but to take you along," he said to her. "But you must be strong. You must have the strength and the courage to come with us. We did not leave you behind, perhaps as we should have. No, we would not trust your safety to a man who is clearly a coward. Now you must repay us by showing bravery."

When the girl didn't respond Francisco

said with emphasis, "You owe it to your sister."

Neither Sheriff Briggs nor I interfered with what was happening. Francisco was doing what he had to, exhibiting a forcefulness that might be the only way to snap some sense of comprehension back into the girl.

And gradually a spark of recognition came to Lorraine. I peered at the sheriff, whose expression remained set and stern, not providing a hint to what he might be thinking. But I was sure that he, too, understood it was imperative the girl be made aware of what we could expect on this trail. While none of us knew she would be of help if we met up with Silvano Ramos and his gang, neither could we afford to have her impede our progress or interfere when the moment of reckoning came.

My own attitude hadn't changed. I understood we were pretty much cornered into this decision, but I still worried that her presence would add to the burden we already carried.

For the next two days we rode with the girl — who was silent, distant, and apparently oblivious to the grief she carried — as we continued our trail northwest, into much rougher territory, just the type of terrain

Ramos and his bunch would likely cross to discourage pursuit. At least that was what Sheriff Briggs presumed. From my own professional experience, I agreed with him. The Ramos Gang's only hope of eluding capture was by navigating a terrain where their tracks could not easily be spotted. And being successful in that attempt meant a lot of traversing across hard sandy surfaces and rocky outcroppings.

Following such a potentially perilous trail would slow us considerably, but the sheriff, riding firm in his saddle with the unlit butt end of his omnipresent cigar jutting from his mouth, was insistent on playing his hunch. Neither Francisco nor I challenged his decision. Our only concern was . . . might this veering off a safer path be a deliberate maneuver planned by the outlaws? Might Ramos, with those keen senses possessed by many who ride outside the law, know he was being tracked and was trying to lead us off course, perhaps away from where there might be water? Maybe his aim was to deplete our resources until he could prepare his own strike.

Silvano Ramos was as cunning as he was deadly. To ensure his freedom, he was capable of any such trickery.

# CHAPTER SEVENTEEN

It continued to be a quiet ride. So far the minimal conversation among the three of us had been welcome, if not outright agreeable. Since leaving Chesterfield City, we rode most of our journey in silence, each of us accompanied by periods of introspection that provided us with a good way to keep our individual focus clear. Or at least that might have been the way we justified it. More likely, we were surrendering to a gradual if inevitable tension. Because, as we carried on since leaving the death and destruction we'd found at the homestead where we had rescued Lorraine, the quiet among us almost imperceptibly took on a dark and ominous quality.

I did not know what my two companions were thinking, but for me, I had the gut instinct we would soon be nearing the end of our journey. That feeling in my belly had been honed from experience and was rarely wrong.

I thought perhaps Silvano Ramos and his bunch understood that as well. Why else would they have snatched an infant, if they weren't motivated by desperation that they might be forced to resort to eating the child? If that were so — and for we who followed the Ramos trail such an abominable outcome could hardly be considered, let alone dwelt upon — it might mean they knew their time was running out.

The gruesome fate possibly awaiting the child troubled me, despite my stringent efforts to repel it. Many times throughout those lengthy stretches of quiet, I found myself saddled with disturbing images, overwhelming me to such an extent that I sought relief in meaningless conversation with my companions. Words might free me from distressing ruminations and possibly provide a connection, however tenuous, among the three of us. We each shared two things in common: a similar objective . . . and an uncertain future.

None of us, though, would be the first to offer his own doubts or reassurances. No one spoke beyond the occasional grunting comment or meager observation. Once more I attributed this economy of words to the dread each of us carried. A burden not lessened by our being accompanied by a girl whose own trauma served as a reminder of the type of men we might soon encounter.

Night descends swiftly in open territory, and its vast canvas of black can be virtually impenetrable. One has only the distant glittering of stars and maybe sun-setting reflections off distant mountain peaks to guide him. While on this night Sheriff Briggs seemed determined to carry on for however long he was able, soon the failing light necessitated an end to the day's search. I heard him utter a curse as he straightened on his mount. He'd been riding hard, and I assumed his swearing referred to another of his sharp discomforts. I have to admit, I'd rarely seen a man push himself so relentlessly.

We found a suitable location to set up camp, just beyond some hilly rises where the land dipped and there was an eastern rocky border affording us some seclusion. A small stream cut across the land, flowing with clean water so we could replenish our canteens and wash the trail dirt from our faces and hands — although I didn't expect to see Francisco venturing too close to the water's edge. I could tell by his displeased expression that he aimed to keep his dirt a while longer. The rest of us went toward the stream to freshen up, Lorraine taking tentative steps and being helped along by Francisco. We were tired and I reckon we all felt a little low.

The choppy, rock- and vegetation-laden trail we had followed had brought nothing to aid us in our search. The sheriff rode a good part of the day leaning over the side of his saddle, straining his eyes in an effort to seek tracks or determine other telling signs in the breaks of sand that might point us in the correct direction. Now he was stiff and sore from all of his abuse to his posture. Once we'd dismounted, he did not even try to conceal his aches and pains — partly because he damn well couldn't; though if either Francisco or I took too long a notice, he'd fix us with a biting glare.

After we ate our supper I stepped away from Francisco and Sheriff Briggs. I caught the curious squint of Francisco's eye as he watched me walk off into the shelter of darkness where I could not be disturbed. The farther I walked, the more engulfed in silence I became, my ears attuned only to the sounds of nature that skirted about me; those I could identify and those I could not. I sat against a large rock, appreciating the solitude, since I needed to figure out my thoughts. Thoughts that troubled me with more emphasis than I'd expected.

I wondered whether our efforts would bring us the results we sought. If so, when might that be? Tomorrow? The next day? Next week? That was the question *I* began to ask. I had never been one to surrender to discouragement (I would have starved to death long ago had that been the case), but with so much time to focus on my ponderings, I began to doubt we would ever catch up to Ramos.

The people I had sought in my work as a witness seeker seldom knew they were being trailed, so there rarely was ever a pursuit. But Ramos was an outlaw — and though I loathed to afford him such credit, he was smart. Clever. He knew how to run and where to hide. And while I did want to see him dead and bring his reign of violence to an end, my other concern was, were we really the group to handle such a challenge?

We had learned much since riding into Chesterfield City, and while I was not a coward, neither was I a fool. Yes, emotion had got the better of me after coming upon that massacre just days before. At the time my blood had coursed through my veins so hotly, I would have rushed blindly into a gunfight with the Ramos bunch then and there. But now I was thinking with more clarity. And the young girl the *banditos* held hostage . . . would we be able to save her in time? Too many questions were populating my thoughts.

I confess the moment was growing nearer in which I might volunteer to take Lorraine back with me to Chesterfield City . . . and return to the woman whom I hoped would be waiting for me. When her vision entered my brain, it was as if I'd been struck by a thunderbolt. Only then could I put aside dark ruminations and relax my muddle of conflicting thoughts.

A welcome sense of calm overcame me as I thought of how J.C. was the only reward that mattered to me. Even the payment Francisco offered seemed . . . insignificant, in light of everything else. Of a sudden it occurred to me that Francisco had been right to have uncertainties about me. It had not been my intention to desert him — or maybe, as he would see it, *betray* him — but I realized I had a decision to make.

I heard footfalls approaching and I looked up hastily, poising my hand near my gun belt.

Francisco stood next to me. I both resented and was uneasy by his interruption.

I sensed he might cleverly understand in that mysteriously insightful way of his what I was considering. I tried to resist his stare without appearing too obvious, but his eyes were fixated on me.

I said nothing. I waited for Francisco to speak first.

"The end is near. Perhaps even tomorrow," he said. His voice sounded strange. He spoke darkly.

I remained silent.

"Silvano knows it, too," Francisco said. "And he has prepared himself."

A chill passed through my body that I could not wholly attribute to the night air.

Francisco inflated his chest and then exhaled strongly.

"And we have come with a disadvantage," he said further.

His words were clear to me.

As was what I started to recognize was his self-reproach.

"It was wrong of me to bring the girl along — to once again be made to face Ramos," he said, and he turned toward Lorraine sitting not too far in the distance. I lifted myself from the ground and followed his gaze. The girl's expression was vacant, her demeanor unresponsive as she huddled under a blanket next to the warm campfire.

And then Francisco shot me a look, his deep brown eyes hooded beneath a knitted brow.

Even though I had objected to bringing the girl with us, I tried to ease the guilt that affected him.

"You did what you had to under the circumstances," I said to him. "There really was nothing else we could have done."

"Left her to die?" Francisco asked severely.

"That likely would have been the outcome," I replied.

He spoke with strain. "Yet I now ask myself, have we done her any better? Or with what is to come, have we condemned her to an even more terrible fate?"

I understood my *compañero*'s dilemma. He had made a choice. He had to know even as he made the only decision he could that it was a mistake to bring the girl. If things went wrong, she would be killed along with the rest of us. And with the Ramos Gang's penchant for torture, the death awaiting each of us would be of a horrific nature.

No, there was no easy way to ease the weight from his conscience. But there was still one other point to consider. And to be truthful, I voiced it mainly to reassure Francisco.

"Alone — or if we'd chanced her welfare to her uncle, we'd never know what became of the girl," I told him. "That uncertainty would stay with us, *amigo,* regardless of what happens between us and Ramos. Our outcome might not be what we hope for. But at least we will not have to guess her fate."

Francisco's expression was one of vague understanding.

I explained as delicately as I could. "Right now she is with us. Safe. She is our concern. If our situation were to become hopeless . . . if it looks as if Ramos will win . . . we can ensure her death will be painless."

Francisco did not immediately grasp my meaning. Or if he did, his first reaction was to pay no heed. I'd spoke my piece with intention. What I suggested was extreme, but ultimately merciful. Finally, his expression grew serious as what I proposed in such an eventuality became clear to his comprehension.

"What you are saying . . . that is not what I intended," he said.

"It's not what either of us — or even the sheriff — intended," I returned grimly.

"I did not bring the girl along so one of us might have to kill her," Francisco said with emotion.

"No," I said with equal intensity. "But none of us may survive this. You know that as well as I. Since the two of us rode out from Santa Rosina, we've found out things about Silvano Ramos that we — especially *you* — never expected to discover. He is not alone. There are others, just as ruthless, that he rides with. If we pursue our course, chances are we all might end up dead. Would you rather she suffer the torture that is their specialty?"

Francisco was perceptive. He had listened carefully to my phrasing of "*If* we pursue . . ." He looked at me and rocked his head slowly.

"Yes. You speak as if you have doubts about going any farther," he said with a humorless smile.

I hesitated with my reply, but thought it only right to be straightforward with him.

"I have considered turning back," I told him. "Take the girl with me."

"To Chesterfield City?"

"Yes."

Francisco's smile broadened into a grin. But it was not an encouraging grin.

"And of course the girl who waits for you there," he muttered. "The newspaper lady."

I didn't have to confirm what he suspected.

"So I was right about you," Francisco said, his expression twisting into a frown. "I did not doubt you, *Señor.* Did not doubt your dedication to . . . my cause. My purpose. Not until we reached the town and you took a fancy to the lady. Yet you tell me not long ago that I can count on you to see this through with me."

"I've had a lot of time to think, Francisco. We all have. And things are different now. We have the girl to consider. I just explained to you what would happen to her if Ramos gets the upper hand. One of us would have to take it upon himself to kill her to spare her from . . . But there's also no way of knowing if we'll even find him and his gang. And what chance the three of us would have against him and his men if we do find him. Or maybe it'll be *him* who finds us. Either way . . ." My words trailed off.

"I have no plan to turn back, my nameless friend," Francisco said. His voice rose in a challenge. "And perhaps if that is what you choose to do, I can finally answer another question I know has been troubling you."

I reckon it was inevitable. It was something that had been building between us since the beginning, when neither of us knew precisely what we were getting ourselves into. When both Francisco and I agreed to the understanding that there could be no complete trust between us — especially on my part. I could not forget that I had been coaxed into this arrangement both by profit and guilt; I had never outright volunteered out of a sense of duty.

Whether it was any of these factors or just long pent-up emotions that proved the catalyst to my aggression, I couldn't say. I only knew my temper had reached a fever-pitch and it was I who had dropped the reins on my restraint — and who threw the first punch.

My hand balled into a fist and, seemingly of its own will, lashed out and connected with Francisco's jaw — and with such force that only after I felt and heard my knuckles crunch against bone did I fear I might have reacted in haste and that I might have made a move I would regret.

Francisco's head snapped back on impact, the *sombrero* flying from his head, and his body twisting in a half turn, his legs starting to buckle, before he somehow managed to regain his balance and keep himself on his feet.

I was flabbergasted. Most of my might had gone into that punch. I considered myself a powerful man. I had knocked bigger men than Francisco to their knees, if not outright to the ground. Yet the little Mexican, after he shook the stardust from his eyes and raised his head, regarded me with a look that almost seemed to dare me to throw another punch.

I had worked out my aggression through that single blow and held myself back. I looked at him with regret. Yet I resisted offering him my hand to help steady him.

Francisco took notice of my disinclination to assist him. He wiped the trickle of blood from the corner of his lips and, to my surprise, nodded his head approvingly.

"You were entitled to that, *Señor,*" he said without acrimony.

I wasn't so sure. I was not quite ready to accept his generosity. From the outset we had been riding alongside each other with a subtle tension, mistrust, and, for myself at least, an overall uncertainty that would occasionally gnaw at my innards. Yet we'd also both come to rely on each other — whether it was through our joint defiance at the reception we'd had at Pawnee Joe's or a growing commitment from what we'd learned along each mile of our travel in our search for Silvano Ramos.

Francisco scooped up his *sombrero.* He gave his head a brisk shake. Then he dared to step over to me. Just a few feet from where I had knocked him backward. He gazed deeply into my eyes with that oftentimes probing and unsettling stare. I could not tell whether he might be contemplating returning the blow. In any event, if that were his intention I was not going to defend myself. I reckoned I was owed a punch in the face by Francisco just as he had deserved one delivered by my own hand.

But it was not to be. Francisco was wily. It was as if he still preferred to play the game his own way — and it obviously had not yet been settled to his satisfaction.

"Perhaps now that you have gotten that out of you, you will reconsider your plans," he said.

I responded with a vague smile.

He spoke his next words in his typically enigmatic fashion. "But if you decide to continue to ride with the sheriff . . . if your doubts about the future between us still persist, *Señor* . . . be assured that moment between us still may come."

And with that — without waiting to see if I would reply — Francisco walked away.

Moments later Sheriff Briggs appeared alongside me, another shadow emerging from the dark. His presence gave me a slight start, since my thoughts were elsewhere and my reflexes still at the ready.

He was gnawing on a bit of hard tack. He didn't speak, just gave me a quick, direct look; then he nodded. As he turned and started to walk away, I felt compelled to say, "Not gonna ask?"

"Nothin' to say," the sheriff returned casually, without so much as a glance back in my direction.

Yeah, I silently agreed after a few moments of thought. There really was nothing to say. While there was a commitment of purpose, between the three of us there also seemed to be no set rules.

There was a sort of distance among our party that night. Not so unusual in itself, but there was that fourth to consider. The girl, Lorraine. Still a tragic specimen. Francisco spent most of his time with her, looking to comfort her in his own particular way. The girl seemed mostly off in the protection of her own solitude and not receptive to his quiet attempts at communicating with her.

I had my own thoughts about that. Whether they were of any value, I could not say. But I felt they were at least worth considering. The girl had witnessed extreme brutality and murders committed by people of Francisco's race. While it was clear he was only trying to reassure her that she could feel safe and protected with him, the girl likely saw things a mite differently; she appeared, at least to my eye, to regard Francisco warily, maybe as a threat, and was guarding herself the only way she could. Perhaps she only pretended not to acknowledge him. While earlier she had been forced to respond to his bluntness, with the reminder that her sister's life was in danger, it was possible the memories of what had occurred at their homestead had resurfaced with an even greater impact, sending her back to a type of oblivion.

I confess I was waiting for the moment when Francisco would edge away from her so that I might have my own opportunity to attempt to reach her. I still hadn't made up my mind conclusively what I was going to do come sunup.

Maybe the girl could help me reach that decision.

As my impatience heightened, I probably could not have been more obvious in my intention. For the longest time I stood just yards from where the two of them sat, my focus steady as I slurped loudly on my coffee, a brew prepared by Sheriff Briggs that tasted as if it had been filtered through the sandy grains our horses had trampled over. Francisco did his best to ignore me, casting only the occasional glance in my direction. Finally, perhaps in exasperation, he looked at me, almost as if in another gesture of challenge. I met his gaze calmly. The expression on his face then lightened and hinted that he seemed to understand I only wanted to share some time with the girl and do whatever I could for her. Despite all else, he had to agree the girl must not be part of what was to come, and that I was the most likely one among us to take her to safety.

Nevertheless, there could be no denying that the relationship between Francisco and me (if that was what it could rightly be termed) had become strained. Even before he learned I might be leaving the hunt for Ramos, I felt a separation between us. I had noticed a gradual shift in his character from the outset, when he was prone to long periods of moody silence — at odds with the man who acquainted himself with me in Santa Rosina. The change in his personality became more apparent when he rode out from Chesterfield City, but that had been offset by flashes of the Francisco I had earlier come to know. Moments that were infrequent but familiar. But he had become almost an entirely different person since we had come upon the desecrated homestead where we had found the girl.

Now there was a nearly perpetual darkness to his character that put him at a distinct distance not only from me, but also from Sheriff Briggs. The sheriff had perceived this and responded in kind. Only with Lorraine did Francisco exhibit compassion.

But once I thought it out more carefully, I understood. Lorraine served as a reminder of what Francisco had lost so tragically. Unlike his sister Felicia, this girl had survived Silvano Ramos's evil. Because of that, Francisco believed he owed her special, personal protection. Which was why he could not leave her to the care of a man of dubious character: her supposed uncle. A man whose "truth" in that regard had left me suspect.

Francisco took it upon himself to see that Lorraine remained safe — even if it meant bringing her to the very threshold of danger.

But the more I mulled the matter over in my head, the more I knew I could not permit him to expose her to Ramos's violence, and that I must take charge of her safety. Whether or not Francisco wanted to think poorly of me — if at some point he might want to seek me out and settle the score — he had to see the wisdom of my decision . . . if only for the girl's sake.

I walked over to Lorraine and greeted her wordlessly, but with a smile. Her eyes slowly met mine and, while the expression on her face remained vacant, I was sure I detected the slightest flicker of acknowledgment in her gaze. I kept my movements slow, for I saw how tentative she was. Her own motions were frequently stiff and jerky, a frightened reflex, as if she were bracing herself against another assault. I could not imagine what she had gone through when Ramos and his gang had invaded her family's camp, but I briefly contemplated that maybe they had not done her such a favor by sparing her life after she'd witnessed their brutality, the horror to which they had subjected her family. The truth was that Lorraine not only had her folks and sister taken from her, but also her youth and likely a future of any happiness.

Yet there was still a slim hope at restoring some of her well-being. And that was in rescuing her sister. If . . . it wasn't already too late.

I wanted to touch the girl. Take her hand in mine. Give her whatever comfort I could. The way she looked down at my hand, I finally determined she would accept the closure of my fingers over hers. But I still approached the gesture with care. I did not want to frighten her. I wanted to allow her the opportunity to resist, if she chose.

I laid the palm of my hand over the back of her hand. At first I felt her fingers stiffen, but I held my own hand steady. I also kept my eyes on her. She didn't return my gaze. Instead, her eyes gradually lowered to the gentleness of my touch. I took it that she understood I would not harm her. There was a slight parting of her lips. I heard the tiniest sigh leave her mouth.

And then — when I delicately rubbed my fingers along the soft smoothness of her hand, she cautiously lifted her eyes toward me.

The expression in her eyes remained dull and even colorless, but I gave her the most sincere, trusting expression I could manage in an effort to encourage some reaction out of her. Even something as minor as a flicker in her eyes, as I'd briefly noticed before.

It was then that I felt other eyes upon me. I was slow to release my gaze from Lorraine, but I turned my focus to the side, where I caught sight of Francisco watching us. The expression on his face was cold. Yet I met his stare, firmly and without hesitation. I felt compelled to rise but, to my surprise, the girl would not let go of my hand. In fact, her grip, as feeble as it was, tightened. I glanced down at her. Her features were unchanged. Blank. Empty. Not a single shift in her face to match the sturdiness of her grip.

Once again I felt as if I was being challenged by Francisco. As if, to his way of thinking, I had intruded into his territory.

The mood between us continued to darken.

Francisco stepped over and separated our hands. The girl did not resist or fight against his pull, even though her eyes stayed fixed on mine. I felt my own fist clenching at his interference and the audacity of his action.

"I have taken responsibility for the girl's welfare onto myself," he said sharply.

"She doesn't belong to you," I said in reply.

The moment of tension broke before it could escalate further. Whatever had compelled Francisco to act in such a fashion instantly seemed to dissipate, leaving him looking ashamed and embarrassed.

"No, *Señor,*" Francisco said gently. "She does not belong to me."

I stood up and faced him directly.

"I've decided that the girl and I will be leaving at sunrise," I said.

He looked at me for a long time before he shifted his gaze to the oblivious Lorraine.

He surprised me when he said very quietly, "Yes. Perhaps that is for the best, *Señor.*"

# CHAPTER EIGHTEEN

Through my work as a witness seeker, I'd had my dealings with deadly night predators during remote campouts. The most loathsome and lethal were snakes. Those belly-crawlers who slithered across the sand in a clever pattern, rarely giving warning of their approach. They attacked their unsuspecting victim suddenly, in a motion evolved from hundreds of years of seeking their prey. They struck without their victim even knowing he had been come upon until it was too late.

The snake was a formidable foe. Yet even its deadliness could be matched by a human reptile — one to whom we had attached a name.

Silvano Ramos.

As we were to discover that night when we fell into slumber, exhausted. Sheriff Briggs volunteered to keep the first watch.

I don't know how long I had been asleep

when something snapped me awake.

My eyes opened to a dirty, grinning face looking back at me.

It wasn't a reptilian night crawler. Perhaps if it were I might have been able to move quickly enough to escape its venomous strike.

But it was a night-shadowed human face that met my gaze, a face confident in its advantage as it held its white-toothed grin against my quick, reflexive attempt to defend myself. The body belonging to that face was powerful and kept me pinned to the ground.

The blade of the long knife that pressed against my throat kept me very still.

I had yet to fully awaken. I suppose some part of me thought this was a dream. Enough had bothered my brain that day so that my imagination easily could have been overworked.

But I wasn't imagining the physical sensation of sharp, cold metal teasing my neck. I realized that just the slightest move on my part would encourage that blade to penetrate flesh and muscle.

The voice that greeted my ears was like a prolonged hiss. The snake about to strike.

*"Shhhhhh,"* it sounded, at the same time releasing the stench of foul whiskey breath.

I forced myself to come awake but not to dare any aggressive action. For one thing, my gun belt, which I'd laid out next to me, had surely been taken. I also had no idea what precisely faced me. Were my companions in a similar predicament as I had found myself?

Were they even alive?

The Mexican spoke in a whisper. "You have come seeking us, *sí?*"

I didn't answer.

"But it is *us* who have found *you.*" He laughed.

I was afraid, yet determined not to lift my stare from his eyes. I understood how bandits thought. They wanted a person to show fear. Calling upon all my will power I was not going to grant this *hombre* that privilege.

"Maybe for the reward money, is that not so?" he said, grinning and nodding his head vigorously.

I kept my mouth shut. That might not have been a smart move, for I noticed the frustration rise in the bandit. His grin slowly faded, and his features drew tight into a mask of malevolence.

I expected at any moment that knife to slash across my throat.

Still, I maintained my defiance and only

hoped he couldn't feel how fast my heart was beating.

He turned away from me, only for an instant. When he looked back his expression was less threatening than inquisitive.

"Do you know who I am, *Señor*?" he said, sounding almost wounded that I hadn't determined his identity.

With that question, only one answer came to me.

I was staring into the face of Silvano Ramos.

The man I had heard so much about. A ruthless killer. A man whose bloody reputation had stimulated nightmares, yet who had also become a legend. The scourge of citizens and lawmen alike.

I never imagined this was how I would be introduced to him, with his face mere inches from my own.

And at that moment I had to accept that I and the others were to die — if my companions were not already dead. What sent a chill sweeping through my body was the knowledge that Ramos and his crew rarely killed their victims outright. They enjoyed toying with them, with taunting, torture, and other acts of brutality. Murder was the eventual end, but first they had their fun.

Finally, I spoke the name. "Ramos."

The bandit gave me a peculiar look, and then he threw his head back and started to laugh wildly.

"The *gringo* thinks I am Ramos," he roared.

There followed other eruptions of laughter from around the campsite. The bandits had crept up on us in silence, like vipers. Now that their presence was known, they no longer felt the need for restraint.

Not until a harsh command for quiet was issued. The men instantly obeyed. Total silence descended over the camp.

The bandit who had been holding a knife to my throat scrambled to his feet and hastened away, like a child in fear of his father's whip. I heard footsteps approaching. Slow, heavy. With purpose. I still dared not to move. But I now knew for a certainty who I would meet next.

A face that might have been pulled whole and horrible from a dark dream. A fierce-looking, skull-featured Mexican. While he had been called *El Diablo,* to my eyes he looked less like the devil than death personified. A man whose mere appearance reflected the worthlessness he placed on human life, be it a man, woman . . . or child.

He looked tall and broad from the angle at which I viewed him. He stood with his legs wide apart, closed fists pressed against his hips. His outfit was flashy: wide, beaded Mexican hat, striped shirt and trousers, gray sleeveless waistcoat, a scarlet bandanna tied loosely around his neck. But despite the fanciness of his attire, his clothes were also dirty from the long trail he had ridden. Most "impressive" from my standpoint were the bandolier belt and holster rig that looped over each shoulder. Bullet loops across the front and shotgun loops across the back. Each of the loops was loaded with cartridges. Silvano Ramos was a man who would not be caught unprepared.

His whole attitude projected a brazen, arrogant authority. Yet I didn't have to remind myself that this lowlife specimen had begun his criminal career by murdering a frightened and defenseless girl.

I could tell by the detached way he seemed to be studying me that Silvano Ramos considered me of little importance. Like a fly he could brush off of his sleeve.

"Bring him to his feet and take him to the others," he ordered in a gruff, accented voice.

And two husky Mexicans were on me before I could even start to pull myself from my bedroll. They took me roughly by the arms. Once I was on my feet, I could finally survey the situation. I counted eight bandits, besides Ramos, milling about the campsite, a lesser number than I had expected, but of course there might have been others outside the camp, perhaps standing watch.

I saw Francisco being lashed to a tree, yet his face maintained a stolid expression. The girl, Lorraine, knelt on a blanket near the campfire, trembling, and it was not from the night chill. She finally showed emotion: terror reflected in her glazed eyes.

I did not immediately see Sheriff Briggs. My eyes scouted the area . . . and then my gaze fell upon the sheriff. He was lying not far from the campfire, motionless. I looked intently at his chest. He did not appear to be breathing. I squinted to get a better look — and that was when I felt as if I had been punched in the gut. Sheriff Austin Briggs, the courageous lawman who had hoped to end his career the way it had begun, with a victory . . . was dead. He'd obviously been surprised while on watch. He likely never even heard his killer approach, as the bandit must have crept up on him with stealth. I saw the wicked gash across Briggs's throat and the blood that circled his neck like a crimson bandana. If there was any consolation, it was that he had probably died swiftly, without even knowing he had been murdered. It occurred to me that Ramos saw there was less need to torture him than get him out of the way. He would save his entertainment for us.

Ramos surveyed the camp and said in a loud, commanding voice, "You can consider yourselves fortunate that I noticed my *amigo* Francisco here after I cut the lawman's throat. Otherwise I would have had my men do the same to you. But now . . . maybe we have some fun, no?"

Ramos looked at each of us, again regarding me with as little worth as he might have for a wad of tobacco spit. I knew he could shoot me dead and forget about me in the next blink of his eye.

Which he might have done. Only there was Francisco, Ramos's boyhood friend. His former brother-in-law. The man whose sister he first had tortured, finally murdered, then violated further by emptying his gun into her. A heartless fiend. Ramos appeared intrigued by Francisco's presence, so I became an afterthought. I was given a "reprieve," as it were.

I heard Ramos say, "But now I ask myself, what do I do with my *amigo*?"

A question he spoke for his own amusement, given the tone of affection in his voice — not so subtly directed at Francisco, whose life expectancy seemed shorter than my own.

I knew Francisco's death would not be swift. Because he set out after Ramos to avenge his sister's death, there was now a personal score to settle. I doubted Ramos would be inclined to be merciful. I tried to keep my thoughts free of the various tortures the insane mind of Silvano Ramos could devise.

My body was thrust up against a tree. My head was held firmly by the forearm of one of the bandits, who had it locked against my jaw. I could not look in any direction except straight ahead. I could no longer see Francisco or the girl. All I was aware of was the whimpering of Lorraine, who I only hoped would once again become lost in the salvation of her own oblivion.

"Do not fret, *amigo,*" I heard Francisco say to me, speaking with a gallant determination. "All is not hopeless."

I managed to twist my head free just long enough to crane my neck and see Francisco. His words might have been strong, his intent sincere, but his prediction was doubtful, as his arms were bound to the trunk of the tree with ropes of rawhide.

Moments later Ramos walked over. He ignored me completely but moved to within

351

inches of Francisco's face. It didn't take me long to see that he was taking great pleasure in toying with him.

"I would not have guessed it would be you, my brother, who would move against me," Ramos said, sounding almost regretful — though in no way sincere.

Francisco responded in defiance. "Once you might have been considered my brother, Silvano, but you insult the memory of my sister by daring to call yourself that now."

"Your sister," he said musingly. Then he drew a breath. "My wife. She would speak against me to the court. There is no love where there can be no trust." He shrugged. "And if there is no love . . . then what does it matter?"

"She did not speak against you," Francisco said emphatically. "Because she would not betray you, you were set free. Why could you not leave it at that?"

While I could no longer see the two men, as my head was thrust forward and held away from them, I listened to the words. I wondered if the truth might come out that it had been I who had escorted Felicia to the town to present the evidence she refused to deliver. The poor girl had been coaxed into that decision by me, in my official capacity . . . so perhaps, if this fact were made known, I would be looked upon as the most guilty by Silvano Ramos.

Francisco was the only one who knew of this, of course. However way Ramos chose to end my life — swift or slow — might be decided if Francisco made the decision to speak up in order to make his own death less painful.

The question was, how much hostility did Francisco hold against me?

Francisco was silent for a long time. I wondered if he was considering what he should say. Was Francisco a man of courage and character? Or would he take this opportunity to betray me?

The seconds that passed could not have seemed any longer if I were standing before a firing squad.

During those moments, my brain damn near exploded with thoughts. Questions of relevance, some now seeming of no consequence. For instance, I still did not know if it had been Francisco's intention to kill me at the end of our journey — if we had succeeded and survived. That was not the situation now. Our outlook was grim. If Francisco wanted me dead, this was as good a time as any. Only I would not die by his own hand.

And then — I heard crying. The crying of

a young child. While I could not move my head, I managed to veer my eyes toward Lorraine, who had recovered enough to gaze off into the dark, looking curiously intent.

And then I knew. She heard the child. Lorraine's sister.

I forced my head free so I could watch the child being led out into the light of the campfire by one of Ramos's greasy *banditos*. She looked to be no older than four years. Again, the thought of what Ramos might have had in store for the girl filled me with rage. Against my will, I resisted attempting to struggle free of the hold on me. But finally the hold on my head loosened so I could see more of what was going on around the campsite.

Ramos turned his gaze from Francisco to look at the child, and he laughed.

"Yes, a tasty little morsel," he said, spitting saliva.

I could hear Francisco curse in Spanish at Ramos.

Ramos spun back around and slapped the back of his hand several times across Francisco's face, severely enough to cut open his bottom lip. Francisco spat out blood.

"You are a fool," Ramos said with disgust.

"And you, Silvano, are the worst kind of animal," Francisco dared to reply.

Ramos had his own cruel way to respond. "The fire is crisp. The child's flesh is tender."

On impulse I began my own struggle against the hands holding me. But my struggle was in vain. I too would be tied to a tree, to keep me as bound and helpless as Francisco while they scavenged through our belongings and debated the most effective way to dispose of us. I couldn't bring myself to imagine what this pack of jackals had in mind for the girls.

But I was not totally submissive yet. I still had a chance — as slim as it was — to break free. Not through force, I had to concede, as any such move would be plain suicide with the odds so heavily against us. No, I determined my sole advantage might be through using my intelligence. To take a gamble on challenging Ramos's pride. It likely would be one shot, all or nothing. I only hoped Ramos's arrogance would prove to be the weapon that might work against him.

I kept my voice even; my words alone needed to be effective.

"You can crawl up on your belly in the dark, slit the throat of the man wearing the badge, hold the rest of us captive." I stopped long enough to take a deep breath because

I detested what I was going to say next. "Then you really show your worth as a man — by dragging out that child. Brag how you're gonna carve out her innards and eat her."

My words were rough, and had enough impact to free Lorraine from her deadened state so that she turned to me with a hateful look. I regretted having to subject her to such a blunt, cruel remark, but I had to play my one ace in the hole.

Ramos scowled at me. I had no clue what his response would be. Once his mood seemed to settle, his stern features relaxed.

And then he laughed.

"You interest me," he said, and for the first time he appeared to study me. "But I ask myself, who is this person?"

"No one who will matter to you," I replied.

"Yes, of that I am certain," Ramos muttered with a slight nod of his large head. And then he said, "Perhaps I am only joking about the child. How can you be sure we did not bring her along as . . . merely a precaution?"

"That is still the act of a coward," I said with disgust.

Ramos ignored the insult. He started to pace, slowly, as if in contemplation. "Would it have been better to leave the child behind?

Her father and mother dead." He turned to look at Lorraine. "Her sister in such an unfortunate way."

It was incredible. He was trying to justify his act with deranged reasoning.

"All of which was your doing, Ramos," I reminded him.

Ramos nodded, unaffected. *"Sí."*

"As with all of those you killed . . . you never gave them a chance," I said.

"This you know for a fact?" Ramos asked, his lip curled in a sneer.

"Yes," I said without hesitation.

"And how is it that you know?" Ramos pressed.

"Because I recognize the nature of a predatory beast."

Ramos frowned and squinted his eyes, apparently not understanding what I meant by my comment.

"I detect something in your attitude, *gringo,*" he said and cocked his head.

I went quiet.

Ramos began waving a finger. "If I am reading you correctly, you might be issuing me a challenge. *Sí?* To give you the chance you seem to think I did not give others."

I stayed silent for just a moment longer before I replied, "I only wonder if you, Silvano Ramos, are man enough to accept such a challenge."

Ramos's face suddenly took on an expression of rage. My remarks were starting to rile him, though in the next moment he regained his self-control so as not to show hostility over mere words. Ramos was too grand to expose such childish emotion, particularly in front of his followers.

Still, he breathed out his next words heavily. "Only a fool dares to question the manhood of Ramos."

Ramos pivoted to look at his men, scattered about the site, each of whom dared not utter a word. Perhaps he was seeking their approval. Maybe his strength existed only in his bravado, and he was not as secure in his influence over his men as he tried to make us believe. I didn't know. In truth, I started to ponder what foolhardiness had prompted me to present a challenge to a cutthroat killer. Ramos was a big man, broad as a door, and possessed of a muscular physique he flaunted by frequently expanding his chest and arms under the tight fabric of his shirt. Even if he fought me fairly, there was every chance that he would defeat me. But then, to a man like Ramos, a fair fight would exclude most common rules. Eye gouging and genital crushing was a common practice among such ruffians as he. Even with those dirty techniques at his disposal, if I ever held the advantage, I knew a knife would appear out of nowhere to plunge into my belly.

Still, engaging him in hand-to-hand battle was the only chance I saw for any of us to get out alive. And that most particularly included the child now crying and struggling feebly against the grip of the bandit who had brought her out into our camp. A man whose mean look suggested that to kill her would be of little matter. These men were not only bandits. They were barbarians.

"*Amigo,* even if you win —" Francisco started to say before one of the thugs thrust his forearm against his windpipe to silence him.

But it made no difference. I knew what Francisco had tried to tell me. Perhaps all I really hoped for was a stall — a vain hope that by a miracle we might be rescued by a delay. That was an unrealistic expectation. I would never be able to keep a fight going with a man of Silvano Ramos's apparent strength for very long — even if there existed the vague hope of a band of Texas Rangers discovering our camp.

"You wish to fight me, *gringo,*" Ramos said. "Very well. We shall fight."

I saw it in Ramos's coal black eyes that his intention was not merely to beat me — but to kill me. He proved this when he snapped his fingers and gestured for one of his companions to furnish him with a knife.

He took the knife and tossed it my way. It was a big knife and it landed on the ground with a *thump.* I was let go and slowly reached down to pick it up. I watched Ramos withdraw his own knife from a sheath at his side. A blade that Ramos handled deftly, to demonstrate his skill.

All I could see when I looked at that knife was a blade awash with invisible blood stains.

I dared to say, "If I should win, I need something from you."

Ramos gave me a peculiar look. "You ask something . . . from *me*?" he said.

"Yes. If I win, you let the girls live. Let them go free."

Ramos considered my words. Then he said, "A noble gesture. But what of yourself?"

I didn't answer. It was an intentional silence. I wanted to give Ramos the impression that I didn't care what happened to me. If I did not express a fear of dying, my opponent might wonder what I was capable of, which might give me an advantage.

A much-needed advantage under these desperate circumstances.

"Yes, a noble gesture," Ramos said again. But then he added: "But an empty one, as you will not win against me. No man can win against Ramos."

Ramos scratched his whiskered chin with the back of the knife blade, the silver gleaming against the reflection of the campfire. The bandits were obviously more concerned with the cleanliness of their weapons than of themselves.

Ramos spoke thoughtfully. "Perhaps I could let you live in that unlikely event. On the other hand, if I let you go free, it is most certain we will meet again. And maybe next time Silvano Ramos will not have the advantage he has now."

"I ask only for the girls to be safe," I said.

"Do not trust him, *Señor,*" Francisco suddenly urged. "The man has no honor."

The bandit standing next to Francisco responded to this remark by slapping Francisco several times across the face, hard.

Ramos turned his head sharply to the aggressive bandit.

"Leave Francisco alone, Carlos," he reprimanded. And then he gave a swift gesture for the child to be released. She immediately ran to her sister, Lorraine. The two girls clutched each other, both sobbing. I was grateful to see emotion come from Lorraine. Ramos ignored the girls. He never lifted his fixated stare from Francisco. Gradually a slow grin snaked across Ramos's lips.

"After all, this man is my *amigo*," he said slowly. "My long time *compadre*. If anyone is to strike him, it shall be me."

And as if to make his point, Ramos moved quickly to Francisco and struck him a hard blow against the mouth with the flat of his hand. Hard enough to again draw blood from Francisco's lips.

I'd had dealings with lawless individuals, but it was difficult for me to understand the makings of a man like Silvano Ramos. In the short time I'd been exposed to him, I saw a man of uncompromising brutality. Someone who possessed no capacity for compassion. He was the personification of pure evil, committed solely to his own survival, no matter what the cost. I could almost understand an outlaw who killed for self-preservation. But it went beyond that with Ramos. Certainly he killed for survival. But he also killed for pleasure. It gave him a twisted gratification. That was why he made no distinction between women and children, the elderly and the helpless. He truly was a spawn from hell . . . and I saw that, despite the odds, I had this one chance to permanently snuff out his malevolence.

If I somehow were to defeat this madman . . . while all of us might then die under the vengeful hand of Ramos's gang . . . I could accept such a sacrifice as I recalled what Francisco had said to me:

*When you cut the head off a snake, the body withers and dies.*

I turned to look at Francisco. And I spoke a summation of those words.

"The head of the snake."

He immediately understood.

"Yes, *amigo,*" he mouthed back to me with a slight smile.

"You have chosen to die," Ramos bellowed. "I am prepared to fulfill your request. But the time must be now."

I stood firm. Ramos needed to see that he was facing a courageous adversary.

"Likely it will be *you* who dies, Ramos," I said.

Ramos glowered at me. A man of his exaggerated pride could not accept such insolence from someone he held in low esteem. Which was just as I had hoped.

He spoke with supreme arrogance, his words meant to intimidate me. "My only question is, do I gut you or maybe cut your throat?"

"You are skilled at both," I said.

*"Bravo!"* he applauded, then he turned to gaze at his men. "This *gringo* has much courage, and that is well. Though I shall defeat him, it will be a victory for which I will feel much pride."

"Yes, because you are fighting a man who will face you," I spoke up quickly. "Because if I should die, it will be with me looking you square in the eye."

"I have killed many men who have looked me in the eye," Ramos said, making a fierce gesture. "I enjoy it that my face was the last thing they ever saw in this world."

"Women . . . and children," I scoffed. "Kill *me,* Ramos, and you will have won a fair victory."

Ramos tightened his jaw and I could see the muscles stand out in his cheeks, the cords of his neck raised. My words were having an effect on him.

He stepped close to me so that he hissed a breath redolent of cheap whiskey directly into my face.

"Perhaps your death will not come so swiftly."

"Would you dare to fight me away from your men?"

Ramos eyed me. I was not sure he understood my request. Or the reason for it.

"Does it make a difference to a man of might like Silvano Ramos?" I said, my face a mask of transparent flattery.

If Ramos saw through my facade, he didn't respond to the insult. Instead, he considered. Then he spoke with vehemence. "I need no audience to watch me dispose of you."

Ramos's enormous ego prevented him from thinking there was anything peculiar or suspicious about my suggestion. But I did have a motive. With my chances against Ramos likely slim no matter where we fought, I was hoping that if we had our fight away from the others, Francisco might somehow find his own opportunity to save himself and the two girls.

It was a slim hope with my *compañero* bound and helpless . . . but it was all we had.

And then Francisco spoke up.

"Silvano. This man who has challenged you — even as you have said, it will be no contest. He is a man not skilled with the handling of a knife. How could you feel pride defeating such an opponent?"

Ramos very slowly swiveled his head toward Francisco, a strange smile on his face.

"What are you suggesting, my one-time

*amigo*?" he said.

Francisco said, "Untie me and fight against a man whose skill matches your own. A man whose blood you would prefer to spill."

Ramos started to laugh.

Francisco then spoke with defiance — addressing the outlaw bunch as a whole.

He said, "Would not you men like to see how grand your leader truly is? Have him prove to you that he is worthy of your respect? Such would not be the case with him killing the *gringo.*"

Not one of the men responded, although I heard slight murmurs coming from some. I felt myself tense, and I didn't know whether I approved of what my *compañero* was doing. Francisco was going to take my place against Ramos, provoking that action by daring to call into question among these ignorant peasants the leadership quality of Silvano Ramos.

It was Ramos himself who answered.

"My men need no proof of my might," he declared, holding his body upright, his posture ramrod straight, with an inflated pride intended to demonstrate his authority over his gang.

Francisco fell silent. He waited for Ramos to say more, but the words were not immediately forthcoming. Instead, Ramos frowned and deep lines embedded themselves in his walnut skin.

"These men have ridden many miles with Ramos," he then said in a snarl, emphasizing his point by thumping a fist against his chest. "They have me to thank for the prosperous lives I have given them. Each has shared equally in the bounty we have obtained."

Francisco's gaze traveled to the pathetic forms of Lorraine and her sister, huddled in each other's arms next to the waning flames of the fire.

"Yes Silvano," he said in a quiet voice. "A plunder so profitable that you now intend to sacrifice a child to fill your bellies."

Ramos fastened Francisco with a cold stare.

I admired Francisco for speaking so bravely, but I feared Ramos would no longer control his patience and might put an end to Francisco's defiance by slitting his throat.

Francisco was attempting the same gamble as I myself had tried. But he was playing his hand at much higher stakes. He was a greater risk to Ramos than I could be.

And Ramos recognized this. Francisco had more to gain out of his challenge. A fierce personal desire for vengeance that could not be taken so lightly by the murderous bandit.

I detected hesitance in the mighty Ramos. He had to make a choice. If he did not fight Francisco, it might be looked upon as cowardice by his men. As each was nurtured in violence, if they saw or perhaps even suspected Ramos was showing weakness, they might turn on him. While individually it was doubtful any one of the peasants possessed such courage, as a group they were formidable and a threat to Ramos.

It was essential for Silvano Ramos to prove to them through this challenge that he truly had the strength to remain their chief.

I watched the man intently and waited for him to speak.

His gang looked eager, as if seeking a profound pronouncement that would satisfy their ignorance and establish that their obedience to Ramos had not been misplaced.

"I am waiting for your decision, Silvano," Francisco said coaxingly. "Either kill me here with my hands bound . . . or let your men see the true *masculino* that you claim to be."

Ramos waved one of his arms in a sweeping gesture. "As I said, I need not prove anything to them. I have earned their respect. I have demonstrated my strength to them many times. I am Silvano Ramos, their leader."

And then one of the men took a tentative step forward. He was a young Mexican, maybe close to the same age as Lorraine. A boy. He timidly and respectfully removed his *sombrero* and held it by the brim in both hands. He took a long look at the girl before he turned toward Ramos and spoke with his eyes lowered.

"I . . . I humbly ask you to fight him, *Señor* Ramos," he said meekly. "To show to each of us how a warrior such as yourself . . . how you can allow this man to die in the honor he requests."

While he spoke his piece well, the boy had made a tragic mistake, and I feared the consequences. Through his words, he confirmed that Ramos had rarely if ever killed any of his victims fairly. He and his band of thieves and assassins sneaked up on those they had chosen to plunder and their actions were swift, ruthless. A man would not be given the chance to defend himself or his family. He would be struck dead instantly . . . and then his wife and children would follow.

Ramos glanced at his men with an almost

jovial expression intended to show his humor at the daring displayed by such a young "soldier."

He walked toward the young man and eyed him speculatively. He placed a hand on his shoulder.

"I cannot be sure if you are a fair man, Miguel . . . or maybe of a sensitive spirit," he said almost kindly.

Miguel didn't not speak. His eyes remained lowered.

The tone of Ramos's voice suddenly grew harsh. "Or if you are brave — or simply a fool!"

And in the next instant, Ramos turned on the lad with an expression like that of a rabid dog.

"You dare to tell me — *Ramos* — what to do!" he snarled, his teeth bared.

Miguel stood motionless, his body trembling. Either out of respect or sheer terror he did not lift his eyes to meet Ramos's intense, insane glower. Perhaps to the lad it would be like gazing into the very eyes of *El Diablo*.

"I — I meant no disrespect, *Señor* Ramos," the boy muttered.

Miguel died instantly once the knife was plunged deep into his chest. Deep enough so that only the hilt was visible. Miguel wore a look of disbelief before he fell face-first into the dirt. Ramos stepped away from the corpse, again leveling his eyes on his group.

I felt my body grow numb and hastened to collect myself, regain my self-control, which was imperative, given the tenuousness of the situation. I would not let my courage waver, even as my hatred for the butcher grew to a fever-pitch. Ramos would surely notice my vulnerability and feast his ego upon it. Yet my momentary weakness was less a reaction to Ramos's kill than shock that he had committed such an act against one of his own people — a boy whose comment was not made as an insult or a challenge. A virtually harmless remark for which Miguel did not deserve to die. I glanced at Lorraine. She had witnessed the killing, too, and was wide-eyed. She held her sister close to her, burying her little face into her shoulder to shield her from the violence.

Ramos stepped over to where Miguel lay. He regarded the corpse coldly before he kicked the body onto its back. Sneering, he bent over and savagely withdrew the knife from Miguel's chest. He slowly, deliberately, and disrespectfully wiped the blood from the blade against the dead boy's shirt.

Once more he stood to his full height, to

present to his men his imposing stature.

"So shall it be for any man who dares to question Silvano Ramos," he proclaimed.

And as if they were listening to the profound statement of some ancient prophet, his band seemed to cower at the strength of the man and what they interpreted as the significance of his words. Ramos himself looked pleased, as he had maintained his authority among his men.

Ramos's move had been calculated. An attempt not just to preserve, but to flaunt, his eminence among his rag-tag band of pissant *pistoleros.* It might have been an effective tactic. But as I saw it, all it did was forestall the real challenge presented to him by a worthy adversary. To suddenly plunge a knife into an unprepared boy showed no courage. No matter how his men regarded the killing, the act was cowardly and likely committed out of desperation.

But that aside, I, Francisco, and the two frightened girls were dealing with a power-crazed madman. I remained apprehensive of what was to come next.

# CHAPTER NINETEEN

Silvano Ramos looked frighteningly empowered by the killing he had just committed, holding and maintaining a posture of superiority, his chest jutting forward under the tight-fitting fabric of his shirt, and he spoke with a boastful, abrasive conceit intended either to inspire or instill fear in his men.

To my mind he was doing both. Just as I'd finally seen firsthand how Ramos enjoyed getting blood on his hands.

"The swiftness and uncertainty of death," he announced. "And when one man controls that decision over life, it is power indeed."

Francisco's voice rose. "A power *undeserved.*"

I watched as Ramos's gaze veered toward Francisco and studied him with curiosity. He then took deliberate strides over to him, sidling alongside Francisco and peering curiously but with obvious amusement at the hands bound tightly behind the tree trunk.

"It never ceases to amaze me how a man so vulnerable can speak with such . . . impudence," Ramos said.

"You wish for me to speak to you with respect?" Francisco said with a scowl.

"In your situation, does it really matter?" Ramos responded with a shrug.

"It is interesting, Silvano, to be so near to you now, after such a long while — to look into the face of a man I once considered *mi hermano* and see only the face of a killer. A man I trusted, who not only took my sister's life, but who also betrayed our friendship."

"You speak of . . . loyalty?" Ramos said with derision.

Francisco didn't answer, just eyed him contemptuously.

*"Sí,"* Ramos sighed. "It is indeed unfortunate that it has come to this. With me standing here . . . and you with your hands tied behind a tree."

"And that is all you can say?" Francisco muttered.

Ramos said in a guiltless tone, "What more is there?"

"What of my family, Ramos?" Francisco asked. "Those years when you had no place to stay, no food to eat, and my mother fed you and often gave you shelter. Look how you repaid her. I should have known even then the type of person you were. But I was blinded by our friendship. Blinded enough to welcome your attraction to Felicia — and encourage her to accept your courtship. Blinded because I accepted your assurances that you would give up your crimes and care for her as a husband should. We all suffered because of you, Silvano."

By the time Francisco finished speaking, a trembling in his voice as he spewed out with passion those final words, I had my eyes steady on Ramos. It was hard to tell by the vacant look on his face if he'd heard even a single sentence. Or if he had, did they matter to him?

Ramos answered my curiosity when he drew a long breath and said, "As a boy I always dreamed of being a pirate. We played such games as children, do you recall? I was *el capitan* and you, Francisco — you were my crew. It was play in those days. We attacked our pretend enemies using sticks for swords and stones as cannon fodder. And always did we win our conquests. And look how it has come to pass." He puffed out his chest. "I *am* a pirate. A pirate of the land. And I command a crew. A crew who obey me . . . but who I must also be wary of."

Francisco was silent. Ramos stepped up very close to his bound captive.

"I notice a strange wetness against the rawhide," he said quietly, out of earshot of his men. He lifted the moistness on his finger to his lips to taste it. He paused. "As I suspected. Blood." Moments later he said, "It is not just your blood that is dripping from your wrists. Do you also recall when we, as boys, pledged our friendship and forged our commitment to that friendship with the sharing of each other's blood? You welcomed it then. Do you now feel, *amigo,* that you have become tainted by our exchange?"

Francisco said nothing. It wasn't necessary. All he felt — his hatred, resentment, perhaps even uncertainty as to his fate — was reflected in his expression.

Ramos's mood turned serious as he considered.

"Yes, my friend, I *could* release you and we could fight, you and I. But now I must ask myself: Would that be fair . . . with you at such a disadvantage? Yet . . . you insist that we fight. It is not right that I should disappoint you. You and I shared blood. To break that bond one of us must die."

Francisco was clearly in considerable discomfort, though he was loath to reveal it outside of the occasional grimace. He must have possessed a high threshold for pain. He also had to know when he'd made the challenge to Ramos that his hands were injured, his wrists cut by the severe binding. While I could not know precisely Ramos's skill with a blade, I recalled only too well how Francisco had manipulated a knife outside the cantina in Santa Rosina. Whether he could manage that skill now, I confess I had my doubts.

But Ramos had just been toying with Francisco, stalling. Waiting until he was confident Francisco's wounds were bad enough so that he, his opponent, would not have a fair chance in their challenge.

Ramos was a devil. He may have been a peasant through heritage, but he was possessed of an evil (what the Mexicans called *el mal*) that provided him with malevolent cunning.

He reproached his men with a loud but devious accusation. "Whoever of you tied this man to this tree did so much too tightly. Yes, I see blood upon his hands. Tell me, how can I fight this man when he is clearly at a disadvantage?" He heaved an exaggerated sigh and then scratched furiously at his brow, giving the impression that he was in a struggle with himself about what to do.

It was an obvious act, but it did bring frowns of concern to his ignorant companions.

After several moments of pretend contemplation, he resumed. "Still . . . this man, my *amigo* since boyhood, has claimed to have a skill greater than mine. And so I think it is only fair to let him prove it." He placed a hand, fingers splayed, against his chest. "Yet I do not want to fight him if any of you feel I have an unfair advantage. So I will leave that up to you men. Do I fight . . . or do we ride from here?"

Perhaps out of fear, Ramos's men were not enthusiastic in their response. There were a few guttural mutterings, but not one of the gang urged him on with enthusiasm. I saw the troubled look on Ramos's face. An expression he was quick to erase so his men would not notice so much as a hint of vulnerability. He walked over to cut Francisco free from his binding.

"I shall finish what I started," he announced grandly.

"I have but one request, Silvano," Francisco said.

"If it is a fair request, how can I deny an old friend?" Ramos replied with mock generosity.

"I choose not to use that blade," Francisco

said, gesturing to the knife that I still had in my grip.

"No? And how do you intend to fight me? Do you suggest we throw rocks at each other?"

"I would prefer to use my own knife," Francisco told him bluntly.

Ramos looked skeptical. "And why is that important?"

Francisco offered his words in a defeated tone. "What matter is it to you? You have already won this fight."

Ramos remained wary.

"As you can see, I have no advantage," Francisco told him. He started to lift both hands, but Ramos used the palms of his own hands to thrust Francisco's damaged wrists downward. He did not want his men to notice the extent of Francisco's injuries.

Ramos sighed and nodded.

"Where is your knife? I will get it," he said.

"*I* will get it," Francisco replied firmly.

Ramos looked dubious.

"I trust you to walk away from me?" he said carefully. "To possibly seize yourself an opportunity."

"It is interesting, Silvano, that it is *you* doubting trust," Francisco replied.

Ramos smiled faintly. "Interesting, *amigo,* when it is you who has more to lose, with me having the advantage."

Francisco's gaze swept across to the bandits grouped together.

"In number, yes," he returned. "But man against man . . . in that we shall see."

Ramos nodded again, then he glanced in my direction. He gave a jerk of his head to the bandit standing nearest to me. Now that the game had changed, the bandit thrust out his hand to take the knife from me. I felt myself hesitant to release the blade. I would be surrendering what might be my one hope at defending myself.

For only a moment I debated. I stood close enough to the bandit that I could stick the knife into his belly. But tempting as it was, that would be a futile move. There were still too many others to deal with. Killing at least one of this gang would provide satisfaction, but the effort would almost certainly lead to all of our deaths in a Ramos-dictated retaliation.

I handed the bandit the knife, with the blade out toward him. He hesitated and gave me a peculiar smile, as if he had suspected what I'd been considering and was reminding me of its ultimate pointlessness.

I was now as powerless as Lorraine and her sister. I could barely look at them. I had made an attempt to save us, but Francisco had intercepted my plan with an idea of his own. Did he even have a plan? Or did he simply realize the folly of my going up against a skilled knife-wielder like Ramos and want to save me from certain death?

Questions likely never to be answered, regardless of the outcome of this long night.

# CHAPTER TWENTY

Francisco looked unsteady on his feet as he all but stumbled toward his horse . . . then he appeared to lose his balance. His body lunged forward against the flank of his animal, against one of his saddlebags.

"*Señor* Ramos," one of the men said, alerting the bandit chief to the situation.

Ramos turned to look as Francisco's body started to slide to the ground, his hands clutching the saddlebag and pulling it free. Francisco still grasped it as he dropped to his knees. Ramos responded with a smirk before he spat on the ground. Another obvious display of his own importance — and a posture still blindly accepted by his band of cutthroats.

"A worthy opponent," he said with ridicule.

I'd reacted impulsively, taking a step forward before I felt the barrel of a pistol being jabbed into my ribs.

The bandit holding the gun grinned at me. "Hold steady, *Señor*. Soon it will all be over and then neither you nor your *amigo* will have any worries."

There was nothing I could do to assist Francisco. With a revolver aimed at my side, all I could do was watch helplessly as my *compañero* struggled to pull himself to his feet. I was concerned that the wounds to his wrists were more serious than I had thought, and that he was losing a significant amount of blood.

Ramos spoke up in distaste. "Perhaps we should stop this play and I will kill you right now, as I intended. Yes, Francisco, give up this foolish bravery and I will grant you that mercy. A fast death."

From where I was standing and with the flickering of the campfire still providing sufficient if waning light, I saw Francisco's bloody hands disappear into the saddlebag. It was then that I knew my *compañero* had something up his sleeve. But whatever that might be, he would have to make his move quickly.

"You cannot fight a man in his condition," another of Ramos's bunch objected. And then he realized he had spoken impulsively, likely remembering the fate of his young comrade, as his face set into an expression of dread.

Ramos turned cold, threatening eyes on the man, but in this instance, for whatever reason, he spared him his life. Grateful, relieved at what he saw as his narrow escape, the tough, rough-hewn bandit nearly collapsed.

"Consider yourself lucky," one of his companions muttered to the man out the side of his mouth.

The bandit could not find the voice to speak.

It was becoming ever more apparent that individually these bandits were cowards and survived only by feeding off the strength of their leader, Ramos. I only wished there had been some way to use that to our advantage.

"This game has gone on long enough," Ramos called to Francisco. "You expect pity from my *compadres.* Your attempts may fool them. But be assured, unless you turn to face me now and give me your surrender, you will receive no mercy from me."

I heard Francisco utter what sounded like, "Nor will you get mercy from me."

In the next instant, he sprang to his feet. He spun around to face Ramos, twirling the *boleadoras* he'd stashed in his saddlebag.

Ramos had not expected this maneuver and it took him by surprise.

When he recovered he responded with amusement.

"You think you can defeat Silvano Ramos with that . . . slingshot?" he said with typical bravado. "Like that boy in the Bible story who slew Goliath."

Francisco said nothing. His eyes were fixed on Ramos as he continued twirling, trying to keep up his strength though looking greatly pained by his effort. I didn't see how he could manage it with the blood that was seeping from his wrists and sluicing down both forearms.

The night was nearly coal black, the glow from the campfire weakening, and none of us could completely define the situation. Including, it seemed, Ramos.

At first Ramos brandished his knife in a threatening gesture, but then he tossed it carelessly to the ground. Instead, he quickly stepped over to one of his gang and pulled a pistol from the man's gun belt — a peculiar move since Ramos had two revolvers tucked into his own double holsters. There was no sense to his action unless Ramos had suddenly become aware of his own vulnerability and the fact that he was finally facing a man who did not fear him. The great Silvano Ramos stood alone against his adversary as not even one of his gang moved forward to support him.

"It is just you and me, Silvano," Francisco said. "As it should be."

Ramos may have felt uncertain, but what mattered most to him was maintaining his pride and his self-professed eminence among his band. To call upon or even to accept help would show him as weak in front of his men, and Ramos had already risked compromising his status that night.

I realized that somehow I, too, had to take advantage of this situation. I had to make a move, if only I could seize an opportunity.

I recalled my experience in the Bodrie Hills — as if events in my own life had come full circle in just a few short weeks.

On that occasion I'd had the assistance of someone prompting me to use gun power. That man, Ed Chaney, made the first move and had died for his effort . . . but I followed through on his lead and survived. Dead bodies lay about me, but mine was not among them. Now, at this desperate moment I was still surviving, although my future and that of the children hung by a thread. I didn't have the support of anyone other than Francisco, and I still wasn't entirely sure what his move would be. Even with Ramos dead, there were seven other bandits for us to contend with.

Until this situation was resolved, none of us — and that included the outlaws themselves — could feel confident we would be alive come daybreak.

None . . . except Francisco, who perhaps had come to accept his fate. This was apparent in his aggression toward Ramos, swinging those bolas with a mad glint in his eyes. Ramos was all he really wanted. Even if he were to be murdered by the others, knowing that he'd first put Ramos in his grave would allow him to die with satisfaction, with the realization that he had fulfilled his purpose and, most importantly, avenged his sister Felicia.

Which was good enough for him. But I was selfish. I wasn't quite ready to share that fate. And neither Lorraine nor her sister deserved to die, either.

Ramos had his pistol aimed at Francisco, who had stepped for protection into the night shadows that wrapped around him like a cloak, enveloping him until his body seemed to be absorbed wholly by the dark.

The voice of Ramos shattered the stillness. "You have no strength. Where is your accuracy? And so now, my one-time brother, *you will die!*"

Ramos fired off a volley of shots. I heard Lorraine shriek and her sister start to cry at the loud reports of gunfire. Ramos's target had become a vague silhouette. Although I could not tell for sure, it was likely that at least some of the bullets found their mark in Francisco. But then I heard the distinctive *whoosh* I had heard once before and watched the bola streak through the air.

My eyes stayed focused as one of the heavy balls struck Ramos on the head — and then another twisted, and that ball too connected with the outlaw's skull. In both instances I thought I heard the shatter of bone. Ramos's body twisted in a half circle and his finger tightened reflexively on the trigger of his pistol, one stray bullet smashing into the face of one of the bandits who fell instantly. The last shot fired from Ramos's death spasm went harmlessly skyward.

And at that moment something shocking and unexpected happened. Was it in defense — or maybe a reflexive maneuver — but at least two of Ramos's bandits withdrew their pistols and fired gunshots into their leader's body, blasting holes into his chest and belly while Ramos jerked about, seemingly held upright by the penetrating impact of the bullets.

It was only after the firing ceased that Silvano Ramos, with a final grimace frozen upon his features, dropped lifeless to the ground.

Then . . . silence.

I didn't know what to expect next. Ramos's men did not immediately react, and I didn't know how they would respond. Soon they started to step forward, slowly, to observe the body of their fallen leader. Even the bandit who'd held a gun to my side lowered his weapon and moved to join them, as did those men who had fired the final shots, each still holding his pistol. Then there came a gradual murmuring, but the men spoke in the language I did not fully understand and so was unable to translate. I figured they were expressing a peasant's amazement that a man of Silvano Ramos's legend and conceit could, after all, be mortal.

With their attention focused away from us, I started to turn toward Francisco. I found myself hesitant, disturbed by what I might find.

Francisco had indeed been shot. I noticed blood blossoming from a chest wound. He remained stubbornly on his feet, his body braced against the same tree to which he had earlier been tied — and being tended to by Lorraine who, miraculously, looked to have regained her senses. Her little sister was next to her, clutching at Lorraine's dress.

I took in a breath and walked over to my *compañero,* who lifted his eyes at my approach and managed a weak smile. When I stood next to him, he took my hand in fingers stained with his blood.

"We have shared an adventure, my friend," he said.

I nodded slowly. "Yes, my *amigo.* One that neither of us will ever forget." I held back the urge to speak encouragingly and tell him that one day we would sit together in a cantina in Santa Rosina and reminisce about our experience. I resisted because he would know my words were shallow and only intended to comfort him. He and I both understood such a time would never come.

"You must see to it that these girls are returned to safety," he said.

"Yes."

I only hoped I was not making a hollow promise to my dying friend. There were still Ramos's men who might have made their own decision as to our fate.

Francisco tilted his head in a direction over my shoulder.

I turned to see one of the bandits break away from the others and start to walk toward us. I was uncertain but did not want Lorraine to notice my apprehension. I summoned all the courage and fortitude I could muster to serve us through these next terrible moments as we waited to hear what the man would say. Or what he might do.

But he did not speak. I managed to keep my gaze steady and neither of us looked away from the other. This went on for what seemed like a long while but was probably just seconds. The bandit held all the cards in the deck, and he knew it. He had only to give a simple nod and Francisco and I would be dead and the girls left to whatever horrid fate he and the others had in mind for them.

He kept his expression void of emotion, providing not a hint as to what his next move might be. Likewise, I would not betray the dread I was feeling.

A standstill. A stalemate — or that moment when a condemned man is permitted to make his peace before his execution. I could not know which — if either — was the reason for the silence between us.

Then — finally, with just the slightest shifting of his features, he turned and walked back to the others. There were still mutterings going on within the group. Yet I instinctively felt the threat was over. The tension eased from my body.

I heard, faintly, Francisco say, *"Señor?"*

I turned to him.

He was smiling wanly.

"The head has been cut from the snake," he muttered.

I understood and nodded. Ramos was dead. The survivors of his gang, for whatever reason, no longer saw the need to torment us. I could not understand why exactly, but neither was I about to question their decision. Francisco, however, seemed to know. Perhaps yet another mystery associated with the man and his past. I knew there was much more to discover about my *compañero.* Sadly, if that were so, I now would never know.

The outlaws would ride off and eventually scatter and in time reach their own destinies. Whatever their fates, they were not my concern. Nor any longer a concern to Francisco, who could face death with the knowledge that because of his bravery the bandits would disappear into the winds.

"They will take their leader and bury him," Francisco said. He then gazed directly into my eyes. "As for me, my *amigo* . . . I would prefer if you would lay me to rest here. It . . . seems appropriate."

Once again I understood.

Francisco then allowed his body to go limp, and he slid onto the ground. His face did not reflect distress, but I noticed how he dug his boot heel deep into the sand and slowly but with effort stretched out his leg in response to his pain.

"There is one more thing," Francisco said in a faltering voice. He urged me a little closer with a slight wrenching of his head. I bent in to listen.

He spoke quietly — for a purpose. "Now that the bandits are leaving, we can consider ourselves fortunate. And you, *Señor,* are most fortunate that they did not search our saddlebags — which they surely would have done had they killed us." He grimaced at a sharp stab of pain and took a moment to recover before he resumed speaking.

"The money I owe you is in one of my saddlebags," he said, his breathing becoming labored. "I ask you to take out what you think is fair payment . . . and maybe with the rest to help these girls."

It was a fine gesture. My lips tightened and I gave a nod. What I would not tell Francisco was that as far as my fee was concerned, I considered myself paid in full. Lorraine and her sister could use that money more than I could.

And yet in those final moments of Francisco's life, there remained one question I'd still hoped he would answer. The question that had traveled with me since the beginning of our journey, the uncertain resolution seeming to shift as frequently as the Texas prairie winds.

But the truth would follow Francisco to the grave. I could not bring myself to ask if it had been his intention to kill me. If he still held me in some way responsible for his sister's death. I justified the decision not to satisfy my curiosity by convincing myself that maybe even Francisco didn't know what he would have done, had the outcome been different.

For now, all that mattered was for the girls and me to be with Francisco while he waited to die. And then to honor his request by digging his grave here, where he had fallen.

Francisco died before daybreak. He had hoped to watch a final sunrise, but his fading vision only managed to catch glimmers of light over the eastern horizon before he took his last breath. The outlaws had ridden off by then, taking the body of Silvano Ramos with them.

While I dug the grave, Lorraine, taking the duty upon herself, cleaned and prepared Francisco's body as best she could. Once in a while as we performed our separate tasks, we exchanged a glance and shared a gentle smile.

The sun was near fully up by the time we laid Francisco in the ground. At my request, Lorraine covered his body with the color-patterned wool *serape* that had kept him warm on cold nights. It was fitting. It was difficult for me since I was not a religious man, but I felt I should say something before I filled in the grave. But what words to say?

I removed my hat and held it before me in both hands. I stared into the hole that now held Francisco's body.

And then — without my even being aware of what I was saying, the words came. I spoke them quietly, with respect and reverence.

"Francisco Velasquez was not a man I knew for very long. But in that short time, I reckon we shared the better part of a lifetime. At least in what we went through together. We came to know each other, yet we did not. I was never entirely sure that we shared a trust between us. What I can truthfully say is that Francisco was a brave man. He carried with him both purpose and determination. He never wavered from the task he set out to do. A task that he accomplished — at the cost of his own life. I regarded him as my *compañero*. But now I feel I can call him my *amigo,* and say that both with privilege and pride."

After the grave was covered, I walked over to the horses. Lorraine and her sister mounted a horse together, with Lorraine taking the reins and the child seated on a blanket behind her, snuggling against Lorraine's back, holding her older sister securely by the waist. I would lead Sheriff Briggs's sorrel with my own horse. I draped the sheriff's body, wrapped in a blanket, over the animal's back. I would take him back to Chesterfield City for a proper burial. And I would also tell the citizens of his courage. I knew J.C. would help with that. Over time the stories of Sheriff Briggs's accomplishments would grow until they would assume the status of legend. A legend of heroism and of much more significance than the legacy of Silvano Ramos.

I didn't think Briggs would have objected to the embellishments. He had earned the honor. Besides, the truth itself might be difficult for some to believe.

And with that, my thoughts turned to J.C. I felt in my heart that she would be waiting to greet me once we rode back to town and that we could start to plan a future together.

I'd decided that my days a[ ]
were over. I wasn't entirely [ ]itness seeker
tions, but I wasn't concerne[ ]of my op-
enced too much too suddenl[ ]d experi-
about my future. What I did kno[ ] worry
I had tired of adventure and was r[ ]as that
settle down. Maybe I'd work with J.[ ]ly to
the newspaper. That was an appeal[ ]on
thought. After all, I shared her love o[ ]g
words, and I could not think of a more
comfortable working arrangement.

But first I had another responsibility. A promise made to Francisco, but one I would have undertaken in any event. I would see to it that Lorraine and her sister were properly cared for. They would have a home that I would ensure would provide a loving environment so that someday this experience might fade from their memory. Especially Lorraine.

We set forth to ride. I indulged myself to a last look about the site. There were disturbing pockets of blood visible, but the winds would eventually whip up sands to bury these tragic markings. One day when people trekked through these parts, they would never know what went on here. They also would never know of the gallant soul that rested beneath the sands. Yet . . . he would never be completely forgotten, for it

was then that ...aine finally spoke, her
words quiet a... were directed at me, they
not be sure...oughtful. At first I could
sounded ...istant, as if she were merely
ruminat...

"Do...ou suppose he did it . . . *for us*?"
she ...d.

...took me only a few moments to compre-
...end what she was asking. But it was a
question I could not easily answer, since I
could not say with a certainty. The real truth
possessed its own ambiguity. Yes, I had my
suspicions about Francisco's motives when
he chose to challenge Ramos alone — and I
was probably right. But did it really matter
now? It would make no difference, and how
better and more meaningful than to leave a
heroic legacy in this girl's eyes.

I looked directly at the girl and said
simply, "He did it for us."

Lorraine appeared contemplative. Then
she cast her eyes skyward and she smiled an
appreciative smile. Oddly, without my even
being aware of it, I did the same. And looking up to acknowledge the heavens didn't
feel as strange or unnatural as it might have
seemed. In fact, I felt overcome with a kind
of tranquility that I could appreciate and
even embrace after what we had endured.

Two men had died on this quest. Two

good men. But we — the girls and I — had survived.

I tilted the brim of my hat in gratitude.

*"Muchas gracias,"* I whispered.

So we started our travel, riding south against a magnificent sunrise, one that spilled a golden glow across the vastness of the Texas prairie landscape.

A new day was dawning and though it was bittersweet, it also promised a new beginning.

# ABOUT THE AUTHOR

**Stone Wallace** is the published author of eighteen books, ranging from horror to westerns, history to biographies. A communications and two-time broadcasting graduate, his career ambitions have taken him along many paths: actor, announcer, boxer, advertising copywriter, creative writing and media instructor, and celebrity interviewer. He finds particular satisfaction in writing westerns, stepping back creatively to a time when the lands were clean, heroes and villains were clearly defined, and values were simple and straightforward. His five previous Western novels have been critically acclaimed, with his second, *Montana Dawn,* being named "One of the Ten Best Westerns of the Decade" by *Booklist.*

Stone resides in Canada with his loving and supportive partner, Cindy, who is also an author, as well as storyteller and children's entertainer.